The Bog Wife

ALSO BY KAY CHRONISTER

Desert Creatures
Thin Places

THE BOG WIFE

A NOVEL

Kay Chronister

COUNTERPOINT ❧ CALIFORNIA

THE BOG WIFE

ISBN 9781640096622

Jacket design by Nicole Caputo
Jacket images: woman © Marta Bevacqua / Trevillion Images;
pitcher plant © Florilegius / Bridgeman Images
Book design by tracy danes

COUNTERPOINT
Los Angeles and San Francisco, CA

Printed in the United States of America

For my daughter

These fragments I have shored
against my ruins

The Waste Land
T. S. ELIOT

The Bog Wife

On winter nights, they burned heavy bundles of dried peat in the hearth and inhaled the scent of sacred ground burning while their father paced the length of the room, reciting the history of the Haddesley compact.

He said, *Our ways are noble; they are ancient.*

He said, *Always the bog has belonged to us and we to it.*

He said, *A millennium ago, the father of our line was thrown into the mire as punishment for a transgression that he did not commit. His hair shorn, his hands tied, his mouth gagged, his clothes packed with stones. But he did not die. No man can tell what strange negotiations were made beneath the surface. But from that day onward, the bog was in him. When he rose from those depths, a woman rose with him to be his wife. You are bound now, she told him in her language, to the care of this land. Your sons' marriages will reseal the compact between us. Your family line must not comingle, must not branch.*

He said, *Purity has been the way of our progenitors.*

He said, *It was unjust suspicions of sorcery that drove our ancestors from the old county, uncountably many years ago. But the first American Haddesley was led by his dowsing stick and the hold of the compact on him to this West Virginian bog's very heart, and in this place he built our home.*

Holding aloft an antique globe with his index finger on the dark expanse of the Atlantic Ocean, his voice reunifying the continents that time had torn asunder, he said, *They are the same mountains. The same veins of water. We are natives to this land. And still the bog's custodians.*

He said, *Always the bog has belonged to us and we to it.*

And they listened dreamily, the five of them, as they melted into a pile of blankets and limbs and lolling heads: Nora's chin on Wenna's shoulder and her feet tangled up with Percy's feet; Eda stroking Percy's bath-damp hair as his small head lay in her lap, her back propped against Charlie's. They were so warm, so close.

Later, none of them could remember where their mother had been while their father told that story.

Summer

Nora

ora found the trespassers sprouting brightly at the bottom of the dry swale, an entire zigzagging row of them, broad-headed and firm as if they'd been maturing there for months although they couldn't have been there more than a week.

Her brother Percy was only steps behind her, rooting out the sedge that stubbornly sprouted and resprouted on the banks of the swale no matter how many times they tore it out. Any minute now, he would see, he would know. His face would transform: his lips sucked inward until they almost disappeared, his eyes low and narrowed like he could see the growth of trespassers from seed to sprout right in that very moment if he only looked hard enough. The deep and focused calm that came over him as he worked in the bog—and sometimes, on the best days, lingered in him afterward—would give way to panic. For the rest of the day, he would be consumed by what-ifs and what-nows. He would spend hours opening and closing their battered old copy of *A Field Guide to Flora of the Highland Fens* in the futile hope that the trespasser's name and picture might somehow appear there. Eventually, he would get up the nerve to inform their father, who would not under any circumstances know what to do to help but might, depending on his mood, reply with a thunderous arms-waving injunction to *do more!* or only nod as if he had already known and sink further into his sickness like it was despair that was eating away his stomach, not cancer.

After that, for the rest of the night, everyone would be polite in a way that was like a membrane stretched thin across their anger, Percy resenting Charlie for not doing the custodian's work that was his firstborn obligation and Charlie resenting Percy for reminding him that he should have been the one doing it, and Eda resenting them both for upsetting their father, and Nora stuck at a silent dinner table, resenting no one, terrified by how fragile were the ties that held them.

With a furtive glance back at her brother, she reached out and grasped the trespassers in her fist and yanked them out by the stems. She felt a heart-hammering little slip of relief as she lifted her hand to her pocket and hid the trespassers there, thinking that the night was spared. Percy would remain in that calm and focused half-dreamy state. He would be able to tell their father he had cleared the swale enough to open the lock that held back the river and flood the bog's thirsty mouth without fear of contaminating it. Charlie would emptily but sincerely offer to help with the bog's flooding, and Percy would tell him it was all right, it wasn't his fault, and he would even mean it. Eda would make something edible for dinner.

But then Percy crouched behind her, and she saw him seeing the torn ends of the stems left in the ground, thin but conspicuous orange shoots that she realized now he could never have missed, and everything was worse than before, because now the trespassers were her fault.

"What is this?" he said.

"I don't know," said Nora blandly, her fingers squeezing around the waxy flesh of the trespassers in her pocket until her hand became a fist.

"Don't tell me you didn't see it."

"See what?"

"Look."

Nora reluctantly turned and made her way back to him. Percy was two years younger than she was, twenty-two to her twenty-four, but so forceful and self-assured in their father's old waders. A foot away from his hunched form, she stopped and crossed her arms before her chest. The small bulk of the trespassers burned in her pocket as if they had grown from her hip.

"What?" she said.

"This is bad." He brushed away soil with his fingers and uncovered the white knob of the trespassers' feet in the dark earth. He yanked the knob loose with an audible snap. A ragged mass of spidery roots trailed from his fist.

"Oh," said Nora, emptily, because she knew Percy would be worried if she agreed that it was bad but angry if she protested that it wasn't.

"They're *new*," he insisted. "I don't even know what they are. Orange stems like that, I've never seen before."

Nora uncrossed her arms then crossed them again. "Well, you got them out. And it's only the swale, anyway."

"Yes, and the swale goes to the bog's mouth," Percy said, as if she didn't know that. "Anything in the swale could get carried to the bog. And I didn't get them out. There's roots."

"Dig out the roots, then."

"You can't do that with mushrooms." He raked his fingers through the small crater left by the trespassers' extraction. "There are roots all through here." Percy was on the brink of despair. "They're everywhere."

Nora fidgeted with the trespassers in her pocket, fighting the impulse to tell Percy to calm down, which never calmed him.

She wished he wouldn't always be so anxious. The fear that animated him only made her tired and limp with helplessness. She understood as well as he did that the trespassers meant something was wrong, but if she really accepted that the bog could be sick enough to die, the world became hostile, the future hopeless, their shared life as precarious and small as the lives of the flies that fell into the mouths of pitcher plants and never came out again. So she did not think about it. They were doing what they could: feeding the bog's thirsty mouth with filtered water siphoned off from the river, plucking out trespassers when they found them, crossing the tender shuddering mat of sphagnum moss around the bog's mouth as rarely as possible, and then only on bare feet.

"Maybe Charlie would know what to do," she said.

They both knew that Charlie did not know what to do. That Charlie was, in no ways that mattered, really the bog's custodian. But by reminding Percy that he was neither the custodian nor even next in line to be one, Nora hoped to discourage him enough that he would go inside with her.

Percy answered her with a dark look. It was an acknowledgment that she'd tried to hurt his feelings, not a concession that his feelings had been hurt. "I have to tell Dad," he said, in the low half-muttered register that meant he was mostly talking to himself.

Nora tore her fingers away from the mash of fungal tissue in her dress pocket and followed Percy back through the pitted landscape of hollows and hummocks, close enough that they brushed against each other as they found their footing with a shared set of instincts. When they got to the house, they stood on the back step to unstick the wet earth from their feet, leaning habitually on each other's shoulders for balance. They were still unsticking when Eda opened the back door and told them their father was dying.

❧

Their father was propped up on a pile of pillows in his four-poster bed, his head and neck sticking out from a mound of flannel blankets. To Nora, he did not appear any closer to dying than he had been that morning. But he was more frantic than she'd seen him in a long time. "Come here, come close," he said to them. "You're wasting time we haven't got. Where's Charlie?"

Nora stood behind Percy in the doorway, her fear of dis-obeying her father edged out very slightly by her fear of moving closer to him. She was certain that somehow he would know about the wad of trespassers in her pocket.

"He's probably in the study, Daddy," said Eda, fidgeting with the pillows on the bed.

"Well, get him!" he said. "Someone."

Nora and Percy exchanged a look, neither of them eager to fetch Charlie. Their silent negotiation ended only when Eda brushed past them with a heavy sigh to do it herself. Nora and Percy stayed where they were, Nora sticking her gaze to the crooked little wedge of hair between Percy's ear and his neck, the mushrooms heavy and portentous in her pocket. Percy was shaking slightly, a full-body tremor that Nora noticed by the way the edge of the doorframe kept vanishing and reappearing behind his ear. She wished he wouldn't try to tell their father things. His voice had just begun to crack loose from his throat when the sound of Charlie's stumbling, uneven stride thudded on the staircase, and then they were flushed into the bedroom as Eda came through with Charlie leaning on her. Awkwardly they shifted back and forth as Eda struggled underneath him. He said, under his breath, "Please, just let go," and she said, "You'll *fall*," and he said, "It's *fine*," and at last she deposited him in a heap on the chest at the foot of the bed, where he sat with a dismayed look on his face, closing his eyes as if he could shut out hurt that way.

Eda threw a quick, guilty glance back at him before she returned to fidgeting with their father's covers, peeling back the blankets that she had just tucked in to put on his slippers. In the dark well of the blankets, their father's sock feet were strangely small and soft and vulnerable, and Nora had the feeling that she should look away, but she didn't, because it would have been too conspicuous, it would only have shamed him more, so they all three endured silently as Eda tried without success to wedge a slipper onto their father's right heel.

"Stop that," their father said, suddenly losing patience, striking at her with his socked foot. Eda flinched backward, chastened, and she held her crouched pose at the bedside as he began to speak, even though there was an unoccupied chair right behind her.

"Now, listen to me," he said. "Things are coming to their natural conclusion. You've got to get Wenna back before the time comes for the exchange."

No one spoke for a long moment. Nora could not remember the last time anyone had spoken Wenna's name aloud.

"Wenna?" Eda broke the silence. "You want Wenna here?"

"Yes," said their father. "All of you must be here."

"I . . . don't know if Wenna will come," Eda said. Sometime

in the past few months, she had begun to speak to their father in the same slow, measured way that she sometimes spoke to Nora, as if they were both wild animals that she had to soothe—but dangerous ones, so that all the time in her voice there was a hint of fear. "She hasn't spoken to us in . . . ten years? Does she even know that you're sick?"

"Wenna will come if she is told," said their father, unperturbed. "She knows her responsibilities."

Nora watched Eda to see what she would say to this, but Eda was staring past her at Charlie, her eyes beseeching him to say something. Charlie, as usual, kept quiet.

"You don't have long," said their father. "Have her here. Have everything prepared. Please." He shut his eyes and seemed, for a while, to hold his breath. It was like seeing how he would look when he was dead, Nora thought, and then she was ashamed of thinking it, as if thinking it could make it happen.

"All right," he said when he came back from inside himself. "That's it. Except: Eleanor, would you get my things from the desk? I would like to write a little."

Nora was startled and yet almost breathlessly pleased to be asked. Her father had never wanted her help with his memoirs before. He only ever asked Percy, supposedly because the dictation of the memoirs was part of Percy's ongoing education but in actuality—they all knew, even Charlie, who would always pretend he didn't—because Percy was the only one of them their father ever wanted to depend on. Nora was not, admittedly, interested in her father's memoirs. The contents had already been thrust upon her—and all of them—in the form of long and meandering story-lectures since before she was old enough to understand them. But she *was* interested in being chosen for something. Her pleasure was shadowed only slightly by the trespassers in her pocket, which seemed all the time to threaten to slip out onto the floor.

She could see from the look on Percy's face that he was hurt and even angry at being snubbed, but he knew better than to say so. He muttered something indistinct and slunk out of the room. Nora followed him out the door, wanting to say that she was sorry, that she hadn't *asked* to be asked, and she didn't even know why her father had chosen her, but he was down the stairs before her foot even landed on the first step.

From their father's study, she retrieved the heavy goatskin volume that she had never before been permitted to touch, checking to ensure her fingernails were clean first. When she returned to her father's bedroom, only Eda was still there. "Can't I please make you something to eat, Dad?" she was saying. "I think you'd feel better."

He didn't answer her. "Eleanor, my littlest girl," he said, looking to the doorway. "Eda, let her have the chair. You needn't be here for this."

Under the heat of Eda's glare, Nora crossed the room and lowered herself into the chair at the bedside. She cracked the spine of the goatskin book and luxuriated in the soft, gluey scent of the paper. Her father, she knew, had bound the book himself. The cover was sewn from the skins of their family's goats. Nora uncapped the pen that she'd taken from the study and held it above the first empty page, waiting. Her father had his eyes shut again.

He was silent for so long that she was afraid he was asleep, then that he was dead, but at last he unsealed his cracked lips and said, softly, "Get out the slip of paper in the front of the book."

Nora did as she was told, flipping back through masses of heavy, ink-stained pages filled with dense columns of Percy's handwriting until she reached the front of the book. She unfolded the paper. *Everything to Charles*, it said, followed by her father's signature, written in an articulate script that she knew his fingers couldn't manage anymore. The paper felt brittle between her fingers. She didn't know what she had been expecting to find, but not this.

"You found it?" he said. His eyes were still closed.

She nodded, then realized he couldn't see her and whispered her *yes*.

"Destroy it."

"You . . . want me to rip it?" she said.

"I want you to *destroy* it. Entirely."

Nora had the fleeting impulse to call Eda into the room. Sometimes, since he'd gotten sick, their father held whole conversations in a kind of trance, speaking meanderingly and too slow, making requests that bewildered his waking self. "I didn't want this," he'd say with disgust, even a tinge of fear, to the bowl of soup or hot water bottle laid out before him, as if they had materialized from nothing. If Eda heard their father asking her to tear the will up, Nora wouldn't be in trouble—at least not with Eda, who was the one that really mattered, lately—when he forgot he'd done it later. But their father had sent Eda away, and Nora decided that she was more afraid of her father's certain wrath now than his possible wrath later. Slowly, so that he had time to stop her if he changed his mind, she tore the sheet of paper lengthwise. Her father waited, his head cocked slightly to the side as if he were listening, until she tore the paper once more.

"I want that burned," he said. "Don't bury it. Now, tear out a new sheet of paper. Do you have it? Good. Write, *Everything to the eldest living son.*"

Nora got a feeling like a cold heavy thing lowering itself down onto her chest. Who was the eldest living son if it was not Charlie? "Why?" she said, before she could stop herself.

"Because," her father said, and he sounded sad now, "I am not certain what will happen."

"To Charlie, you mean?" she whispered.

Her father stiffened. He opened an eye. "We don't have time to waste. Write it out. *The eldest living son.* As I said."

Nora scratched the words out, wondering as she wrote if she should change her handwriting so no one would know for certain that it was her. They would figure it out anyway, she thought, and they would blame her once they did, and she again wished that Eda was in the room. "Should I—sign for you?" she said when she was finished.

"Should you sign for me?" her father mimicked, contemptuous now, making Nora startle. "Hand it here. Hurry up now."

His fingers were already trembling even without anything in his grasp. Gently, Nora set the volume in her father's lap, settling the pen into the crook of his hand. His hand clenched and then slackened against the pen. It slid down into his fist so that he held it like a child as he began, with painstaking effort, to etch the letters of his name. He was not yet finished when his fist loosened and the pen fell; he gasped for breath as if he had climbed a steep incline.

Nora held still with her hand suspended above the book and the fallen pen, unsure whether he wanted her to finish. Her father's entire body was shaking.

"Thank you," he breathed, with something like relief. Then,

as if he had never been cruel to her at all, he said, tenderly, "Eleanor, my littlest girl. You'll write to your sister, won't you? I want you to be the one to sign the letter. She'll come back for you. You know, she wanted to take you with her. She loved you most."

There was nothing he could have said that would have surprised her more. She wanted desperately to ask how he knew, and why Wenna hadn't taken her, if she'd wanted to, but Nora knew her father wouldn't answer. "If you want me to," she stammered.

"Good," he said. "All of you must be here."

❧

Even though everyone acted as if they didn't know where Wenna was, they had her mailing address. Every year, she sent a Christmas card—heedless of the fact that the Haddesleys had never celebrated Christmas—with an impersonal and unsigned message that could have come from anyone. She stamped her name and return address plainly on the envelope. Eda always opened the cards and left them in the kitchen for a week as if letting them air out, then tucked them back inside their envelopes and deposited them in a cardboard box in the attic with all the other remaining evidence of Wenna's existence. That night, Eda extracted the latest one from the *Wenna* box and brought it downstairs. They met in the dim foyer beneath the west-wing staircase, speaking in whispers by unspoken consensus, furtive and urgent as if they were making mischief. What they were doing was not even a secret, but Nora liked how it felt to be huddled around the piano bench they were using as a makeshift table, Percy on one side of her and Eda on the other and Charlie standing at her shoulder, the four of them bent toward the same purpose. They were never together like this, not lately.

Eda sighed. "Let's get this over with," she said, picking up a pen. Nora almost let her do it. Eda hated to not be in charge of things. But the letter was too important to be sullied by Eda's spelling errors or her long-simmering anger with Wenna.

"Dad said I'm supposed to write it," Nora said, almost in a whisper.

Eda's eyes narrowed. "You? Why?"

"Because Wenna liked her best," said Percy, before Nora could answer. "And Dad thinks it'll get Wenna to come back."

Nora was pleased to hear that Percy thought Wenna liked her best, although she didn't like the way Percy said it, as if it were embarrassing or even treacherous. "That *is* what Dad said," she admitted.

Eda opened her mouth to protest but changed her mind. She slid the sheet of paper across the bench to Nora. "You write, then," she said.

Nora took up the pen. "Should I write *dear*?" she said, her hand hovering above the empty page.

Percy snorted. "I don't think we're dear to her."

"But she's dear to us. Right?" Nora looked to Charlie, but he only worked his mouth, unsuggestively. No one would concede that Wenna was dear to them. Nora had already etched the first line of the capital *D*, but, with a decisive motion, she sutured the stroke into the first curve of a *W*.

"Please come home," she narrated. "Does that sound stupid?"

"I mean," said Percy, "it's not really *her* home anymore. Is it?"

"'Come home' is fine," said Eda, impatiently.

Nora glanced again at Charlie. He nodded, leaning his weight back and forth on his cane, inclining himself longingly toward the hallway.

"Dad is dying," she said, and the pronouncement of the words wrenched something out of her. She rubbed her bleary eyes with her palm. "What if he's actually not?" she said.

"He is," Eda said.

"But if we carry him down too early, what would happen?"

"We won't do that," said Eda. "We'll know when it's time."

Percy was nodding in agreement.

"Dad is dying," Nora conceded. She went on: "We need you for the buriel rites."

"It's *burial*, with an *a*," said Percy.

"It's not."

"It is," said Charlie, reluctantly.

Nora hated being corrected, but she held back her frustration because she knew if she complained they would leave her to write the letter alone. She scratched out the word *buriel* and then the entire sentence and began again. The flat of her left hand smudged the crossed-out words into a blur as she maneuvered painstakingly across the paper. "He says, please come as soon as you can," she finished. "Is that spelled right? Is that good enough?" She did not know how to plead with the Wenna that Wenna would have become in ten years. She did not know what that Wenna wanted or believed or loved. She wondered if Wenna still loved her best, or at all.

Eda looked at the ceiling. "She's not going to come because you convinced her, Nor," she said wearily. "She's going to come because she knows there won't be a bog-wife for Charlie if she doesn't."

"*I know*," said Nora, although she didn't think that was true, because if it had been, her father wouldn't have been so particular about asking her to write.

That night, Nora stayed downstairs until everyone else went to bed, reading an old issue of *National Enquirer*—the cover story was a state senator's secret conjoined twin, a tiny scowling figure that was said to cast votes for him sometimes and appeared, from some angles at least, to be a shadow on his suit jacket; it was not a particular favorite, but that was the only issue she could find downstairs—and fidgeting with the trespassers in her pocket until they were shredded into waxy little crumbs. When she was satisfied that she was the only one awake, she crept out the back door and emptied the contents of her pocket into the palm of her hand and hid the trespassers underneath the back step, where they could not be traced back to her.

PERCY

Percy couldn't think about anything else but the orange trespassers in the swale. The headless sprouts were not like the other trespassers that had come before them: not the bull thistle that threaded the property-line, fast-growing and inexhaustible but so shallow-rooted that you could yank it out like hair; nor the out-of-place maples that sprouted close to the bog's mouth, doomed from birth because the earth was too wet to anchor them there; nor like the little flowers that impersonated sedge until their buds opened, revealing blossoms pink and sun-hungry and unembarrassed that made them easy marks (and satisfying) for culling. The orange sprouts had not disguised themselves, but they had met him with a sinister indifference when he tore at them. *Tear me out*, they seemed to say. *You won't get the heart of me. That's somewhere you can't reach.* He had clawed at the earth beneath the ripped-out stems but realized quickly that there were no roots to be found—at least, not roots that he could see. The trespassers seemed to have sprouted from nowhere, to have succumbed so easily that they must not have succumbed at all, and the whole swale felt compromised by their presence.

He searched for them in the *Field Guide to Flora of the Highland Fens*, holding a handful of leathery stems against the brittle pages, but he knew already that he would not find them there and he was right. There was nothing orange-colored in the guide. He suspected from the start that they were a variety of mushroom, but he wished that he'd seen their heads. He had an unaccountable suspicion that the trespassers had devised some way of getting rid of their identifying heads, like a salamander might shed its tail to make a quick escape. If he'd only seen the heads, he might have been able to figure out conclusively what they were. He would have known the depth of the crisis that lay before them.

After three days, not knowing what else to do, he brought the stems to his father.

Charles Haddesley the Eleventh was a small man, inches shorter than Percy, his shoulders even narrower than Charlie's always-hunched shoulders. Sitting upright in the enormous mahogany four-poster bed that had slept all the American Haddesley patriarchs, he looked even smaller. For a long time before he entered, Percy stood in the hallway looking at his father through the crack in the door, trying to rearrange the small gaunt man back into the patriarch. He had spent his whole life learning a version of his father that was gone, and he didn't know how to behave around the man that his father was now. His father used to slam his fists on the dining room table for emphasis when he told stories. His father used to sing ballads in a thunderous voice, pronouncing the ends of the lines as if he were angry at them. His father used to wring the necks of chickens in one deft motion. His father used to pace the lengths of rooms until he wore down the carpet because stillness bored him. Now his father sat staring at the floor to the side of his bed with a look of helplessness and bewilderment. For such a long time, he only stared. Then, as if he sensed Percy was there, his head lifted and his gaze sharpened and he was Charles Haddesley the Eleventh again, and Percy pushed open the bedroom door with the trespasser's stems limp in his clammy fist.

"Percival," his father said, companionably. "Sit down."

Percy sat down.

"Look me in the eye," said his father, and Percy did, forcing himself to keep his stare flat and focused. His father had the Haddesley eyes, green-gray, a point of hereditary pride underlined by the portraits hanging on the walls in which every Haddesley patriarch appeared with the same pond-colored irises. Of the five of them, only Wenna had inherited those eyes, which was ironic because Wenna had decided not to be a Haddesley.

His father's eyes watered, but he did not blink. "That's the difference," he said, after an indeterminate length of time had passed, with the air of someone continuing an ongoing conversation, "between you and Charlie."

Percy let his eyes wander to the door, feeling uncomfortably implicated in whatever crushing and unfair and probably true thing his father was about to say loudly enough for anyone in the hallway to hear, but also longing for his father to go on. A small and spiteful part of him liked hearing that he held up to his father's scrutiny better than Charlie. The trespassers, he decided, could wait a little while longer.

"Charlie," his father went on, "will never look at you. Always hanging his head as if he's just been caught abusing himself in the bushes. Well—not that he could, now. But you, son, you know how to look a man in the face and dare him to look back."

Percy squeezed the life from the stems of the trespassers, agonized and pleased. There was nothing he could say back that was not either an outright betrayal of Charlie or a rejection of his father. "Thanks, Dad."

"You do," his father said, with a vigorous nod. "You do, I see you. Listen to me, Percival. You need to end your brother's life."

Percy thought he must have misheard. He held still, waiting for his ears to untangle his father's words into something other than what they had been. "You want . . . ," he began, when he could not untangle them.

"It need not be violent," his father admonished, as if Percy had said that he intended to bash Charlie's skull in. "It's not about punishing him. It's about what has to be done for the good of the family, the family and the land."

Percy nodded, because his father liked to know they were paying attention when he spoke to them and was prone to speaking with more and more force and volume until he got some kind of indication that he had an engaged audience. It had been a mistake not to close the door when he entered the room. At any moment Eda would come with their father's breakfast or Nora would come looking for him and they would be overheard. At least, he consoled himself, Charlie still could not easily manage the stairs.

"I always had reservations." His father's eyes grew distant, and he no longer seemed to be addressing Percy. "From the first. But maybe he would have been all right, if not for—well. You know."

Percy did know. His father did not need to say that a hemlock tree had fallen like a hundred-foot-long inarguable articulation of the bog's displeasure onto Charlie's firstborn pelvis. "Yes," he mumbled, because he didn't want to say it either.

His father scrunched up his face. "Speak up, Percival."

"I said, *yes*," Percy repeated, feeling as conspicuous and clumsy as a child.

"Well, good," said his father, prickly now. Everyone, including probably their father himself, knew his hearing had faded.

But he wouldn't admit it, so instead he accused them of whispering or pretended he didn't care what they'd said in the first place. "You must act quickly," he went on, regaining mastery of the conversation. "What we don't want is to confuse the bog about who is inheriting."

"You want *me* to marry the bog-wife?"

His father sneered. "What did you think I was saying? Yes. Someone has to." His sneer loosened. He looked weary then, reduced. His lips trembled. "The line," he whispered, "cannot be allowed to lapse."

Percy looked again to the door. Perhaps Charlie and his father had decided to test him, to see what treachery he might be capable of. If he said *yes,* Charlie would appear in the hallway bearing one of the gaudy rusted-out broadswords that hung on the wall in the great room downstairs and challenge him to a duel as if they were in one of those chivalric romances that Nora read. This was no more inconceivable than the idea that Percy could just step into his brother's place as if he and not Charlie were the firstborn son. He could not really let himself imagine what it would be like to usurp his brother's role, because both his fear and his longing became unbearable when he did. Hesitantly, he said, "Couldn't I . . . do it . . . without, *you know* . . ."

"Don't you think I would have said so?" his father snipped. "It gives me no pleasure to ask such a thing of you. But there has never been any case of a younger son inheriting while the elder lives. It would be a betrayal of the compact."

Percy was quiet for a long moment that was made endlessly longer by the way his father's eyes held him. What his father was asking him felt unthinkable. He had never even casually tussled with his brother, much less raised a hand to him with any kind of serious intent. He never needed to. Charlie did not compete for things. He either got them by default or relinquished them without resistance. He imagined, grotesquely, his brother receiving a fatal blow with arms hanging limply at his sides, the expression on his face one of glum resignation.

"Percival," his father said, when he did not answer. "Tell me that you understand."

Percy did not understand, but understanding had never once in his life been a prerequisite to obeying his father. He leaned closer so he could speak under his breath and still be heard. "How would I . . . do it?"

"Well, that's up to you," his father said airily, as if the subject was not an interesting one to him. "You're stronger than he is, you know, especially now. But if it were me, I would use poison."

"Wouldn't everyone know?" He imagined Charlie expiring over a bowl of cowbane-laced SpaghettiOs as Eda and Nora sat on either side of him. The expressions on their faces. Wenna arriving a few days later, asking incredulously, *what* did you say happened to him?

"They may realize," his father said. "But they are daughters. These are not burdens for them to shoulder." He looked sternly at Percy. "Don't tell me that you won't be able to manage your household, once it is *your* household."

"I can," Percy said, although really it did not seem possible that any of the five of them other than Eda would ever manage the household. Right now, he could not even get his sister to let him put peanut butter on the grocery list. "I *will*," he added.

His father did not look confident, but he seemed to have tired of the conversation. "Good," he said. "Now, what did you want?"

The problem of the trespassers in the swale felt dwarfed and silly now, but it also took on new significance. If Percy—not Charlie—was going to be the patriarch, he needed to know how to manage the land. He could not let terror of his father's disappointment get in the way of his obligations.

"I found something in the swale," Percy said. He held out the stems for his father to see. His heartbeat thumped in the heel of his hand beneath the trespassers.

His father shifted so he was propped more securely on his mountain of pillows and leaned closer to Percy's outstretched hand. "Hm," he said, after a while.

Percy swallowed his impatient *what?* His father did not like to be hurried, especially now that he moved so slowly.

His father craned his neck to see closer, and then abruptly he pushed Percy's hand back. "Flood the swale," he said.

"That's it?" Percy failed to hide his dismay. The whole reason he brought the trespassers to his father was because he thought it was dangerous to let water flow through the swale to the bog's mouth if some hidden fragments of the trespassers might be carried along with the current. Besides which, he had measured the depth of the bog's mouth, and it was not yet low enough to be flooded.

"What else?" his father said.

"Well—what are they?"

A look of unease crossed his father's face. For an excruciatingly long time, he didn't answer, and Percy couldn't tell if he didn't know the answer to Percy's question or if he didn't even remember what Percy had asked him. Then, scratching at the ceiling of his thin sickbed voice, he said, "Just flood the swale!"

"Yes. I will." Compared with the other demand his father

had made of him, it was easy, eminently feasible. It cost him nothing to comply. But when he returned to the bog, he found a row of trespassers sprouting where the swale met the hinged door to the Cranberry River. These trespassers retained their heads, and Percy knew as soon as he saw them that his suspicions were correct; they were mushrooms. His heart sank. He sometimes saw mushrooms in the sparse forest on the west end of the property, modest white-headed clumps strewn across the soil or fringed gray dishes sticking out like frills from the trunks of trees. But he had never seen any of their ilk here, where the soil was not mushroom soil because it was *bog* soil, a dense wet batter that supported only the shallow-rooted and perpetually thirsty.

They should never have tolerated any of the mushrooms, Percy thought. The mushrooms had all been trespassers. He tore out the orange mushrooms and gathered up the torn stems for burning, but he knew it wouldn't make a difference. Mushrooms could not be dug up. They could not be evicted. He wondered if his father had known and had not wanted to admit to him the hopelessness of their situation.

For a while he stood over the swale, paralyzed by indecision, feeling that what he did now would prove whether he was really fit to be patriarch. He should have been able to take command of the land. Or he should at least have been able to confidently obey his father. Instead, he yanked the lever that held closed the door between the river and the swale as if it were his only recourse, feeling a sense of resignation.

As soon as the door lifted, water rushed out of the Cranberry River and bounded down the swale, twisting in the narrow furrow, lapping at its edges, white-tipped and propulsive.

Percy stood with his hand on the lever, watching the water flow. He counted to sixty, like his father had taught him. When a minute's worth of water had entered the swale, he took his hand off the lever. But the door stuck halfway open. Water broke violently on the iron plate and then dug underneath it. The flow into the swale persisted. Too much water was hitting the bog's mouth, all of it possibly contaminated, and yet Percy stood frozen for precious seconds before he leapt into the swale, heavy clods of wet earth following him down, and pushed the door down with as much force as he could muster.

The door shuddered beneath him but did not budge. Water rushed furiously at him, through him, swirled at his waist and between his legs. "Hey!" Percy cried, though he knew no one would hear. Even if they had heard, they would not have come. No one else felt responsible. He leaned his whole weight into the door and hated his father and Eda and Nora and *especially* Charlie, who made everyone feel sorry for him even as he dodged the burdens that were his birthright, who sat complacently with a dour look on his face inside the house all day and did not offer to pick up the chores that had been Percy's even though Percy had now picked up all the chores that had been Charlie's.

Seconds or minutes or hours passed before he accepted that the door was not going to close. He scrambled out of the flooded swale and began gathering up sticks and undergrowth, breaking off alder and rhododendron branches, kicking down loose earth. It was punishing work, slow at first, the river water rushing defiantly through and even ferrying along the sticks that were supposed to be forming a dam. But eventually the flow was arrested, only thin rivulets of water seeping through. The swale slowly emptied.

With dread knotting his stomach, Percy followed the swale's winding path to the bog's mouth. Water rose above the toes of his waders. As he feared, the bog meadow had become a shallow pond. The bog's mouth gaped open, flooded more in minutes than it had in successive days of heavy rain.

Percy stood in the flooded-out bog, feeling the ground dissolve beneath his feet. He twisted the trespassers in his pocket as if the punishment he inflicted on their limp bodies could do anything to rescue the bog from the trespassers' infinite laying-down of roots. Then he went back toward the house. From their paddock, the goats fixed him with twin pitiless stares as he lit a match and burned the trespassers in the bald circle of land reserved for the purpose. He held his breath so their smoke would not enter him. His fingers black with ash and his clothes still soaked with river water, he went inside. Charlie sat at the table, fidgeting with a spoon and an empty bowl of oatmeal, and pretended not to have watched him.

"You need help out there?" he said emptily, not looking at Percy.

"I handled it." Only for a moment, Percy thought, *I could kill him.*

CHARLIE

I n the first weeks of his father's illness, when no one yet knew he was dying but the idea that he would one day die became real, Charlie spent hours walking the bog meadow, thinking incessantly and with some terror of the woman that would one day emerge from the peat to marry him. In his head, he played through the stages of the exchange as his father had explained them. His father would be buried. The next morning, Charlie would rise before the sun and go to the bog's mouth, carrying with him the dowsing stick that hung on the wall in the study above the desk. He would wash himself in the peat of his father's burial ground until he was covered from head to foot. He would rise from the bog and close his eyes and follow the pull of the dowsing stick, and it would lead him to his bride. When he found her, he must spit onto her mouth to unseal her lips.

("Ew," Charlie had said at five or six years old, hearing this for the first time, not understanding that he was not allowed to say *ew* to the sacred.)

Then, his father said, he and his new wife would lie down together and consummate their marriage. He always used this word, *consummate*, and only this word, and so until Charlie was well into adolescence—long after he had grasped what the goats in the yard were doing to produce more goats, and even after he'd grasped that he and his wife would have to do essentially the same thing to produce more Haddesleys—Charlie thought that to consummate a marriage was to lie side by side, possibly holding hands, and that the act of lying outdoors, with ritual solemnity, was the thing that joined two people inexorably together. He carried this innocent assumption through so many explanations of the wedding rites that he was shocked and vaguely repulsed when his father at some point exchanged the word *copulation* for *consummation* and seemed not even to notice.

"You mean, we have to . . . do that," he clarified, anxiously, "outside? When we've just met each other?"

His father's expression took on a familiar weariness. Charlie was too stupid to be the Haddesley patriarch, that expression said: he didn't hold the spade at the right angle when he cut peat, no matter how many times he was shown, or he didn't ever get the hang of reading old French, or he couldn't make Wenna and Percy and Nora listen to him, or he was in some other way completely insufficient. "Yes," his father said, lips sealed around his teeth as if he were holding his contempt inside his mouth. "Otherwise, you will not be married in the eyes of the bog. The exchange will be unfinished. Did you never understand that?"

What else, Charlie wondered, was he not understanding? He could tell by the look on his father's face that his father was thinking the same thing. Most of the time, he tried not to think of the bog-wife, or his future marriage, at all. Only in those first weeks of his father's sickness did he begin to consider her as something real, not a talisman on whom the vague gestures of ritual were performed but a living person who would want coffee or not in the morning, who would brush her teeth over the basin that was only his for now, who would have to cut her toenails. Who would know him, and look at him, and think something about him.

He tried to imagine teaching the bog-wife to speak, her inert gray tongue—the only bodily evidence of her origins that would outlast the marriage rite, as he knew from his own mother—forming English consonants with a lingering uneasiness. He tried to imagine the words she would say to him. Would she say that she loved him? Would she say that she found him hideous, or boring, or stupid? He tried to envision her saying ordinary things, like, *We have to plant the tomatoes*, objecting when he pointed out there might be another frost still. *I know better*, she would insist, and she would be right; how could she not be right about something like that, having been herself hewn from water and earth? But he would resent that she spoke with such authority when he had tended the garden all his life and she'd barely had any life to speak of. He would even momentarily regret teaching her to speak.

What Charlie realized was that when he got anywhere past toe-deep into fantasies of married life, he could only ever imagine conversations and fights his own parents had already had. He could only ever imagine the bog-wife as a warped version of his mother. And he himself always melted slowly and inexorably into a shadow of his own father, volatile and mean and prone to making pronouncements about the needs of the bog even when speaking to someone who had once been part of it. And so the prospect of his marriage to the bog-wife began to feel, in some sense, like another kind of exchange than the one it was supposed to be: not an exchange in which Charlie's father died so his wife could be born, but one in which Charlie evacuated his own body and his father filled it.

❧

33

When the hemlock tree fell, it was Eda who found Charlie pinned beneath the muscular black trunk. But she screamed and then everyone came to help him, Percy, Nora, and his father lifting the hemlock while Eda pulled him out from underneath. Together they brought him down the stairs and laid him out on the kitchen floor, their movements coordinated as if the extraction of the eldest son from a felled tree was an old Haddesley ritual they'd all known about and only Charlie had forgotten. He fell through hideous dreams while Eda and his father, blurs in his periphery, uttered the words *internal bleeding,* the words *organ rupture,* the words *fractured pelvis.* They cut him out of his sodden clothes as his father said, *He'll never . . . not in this state.* Someone, maybe Eda, began to cry.

When he woke again, he was not in the kitchen anymore but on a mattress in the study, his grandfather glowering down at him from a gilt-framed portrait. Eda came into the room with a cup of chamomile tea and a bottle of expired cough syrup, which she acknowledged would do nothing for the pain but would hopefully put him to sleep if swallowed in great-enough quantities. She had already been dosing their father, occasionally, with the same. Charlie nodded limply and uncomprehendingly. He washed the aftertaste of the cough syrup out of his mouth with a tongue-burning swallow of tea. In his periphery, he kept seeing the hemlock tree bursting through the roof and careening toward him, although he had not seen the hemlock when it fell. He had been asleep.

Two days passed before he realized it was not only his pelvis that had been shattered in the accident.

The loss sat soundlessly in the room with him, looming and improbable and yet *there* in the shocks of pain that blossomed from his groin whenever he shifted. He feared he could no longer father children. The entire point of him was to father children.

He was afraid to face his family, but in the weeks of his convalescence, Eda was the only one who visited with any regularity, carrying trays of the bland food and weak tea that she learned to make up for their father, staying a while after he ate but saying nothing, not even that he would be all right. Sometimes she would open and close the curtains at random, as if to have something to do. She changed his bedpan until he was strong enough to get up from the mattress and empty his bowels in a chamber pot. In her care, he felt wretched and small and geriatric. But when she left him, he was alone. Nora and Percy came to see him rarely, always with slouchy, bored reluctance, and their father was entirely absent from his constricted sickbed-universe. In moments, sunk in a haze of medicine or pain, Charlie thought that possibly his father had died and everyone forgot to tell him that he was now the patriarch.

When at last his father did materialize, it was the middle of the day and Charlie was lying prone on his mattress, dozing with the sludgy indifference of someone who never really had to be awake if he didn't want to. Charles Haddesley entered the study without knocking, without speaking to Charlie, and began rifling through the papers on the desk as if no one else were in the room. Charlie felt rather than saw his presence. He was confused at first, because in all his dreamed-of renderings of his first reunion with his father, his father always came to the study specifically to see him. Now it seemed that his father had not intended to see him at all but merely happened to be in the room with him.

"Dad," he said, after the shuffling noises persisted for a while. He heard, and hated, the tremor in his voice, the nakedness of his hunger and need.

His father retrieved whatever he'd been searching for and crossed the room slowly to Charlie. He stood at the head of the mattress. For a long time, he stayed there. Then, without uttering a word, he left the room.

WENNA

The man in the seat to Wenna's left was a talker. He twisted his hands restlessly in his lap and swung his feet. The length of the journey, the dark indistinguishable quality of the landscape out the window, seemed unbearable to him. He was not deterred by the hood that she pulled up around her face, nor by her whispered suggestion that it was the middle of the night and other passengers might be sleeping. Though, in truth, most of the seats were empty and the few passengers looked resigned to their fate. After Pittsburgh, the Greyhound became a changed beast, a kind of purgatory for the unlucky souls heading to the same place as Wenna. The man asked if Wenna had ever gone to the Pocahontas County Fair, because that was still going on for another week. He asked if she was looking forward to the fall colors that would be coming in soon. He asked if she happened to be a Baptist, then apologized for such a personal question, then chased the apology with a slanted look and a hesitating, "Well, *but . . .*"

She considered confessing to her last name to see if it would silence him. If her father was to be believed, the Haddesleys were still the terror of Marlinton, lurid and exaggerated stories of their hereditary monstrosity a lasting mainstay of local lore. But it seemed doubtful to Wenna now that anyone in Marlinton had ever been so preoccupied with a house of recluses; and even if they had, she suspected that by now the Haddesley name would not evoke fear but only curiosity, the vague memory of a campfire story, and that admitting to her identity would only make the man more interested.

"I'm not Baptist," Wenna said, and she dropped her head back and shut her eyes.

Soundlessly, her lips barely moving, she counted to five and then back, repeating the exercises that Alyson, her therapist, had instructed her to do to steady her pulse. She loosened her muscles and deepened her breathing. Wenna tried to contain inside her body everything she felt, Alyson said, but her body could not hold all of it.

"You all right, ma'am?" The man prodded her with an elbow. "You having some kind of panic attack?"

"I'm all right." Wenna opened an eye to find him unbearably, unaccountably close to her face. "Just trying to get a little sleep."

"It's only two hours yet," he said. "Don't think I'll sleep a wink. I've been away from home for almost eight years now. Don't even know what it'll look like. I heard Marlinton's got a Walmart now. Kmart's gone but Walmart's there. Don't know if that's a trade-up or not, but it means something, I think. Did you say you grew up in Marlinton?"

"Outside town," Wenna said reluctantly. With every answer that she volunteered, she felt more complicit in her own badgering; another person, she felt sure, would have shut him up immediately, gotten to her feet even as the bus barreled down the interstate and extricated herself from the entire situation. Her husband, Michael, always said she didn't speak up for herself.

"Whereabouts?" the man said. "Got a school friend who they bussed in from Williams unincorporated area. You out there?"

"Close to there," Wenna said, although she had no idea where

Williams was. She had only been to Marlinton itself once, on her way out of West Virginia.

"Got a lot of family still there?"

"Some," she conceded. More conspicuous, she thought, to pretend that there was any other reason for her to be in the area.

"Hey, why don't you shut it?" a woman in the row behind them interjected. "She doesn't want to talk to you."

Wenna, half-embarrassed and half-relieved, threw a thankful glance over her shoulder at the woman, who had the sleeve of her sweater over her eyes and seemed uninterested in commiserating. Cowed, the man slumped to the side and pressed his forehead to the dirty glass of the window. Wenna pretended to sleep. She too was restless, although she could not have said she was excited. She had practiced the line, "I am going home for a funeral," but she had not once used it and now she thought she probably wouldn't need to.

When they came to the Greyhound station in Marlinton, the sun was rising. Wenna permitted herself to look once at her phone and see that there were no calls, no texts. Her head swimming from sleeplessness, she stepped down into the town that she had only ever seen by moonlight, in the furtive few minutes that she had passed before the bus arrived at the station. In daylight, no longer a fugitive, she was startled by how small it really was. The main drag was a quarter-mile string of mostly shuttered storefronts. A hardware store and coffee shop persisted. Fourth of July bunting still hung from light posts, although it was late August. Wenna stood for a moment in the middle of the sidewalk, trying to remember if she was early. The correspondence with her brother had been short and fragmentary; Charlie could access email only by going into the Marlinton

Public Library, and he seemed not to go very often. But when she forwarded her ticket reservation to him, he said he would be there, and she had never once known Charlie to say something that he did not mean.

It was not ten minutes—two glances at her phone, almost a third—before Wenna saw the battered fawn-colored station wagon of her childhood bumping down the roadway toward the bus station. She was not surprised that they'd kept the car, but she was a little surprised that it still worked. Charlie pulled the station wagon to the curb, and she opened the door, slid onto the atrophying leather bench.

"Welcome home," Charlie said tonelessly, and he seemed to try to smile. Wenna tried without success to smile back. She was dismayed by his appearance. In ten years, her brother had become hunched and gaunt. His limbs were thin, but a belly protruded from beneath a worn flannel button-down that she recognized as their father's. He sounded vaguely congested. He kept the radio on at a low volume as he drove, tuned to some inflammatory talk show that she doubted he really listened to. The New England accents of the pundits rattled monotonously above the sound of the car's struggling engine.

"How is everyone doing?" Wenna overcame her instinct toward politeness enough to punch the radio off. "You know, I mean, considering."

"They're okay," Charlie said, after a solid minute of deliberation. As the mist thickened ahead of them, he flicked the car's headlights on; only one lit. "Nora's excited to see you," he added.

She was almost amused he didn't pretend anyone else was excited. "And you?"

Charlie seemed blindsided by the question. He deliberated

again. Outside, the mist shrank the world beyond the confines of the station wagon to a narrow strip of road and new-growth forest; they were, all at once, in a world isolated even from Marlinton. "It's good that you're here," he said, which was not, Wenna thought, really an answer to her question. "Dad was worried that you wouldn't come."

In fact, she had been determined not to come. When Nora's note arrived, she read it with alternating currents of anger and pity, thinking that Alyson would say the note was an effort to draw her back into unhealthy old patterns by people who had never gotten out of them. Still, the accusation bristled.

She changed the subject. "Are you excited? To meet your wife?"

Charlie let the stupid irrelevance of the question hang in the air for a moment before he turned the radio back on. The exchange of hostile voices carried them from the foothills to the raised lip of bogland where the Haddesleys lived. At some point, Wenna's phone lost signal.

s

Before her return, Wenna thought many times about what it would be like to see her family again and a few times, with half-guilty yearning, of how it would feel to see the land where she had grown up, but she had not considered how it would feel for the land to see *her*, and now she thought that was what she should really have been worried about. The bog looked eyelessly; it felt knowing. The white pines and maples, leaning on their above-ground roots, seemed to incline their heads toward the car.

Michael would have said she was *anthropomorphizing* the plants. The first time he used that word, she asked him what it meant. He shrugged. It was a word he'd learned in school. *Acting like things that aren't human have human intentions*, he said. *Everyone learns that?* Wenna asked. *In school?* She'd tried, after that, to see the vacancy in everything, but she felt now that Michael was wrong. The bog was not vacant. It had presence and intelligence, and, she realized, it had changed while she was gone in ways barely perceptible and too subtle to name. Were the trees farther apart? Were they taller? Had the moss on the trunks thinned some?

When the car rounded the driveway's final corner and the house came into view, Wenna drew in a breath. The Haddesley manor was a massive old heap of stone that had been crumpling for longer than Wenna had been alive, but now almost the whole west wing was collapsed. The trunk of an enormous tree stuck through the roof and impinged on the front second-story windows. The east wing was intact, but just barely. The entire house had the look of a rotting vegetable. The ground was puckered up around the foundation. Years' worth of rotted leaves and soil lapped at the rubblework stone walls. Mud piled up before the front door.

"We usually go in the back," Charlie explained.

Wenna opened the passenger door and was almost flattened by the stench in the air. She closed the door with the quickness of a reflex. Charlie had gotten out of the car already. He seemed not to notice or to care about the smell. Cautiously, second-guessing her own senses, Wenna opened the car door again. The stench remained. It was an unwholesome, poisonous odor. The bog had never smelled like that to her before. Bogs were, in their own way, exceptionally clean places, all the stink of vegetable death sealed discreetly away under the surface. There was something wrong with a bog that had a perceptible odor.

She was momentarily annoyed that Charlie didn't offer to carry her bag to the door, until she noticed he was leaning on a cane that he'd gotten out of the back seat, his face wrinkled with an expression of intense focus. "The back door's unlocked," he said, before she could ask what had happened to him. This announcement was also the end of any conversation between them. Wenna carried her bag to the door.

In the kitchen, it was the almost-comforting house-smell that she registered first: something between the musty paper-and-glue odor of an unkempt library and the putrid scent of vegetables left to rot in darkness. After a moment, her eyes adjusted. Every visible surface was so crowded with objects that Wenna could only register the whole as clutter. Even the stove was mostly covered, old magazines spilling from the mouth of a saucepan, a single burner perfunctorily cleared for use. Racks of dried herbs and greens hung from the ceiling, so long forgotten that they trailed dusty strands of cobweb; Wenna wouldn't have been surprised to learn they had been harvested the summer before and left there through the winter. The floor was streaked with a palimpsest of dried boot prints. From one corner, a white possum regarded her warily.

"Did you know that was in here?" Wenna said with a nod to the animal. She had a suspicion that the possum was a full-fledged member of the household.

"It's Nora's," Charlie said. He shifted uneasily from one foot to the other. "Eda said there was no point in cleaning, so."

He was embarrassed; Wenna was not hiding her disgust

successfully. "I'm sure it's been difficult," she said, at a loss for any other vaguely appropriate response.

"Sort of." He cleared his throat, girding himself to say something else, but then Nora and Percy came thudding down the stairs.

Her siblings had gone through growth spurts and puberty in Wenna's absence and become young adults. They seemed to Wenna to have uncannily grown into each other, even more alike now than they had been as children. Their upturned Haddesley noses and indignant sharp Haddesley chins; even the feathery mushroom-colored hair that they wore in a cloud around their ears. Only, Percy wouldn't really look at her, and Nora was looking at her as if her gaze could fix Wenna in place.

"You came home," she said, with a kind of awe.

"I can't stay long." Wenna was surprised and vaguely appalled by her impulse to disappoint her sister, but Nora's happiness felt oppressive. No one was supposed to be so affected by her coming back. "Just for the burial," she added, lowering her voice as if it were a secret that their father was right now lying in bed dying.

"I know." Nora's voice carried a defensive edge. She glanced sideways at Percy, as if checking to see whether he had noticed. Regaining herself, she asked: "Do you want something to eat?"

"What have you got?" Wenna hadn't eaten since getting on the bus, but she was less than confident that anything passably edible could be prepared with the kitchen in its current state.

Percy went to the refrigerator, a 1980s behemoth that had been with the house since the Haddesleys, forty-some years late to the game, first acquired electricity. "Pickles," he said. "Swiss cheese. Eggs."

"We should make eggs," said Nora. "Eggs are for breakfast."

She sounded as though she were reciting something she'd read in a book but had not personally experienced. "Do you want coffee, Wenna?"

"She can't have both," said Percy. "Not at once. There's only one clean burner."

"I'll have whichever," Wenna said, and she settled into a spindly little dining chair that she recalled from childhood. The kitchen table was from the same familiar set, but it was now so deeply buried in clutter that barely any of the tabletop was visible. As Percy and Nora negotiated the single functioning stove burner, she fidgeted with a paper box of spoons, some of them ornate and expensive-looking, others bent and tarnished and otherwise unremarkable. All of them glossed by dust. She hoped these weren't the dishes they used.

"Do you want salt on your eggs, Wenna?" Nora asked from across the kitchen.

"And pepper, if you have it."

"We don't have pepper," said Percy.

"Can you still eat them?" Nora asked, worried.

"Of course. You really don't have pepper?"

"No one buys it," said Nora. "It's Charlie who goes to the store."

Only then did Wenna absorb that Charlie was no longer in the room, had possibly not been there for a few minutes. He'd slunk out without making a sound. Percy set a plate of relatively cooked eggs in front of her, and Nora hurried to put water on for coffee. The two of them sat across from Wenna as she ate, their eyes politely averted, even their breaths measured. As if she were a wild animal they'd been lucky enough to stumble upon in its natural habitat. Only when the kettle began to shriek was their attention diverted. Nora rose and poured coffee for all three of them.

"If we had milked Matilde, you could have had milk," she said as she set Wenna's cup before her. "But Percy is supposed to do it, so—"

"I didn't have time," Percy insisted. "I had to do *Charlie's* chores."

"It's no trouble," Wenna said, to head off whatever meaningless bickering was brewing. At least that much had not changed. She looked down into the cup, at the grounds adrift on the surface. "By the way, what happened to Charlie?" she asked, putting off her first sip.

Nora's eyes searched Percy's as if he were responsible for the answer. Percy drummed his fingers impatiently on the table.

"Is he all right?" Wenna heard the panic in her own voice. She hated that already she'd become entangled. She'd been in the house for ten minutes.

"Well," said Nora. She hesitated. "Did you see the tree on the roof?"

"Of course."

"The place that the tree fell was Charlie's room."

Wenna looked at Percy, who only nodded.

"And he got hurt," Nora continued. "He can walk now, but he can't really do stairs and he mostly stays in his room."

"The room where the tree fell," Wenna said, incredulous.

"He sleeps in what used to be the study now," Percy clarified.

Wenna couldn't even decide what to ask first. She felt as if she should have been told as soon as the accident happened, as if she had somehow been lied to, even though she would have said that she didn't want to know. "What did he hurt?" she asked.

Percy and Nora exchanged glances again. Neither of them answered her question before Eda came down the stairs, bearing a tray piled with empty dishes.

It hurt to look at her older sister. In the malnourished light that the windows admitted, Eda might have been sixty instead of thirty-three. Her skin had the same waxy lusterless quality as Charlie's. The dark half-moons beneath her eyes formed furrows down to her cheekbones.

Wenna didn't know whether she was supposed to embrace her sister or shake Eda's hand or take the tray from her, and in the end she did nothing, paralyzed by the sensation that she and Eda were about to resume a fight they hadn't finished ten years ago.

"Wenna," her sister acknowledged, as if she had been asked to identify Wenna in a lineup. Then, after a long and conspicuous silence, "Dad wants to see you."

Wenna steadied herself in her chair. She had not prepared herself for the trial of interacting with her father outside of the mercifully scripted context of the burial rites. "Does Dad know that I'm here? I mean, did someone tell him that I was coming?"

"He knew that you were coming for the burial," Nora offered.

"Right, but—"

"He might not be happy to see you," Eda interrupted, sounding more exasperated than Wenna thought she had any right to be. "If that's what you're asking. He's not happy to see *me*, most of the time, and I've been changing his bedpan for the past month."

"I didn't have to come out here," Wenna said.

"Didn't you?" Eda said, with a dismayed little huff of laughter. "Don't go up there, if you don't want to. Just know that he heard you downstairs and asked for you."

❧

Wenna ascended the stairs with the grim sensation that she was proving something. Her father's bedroom was the first one to the left, the door open. She stood for a second in the hallway and absorbed that the figure on the curtained bed was really her father. It occurred to Wenna that she didn't know what he was dying of. His skin had the same blanched waxy quality as Charlie's and Eda's, but worse. As she entered the room, his eyes narrowed, became unfocused, then regained their intensity.

"Tell Eda that I don't want more peas," was the first thing he said.

"I will," Wenna said, too taken aback to protest. She took a deep breath, fortifying herself. It would have been easier if only he had been dead already.

Her father's eyes drifted from Wenna's face to the other end of the room, the opened door, the dark hallway. He wanted something other than her. "Easier for everyone," he said dreamily, "if I am empty when I go."

Wenna lowered herself into the dining chair at his bedside, awkwardly folding into her lap the worn old throw blanket that had previously occupied the seat. Everything in the room emanated a scent fainter but no less morbid than the rancid odor outside. "Empty?" she repeated.

"My stomach," he said, assuaging any fears she might have had that he was becoming philosophical at the end of his life. "People shit when they die, you know."

"Right," Wenna said. "Do you think," she ventured, knowing that she was being impolite but deciding that maybe they were past that now, "you'll die today?"

"It must be soon." He looked entreatingly at her. "I have dreamed," he said, with urgency, "of meeting on the road a man walking with a cart pulled by a mare impaled on a post."

Wenna crossed her arms to hide the gooseflesh that lifted on them. "I don't know what that means," she said firmly.

"I should have gone a long time ago," he whispered. "It never was right, after her."

Wenna's throat closed as rage tightened her belly and her lungs. She could not think of one single thing to say that Alyson the therapist would have approved of. "I'm sorry that you're dying," she managed at last, staring ahead, inwardly cringing at herself for saying something so transparently insincere, when what she wanted to say was *I am never going to forgive you, not even after you're gone.*

When she dared to glance over at him, his gaze was distant. "You cannot go back, you know," he said, "to wherever you have been. They need you here."

Wenna was perversely impressed. She should have known that the summons to bury her father was only a pretext. Of course she could not simply come back and then leave. She had been stupid to think that she was ending anything by coming here. But even her father could not possibly be so brazen as to think that on his deathbed he could make any demands about what she did or where she went after she had already squirmed free from the Haddesley noose once.

"What right do you have?" she said under her breath, not really wanting or expecting an answer.

"Tell me," whispered Charles Haddesley with the rhythm of an incantation. "Tell me you will stay with them."

Wenna lost her patience. "You can't ask me for things! I

came for the exchange. That's all you get. And it's more than you deserve."

Her father's look became urgent, almost wild. "I never hurt her," he said imploringly. "You must know."

Wenna's stomach turned. "If you didn't do anything to her," she said, slowly, "then where did she go?"

Her father hesitated, and for a second Wenna felt a small gasp of hope that he was going to really answer her, that somehow there'd been a misunderstanding left for ten years uncorrected. But instead he exhaled, and a terse silence unspooled around them. He had no answer for her.

"Like I thought," said Wenna, and she stood to go. She hesitated at the doorway, thinking how disappointing it was that those were the last words she might ever exchange with her father. She did not look back at him.

EDA

hey had readied themselves for months, but the burial still caught Eda off guard. In the excruciating boredom of the long decline, there was never stillness, only a constant succession of cups and plates carried up and down the stairs, a continual adjusting of the curtains to admit or exclude light, an endless cycle of lowering and raising their father's body into and out of the bath and into and out of his pant legs and into and out of bed, and now they had to be ready to lower him into the grave. And Eda was not prepared, and naturally no one else was either.

When she had gone to him that morning, carrying the oatmeal and the cup of cough syrup that were his habitual breakfast, he had been lying awake in the middle of the four-poster bed with his eyes wide and his fingers splayed on the dark quilt like the legs of a white spider. For a second, she thought that he'd died in the night and that they had missed their chance to do the rite of burial. Fear staggered her. Then he said, "Eda," in a soft and pitying tone that she barely recognized, a *fatherly* tone, and she almost laughed.

"When does Wenna come?" he asked. He had been asking the same question and receiving the same answer for the past three days; he could not remember anything lately. Eda didn't know whether this was part of his disease or a side effect of his heavy cough syrup use or only a side effect of being a bedbound man glimpsing through a curtained window the ruin of his legacy.

"Today, Daddy," Eda said, taking his untouched bowl of oatmeal from his lap. "She'll be here in a few hours."

Her father lowered himself back onto the pillows and shut his eyes. Slowly, he said, "Someone really must deal with Charlie."

Eda tried without success to guess at what this could possibly mean. "I can go and get him," she said at last, "if you want."

She doubted that he wanted her to go and get Charlie. The two of them were barely on speaking terms. But the best way with her father, she had learned, was simply to always come up with something not directly confrontational to say to each of his remarks, no matter how preposterous or cruel, until he considered the conversation ended. This strategy had kept her out of trouble since childhood, and she felt safe now in assuming it would carry her through her father's death.

"My firstborn son," her father went on, with a nasal snicker. He was already feeling the cough syrup, thought Eda. All at once, an urgent look came over his face. He grasped her wrist. "Charlie can't be buried like a patriarch; I want you to see to that. Bury him upside down without his eyes. Not in the bog. Will you promise me?"

Eda could not fault her father for hating Charlie. She sometimes, even often, hated Charlie, who from birth had treated his sacred hereditary obligations as chores that could always be deferred to someone else if he didn't feel like performing them. But she could see no reason to be so gruesome about it. As far she knew, no one in the history of the Haddesley family had ever been buried like that.

"Promise me," he insisted.

She promised, not meaning it. She tried to hold his hand and he yanked loose in a convulsive, panicked motion. His gaze became unfocused.

"Laibhaen?" he said.

Eda flinched. "No," she said. "It's Eda, Daddy."

"How did you get here? I never found . . ."

Eda got to her feet. The spoon rattled in the dish as she carried the tray downstairs in trembling fingers. Nora, eating dried cranberries with her fingers at the kitchen counter, looked impassively at her. Upstairs, they could both hear their father calling for their dead mother.

Six hours later, he asked her to bury him. Eda searched herself and found no feeling. The sensation was of a door repeatedly shutting. She was not grieved, nor was she excited to be released from the work of caring for him. "Of course," she said. "If you're ready." She went down the stairs and felt aghast that she felt nothing. "We need the garments," she said to no one in particular. Nora and Wenna and Percy, sitting around the table, blinked back at her. She felt as if her siblings were moving through some liquid thicker than water, their motions slow and labored.

"I think they're in the cellar," Nora said. After what felt like an unreasonable amount of time, she took the hint, got up from her chair, and went to the cellar. Eda tried without success to unclench her jaw enough to breathe deeply.

"Charlie's not here," Percy observed.

"Then go and get him," she said, more violently than she intended. He scrambled into his boots and out the door with at least a feigned sense of urgency. And then she and Wenna were alone.

"I should say goodbye," Wenna said, but she made no move to get up from her chair.

"If you want." It was exhaustingly true to form that Wenna had come back almost exactly when their father ceased to be a belligerent, needy old man and became instead a patriarch, a ritual object to whom you could pay your respects without getting a snide rejoinder back.

Wenna's eyes, ringed in shadowy pools of smudged makeup, drifted inattentively across the table. She grasped the seat of her chair with both hands as if she were at risk of falling off. She did not say goodbye to their father.

Nora returned with a bulging cardboard box in her arms. She set it down on the floor and pulled out a sheath woven of sphagnum moss fibers. "There's spiders in them," she said, and she shook the garment out, sending a small cascade of dust and dead insects to the floor. "Are we supposed to have washed them?"

"We can't wash them," Eda said. "And it's only for a few minutes. Just put it on, Nora. We have to do it before he's . . . gone."

"Over my clothes?"

"No clothes. You know the rules. Ritual purity. Wenna, you too, please."

Nora retreated sulkily into the corridor with the sheath in one hand, its moth-eaten ends trailing on the floor. Wenna followed. After an intolerable amount of time, they returned, looking older and wilder, in their ceremonial clothes.

"We need the cowbane," Eda said to Nora, crossing the kitchen in long strides, shoving aside a pile of ceremonial goblets. They had, somewhere, other saucepans, but there was only one that anyone had used to cook anything in recent memory. As Nora went out the back door to get the leaves, Eda's eyes swept across the wall of junk and found the saucepan on the front burner of the stove. A crusted layer of old coffee grounds coated the bottom. Nothing, she despaired, could ever be done simply or easily. She was still washing the pan when Nora returned bearing fistfuls of cowbane leaves and Percy entered with the spruce plank that Charlie had carved for their father's passage.

"Robes," Eda said to him, prodding the cardboard box with her foot. She held out her palms to Nora for the cowbane leaves and hurried back to the stove, the now passably clean saucepan, the security of having something solid to do. Her siblings shifted restlessly in their ceremonial clothes as the sour odor of the tincture rose in a waft of steam from the stove.

When the cowbane was boiled down into a mash, the five of them arranged themselves around the plank, Eda and Wenna at the front ends and Nora and Percy at the back. Charlie stood in the middle, his hand resting on the wood, his body shaking with the effort of standing. Without speaking, they lifted the plank and bore it to the stairs.

As she and Wenna heaved the plank up the first step, Charlie uttered a hesitating sound. Nora and Percy stalled behind him. He couldn't get up the stairs, Eda realized. Not unassisted. Panic jolted through her. This was how the rite had to begin. They had to carry the patriarch down to the bog. And their patriarch was upstairs.

I should have moved Dad to the first floor while he still could walk, she thought. *Then, Charlie should have figured something out. He should have been ready. He should have known he would need to do this.* Frustration almost choked her.

"What's going on?" Wenna asked.

"Charlie can't walk up," Percy explained.

"I'd need help," Charlie said quietly.

Wenna considered this. "Okay," she said. "Then we'll help. Nora, do you have your side?"

"No!" Eda cried. "It's supposed to be all of us. All of us carrying."

She didn't need to see Wenna's face to know she was wearing that impatient half-confounded expression she always wore when Eda enforced rules that she didn't think were worth following. "It's not going to be all of us," Wenna said. "It's going to be four of us, and Charlie stays down here, or three of us, and he comes up."

"I can help him," Nora asserted, "and keep my hand on the plank. I think."

"Never mind," Eda said. The burial had already gone wrong and they had not even begun. She wanted to fling the plank down and abandon the whole thing. But she knew she had to be the one to drag things along to some pitiful approximation of their rightful conclusion. No one else was going to do it. "Charlie, you stay down here," she decided. He would be there in the bog, at least. Hopefully that was the important part.

Charlie didn't protest. He hung back at the foot of the stairs, his eyes on the floor.

In his bedroom, Charles Haddesley sat propped on the stack of pillows that Eda had arranged, staring straight ahead. His face betrayed no fear. He did not ask where Charlie was. Eda crossed the room to her father's bedside and got to her knees. Gently, she pressed his palsied fingers around the glass holding the tincture.

§

The four of them carried their father down the stairs and toward the back door, bearing the spruce plank on their shoulders. In the kitchen, Charlie rejoined them. When their father saw him, a stricken sound escaped his lips that might have been grief or fury or only a dying body's cry for release. Outside, the rising wind threw twigs and leaves to the ground and whipped Wenna's long loose hair. When her sister's red-rimmed eyes searched hers out, Eda turned around to face ahead. They only had to finish the rite and then Wenna could vanish again. That was clearly what she wanted, and after today, there would be nothing binding her to this place anymore.

Slowly, careful not to jostle the body on the plank, they descended the slope into the bog, crossing from threadbare slender-rooted sedge into dark pitted mire. Their bare feet sank into the earth and withdrew with the gummy *smack* of coming unstuck. Once, then again, someone stumbled on a raised hummock. When that happened, the rest of them stopped, steadying the plank on their shoulders. Then trudged ahead. The soil subsided into a loose fabric of sphagnum moss at the edge of the bog's flood-swollen mouth.

Their father coughed and retched, lifting his head from the plank and then sinking back down. Eda had set the traditional crown of dried alder branches on his head, but underneath, his disheveled hair was plastered to his skin. *We should have brushed his hair*, Eda thought. *We should have bathed him again, changed his clothes, readied him for immortality.* She was afraid that she'd forgotten a necessary part of the burial rite. Underneath, quietly, she was more afraid that the bog knew she was an interloper, and that even if the rite was done in perfect accordance with tradition, it would have no potency. It should have been Charlie. Tradition said everything should have been done by Charlie.

Eda counted to three. With one slow and coordinated motion, they heaved the plank forward onto the wet mat of sphagnum. Their father uttered a low moan. Spit bubbled out from his mouth and dripped sideways down his cheek. The crown of alder slanted precariously to one side. But they could not touch him now.

They stood still as their father sank unhurriedly into his dark, glistening grave. Wenna began to cry, her sobs making her entire body convulse. No one else made any sound.

After a few hours, it became apparent that no one knew whether the rite was done. At some point their solemnity became awkwardness. Moisture lapped at their father's face, but the peat underneath held him, and he did not sink further down. It would be days or weeks, Eda knew, before he vanished altogether.

She could feel her siblings' restlessness. From the corner of her eye, she saw Nora's snuck glances, her fidgeting in the peat, her sulky little exhalations. Charlie wavered, unsteady on his legs still, but they all held their formation. Eda felt that she could not let the moment end. Although she had not wanted Wenna here, she felt the ceremonial rightness in the five of them bent around the body of their father. She did not know what was supposed to happen after they parted. She had inclined herself toward the burial for so many months without ever really conceiving what might come afterward. It did not seem real that tomorrow she would wake up and her brief, inglorious tenure as head of the Haddesley household would already be over, a woman having risen from the bog to marry Charlie and supplant her.

"Should we . . . ," Wenna said, glancing at the others. When no one ventured to finish her sentence, she concluded, reluctantly, "Should we go in?"

Nora toed the lip of the water. "What if he's not gone?" she said.

"He's not breathing," Charlie offered.

"We did everything right," Eda said. "We did enough." She glanced upward. The horizon was wind-torn and fleecy. She thought she could smell moisture on the air. "We did enough," she said again, firmly.

Wenna was the first one to make for the house, pushing gracelessly through the mud without waiting for anyone else to follow. But they did follow, first Charlie and then Nora. Only Percy stayed, his entire body shuddering, his eyes on their father's body in its green sphagnum blanket.

"We did it right, didn't we?" Eda said to him.

Percy grimaced. "I don't know," was all he said, and she couldn't tell if he was lying to spare her feelings or if he really wasn't sure. He was trembling or shivering or both. "It's not fair," he added, and his voice was knotted with rage.

"I know," said Eda. Everything would have been so much more salvageable if only Percy had been born the patriarch. "It should have been you," she said, as if that were any consolation when it wasn't him.

Percy said nothing. Beside them, their father's body released a sound that might have been a gasp for breath. They both whirled to face him, but he was still. The gasp-or-not-gasp fractured in the tree branches and then faded. The peat held him.

WENNA

They came to the back door with feet mud-caked, their ceremonial shifts trailing threads of dried moss. Wenna expected the others to tromp through the house without stopping to clean up, but instead Charlie gingerly pulled clods of mud from between his bare toes and then went inside to get a bucket and a towel for the rest of them. It was like a foot-washing, Wenna thought. Michael said that foot-washing was holy. He'd made her go to church with him on a day when they would be doing it, paint buckets of sudsy water and bleach-faded hand towels in front of everyone's chairs. She had refused to participate.

"You're afraid of everything sacred," he'd said in the car on the way home.

"How is it sacred if you're not afraid of it?" Wenna had answered.

No one washed anyone else's feet now. They took turns purging the filth of the bog from themselves with impatience, in tense silence, then emptied the bucket of mud into the yard and went inside. Debris stuck to Wenna's damp feet as she crossed the kitchen. She had never wanted more desperately to mop something.

In the old parlor, a room forbidden to them as children, Nora curled up in a high-backed armchair and Eda sprawled out across a crusty pale-pink divan that had probably once been some Haddesley sister's fainting couch, while the boys claimed a cat-scratched velvet sofa, Percy making a conspicuous and unnecessary effort to leave a wide berth between himself and Charlie. Wenna could not make herself sit. She stood at the sideboard with its century-old bowl of wax fruit, its dust-glossed crystal decanters; she regarded her siblings indirectly through the concave eye of the mirror on the wall.

"It's been hours and hours since we've eaten," Nora said.

"Dad is *dead*," Eda said, as if it were impolite to be hungry under the circumstances.

"Well, I'm not."

"Dad would have wanted us to eat," Percy decided.

"If anyone had helped with anything today," Eda said, "I might have had dinner ready earlier."

It was strange, Wenna thought, how they talked exactly as they had talked ten years ago.

"You know, you're not even the one in charge," Nora said to Eda. The white possum had slunk into the room and climbed onto the back of her chair and curled into a ball, forming a kind of disheveled crown for her head. "It's Charlie, now that Dad's gone."

Charlie flinched at this assertion of his authority, but he said nothing.

"*Is* Charlie in charge?" Eda asked, her voice rising. "It doesn't feel like Charlie's in charge. Charlie could do one single thing to be in charge, if he wanted."

In the mirror, Wenna watched her brother crumple slowly in on himself, his shoulders drawing inward and his head lowered, even as his face remained stubbornly blank.

"Ease up, Edd," Wenna said. That was her line: her contribution to the everlasting recurrence of fifteen years ago.

Eda lifted her head to regard Wenna with blazing eyes but did not say anything. Percy abruptly got to his feet and excused himself without giving any reason. The four of them watched him go, more to have something to do than out of any real interest. They listened as he put on his boots, then as the back door opened and shut behind him.

"Well, the burial's ended," Eda said, in the silence that followed. "Those of us who don't live here can go home whenever they want now."

"Let her stay," Nora interjected. "Please, Wenna, can't you stay?"

Wenna didn't answer. She closed her eyes and imagined herself begging a ride to the Greyhound station from Charlie, whiling away the hours between now and the arrival of a bus bound for Pittsburgh on a hard-backed bench with a comfortable buffer of thirty miles between her and the Haddesleys.

"If you stay, you're going to have to sleep in the east wing," Eda said.

"She can't," Nora protested.

"She has to. Unless she wants Dad's room before I've even had time to change the sheets."

"The east wing is fine," Wenna heard herself say, with the jarring sensation that she had not decided to say it. Still, it had been said, and apparently by her own voice.

"The east wing is flooded," Nora said. "There's no electricity in there. Something happened when the tree fell. I don't know." She flinched away from the words with a quick sidelong glance at Charlie, who did not look back at her. When no one spoke for a second, she added, "You could share with me. Like we used to."

Wenna wavered. She had crossed some kind of threshold

that she could not step back across now, but she did not want to go further.

"I don't think you'd both fit in that bed anymore," Eda said.

"She can have the bed." Nora lifted her eyes and fixed them on Wenna. "I really don't mind."

"You don't want your privacy?" Wenna asked, as if anything like privacy had ever existed in the Haddesley household.

"I know that I used to annoy you," Nora said. "I won't now, I promise."

"Fine, so it's settled then," Eda said, losing interest. "Now I have to cook something. Unless someone else is planning to do it. Soup?"

"We only have cream-of-mushroom," said Nora.

"That's not really soup," Wenna said, with the suspicion that she was delivering bad news to her siblings. "You're supposed to mix it in things."

"We could have cocoa," Nora suggested. "I know how to make cocoa."

"Cocoa's not a dinner," Eda said. "I'm sure Wenna is used to regular meals."

"Do whatever you'd do if I weren't here." Wenna had forgotten how precarious eating was in the Haddesley household. Cooking was supposed to be the work of the patriarch, but their father had always performed his duties halfheartedly, producing cauldrons of muddy-looking stew meant to last the week that never lasted the week or advising Eda to make sandwiches. It seemed that Charlie was furthering this tradition. "I can always go scrounging later," she said.

"I bought ground beef last week," Charlie said, speaking just a notch above a whisper.

That seemed to conclude the discussion. Dinner was to be cream-of-mushroom soup and ground beef. Eda retreated to the kitchen.

"I hope she washes the cowbane pot," Nora said absently.

⁂

In Wenna's absence, Nora had filled the bedroom they used to share with animals, all of them bogland foundlings: a salamander in a canning jar, a clutch of baby mice in a fishbowl strewn with sawdust, a swallow in a badly bent antique birdcage, and the possum from downstairs, who seemed to have the run of the house. The odor that the room released was a meaty, sour, more organic smell than the faded-paper scent of the rest of the house, although that scent was represented here too, in the form of a four-foot-high pile of water-damaged, crispy-looking back issues of *National Enquirer.*

Underneath the animals and their detritus, the room was unchanged. The walls of paneled wood were strewn with taped-up pictures that Nora and Wenna herself had drawn when they were small. Ropes of dried comfrey and lavender strung by a long-dead Haddesley sister still hung in gentle half loops from the raftered ceiling; a long-unused loom sat in the corner, obscured by a pile of dirty clothes. A braided rug and the narrow oak bed they once shared remained in their accustomed places. Wenna stood in the middle of the room as the possum crept suspiciously around her feet to the closet and tunneled into a ripped-open sofa cushion. She watched the possum work and inhaled the scent of rodent urine and tried to figure out what to say to her sister.

Nora made no apologies or excuses for the state of the room. She hovered for a moment by the door, then clasped her hands together and strode along the wall, her fingertips sliding over bowls and cages and jars as if assuring herself that they were all still there. "You want to meet them?" she said, magnanimous and hostessly, her whole body vibrating.

"Okay." Wenna understood it wasn't really a question she could say no to. She was relieved but also hurt that Nora didn't seem at all curious about her life beyond the property-line, the ten years that Wenna had lived out of her family's sight. She had spent half the Greyhound ride deciding what needed to remain a secret and what she could confess, and she was beginning to suspect she'd wasted her time. No one was going to ask.

"That's Buz Lukens," Nora said, of the possum. "I just call him Buz, sometimes. He only has three feet. He didn't have a mother, or she didn't want him. And that's Barney Frank." She pointed at a salamander in an old canning jar. "Broken leg. Percy's fault. He was underneath a rock that Percy threw over." She lifted a smaller canning jar to the light and tilted it slightly, so Wenna could see the two fat-bodied black beetles maneuvering a terrain of leaf litter inside. "Callahan and Sonny," she explained. "They were almost drowned when Percy flooded the swale. *Most* of the animals are because of Percy."

"What is the swale for?" Wenna interrupted. She had felt something cleave inside of her when she'd seen that furrow carved into the peat, deep and too precise to be anything but man-made. Her first thought had been, *They're not even going to hide it?*

Nora shrugged. "We're just supposed to," she said. "The bog doesn't stay wet enough, by itself. So Percy keeps a measurement of where the mouth's edge is, and when it gets too low, he floods it." She drew a tailless field mouse out of a fishbowl and offered it to Wenna. "Arlan Strangelands," she explained. "Caught in a mousetrap but wasn't dead."

Reluctantly, Wenna opened her hands and let Arlan Strangelands drop into her palms. The mouse was as light and as downy as a ball of dust. She could feel its heartbeat throbbing through its belly, fast and urgent.

"Where does the water come from?" she said.

"*I* don't know. Ask Percy," Nora said. Her attention was elsewhere already. "This is John Kennedy Jr." She crouched before the hulking terrarium on her bedside table. "You see him?"

Wenna stepped closer, Arlan Strangelands clinging with his needlelike claws to the palm of her hand, and acknowledged the turtle on the other side of the humid glass. It was clear that she was not going to get any real information out of her sister. "And what was his problem?" she asked.

Nora grimaced. "He had a fungus. Patches all over his shell. When we found him, he was mushy and defenseless. *Percy* thought we should kill him, because the fungus might spread, but I said I'd just keep him here. I sponged him every day with salt water until he got better. But he can't go back to the wild now."

Arlan Strangelands squirmed in Wenna's hands, prodding at the bars of her fingers. She held out her hands to give him back to Nora, but Nora didn't take him right away and instead he fell, twisting frantically in the air until he landed on his side, looking stunned and breathless. Nora, unfazed, bent and collected the mouse in her hands and lifted him to her face so she could examine him.

"He hurt his foot," she concluded.

"Oh, Nor, I'm so sorry," said Wenna, although her sorriness was braided with irritation; it wasn't as if she had wanted to hold the mouse.

"It's not your *fault*," Nora said, her voice pitched a note higher than usual. "I'll just make a sling for him." She dropped Arlan Strangelands casually back into his fishbowl and brushed her palms together as if sweeping the mouse from them. She crossed the room and sprawled out on top of the bedcovers in her still-damp moss sheath, her bare toes on the pillow, and propped her chin on her knuckles. Apparently she had forgotten what she'd said about letting Wenna take the bed. "You know, I'm so glad you came home," she said. "You came at just the right time. It'll be peat-cutting time soon, and then the cranberry harvest, and—well, it's just been hard to get everything done, since Dad got sick and Charlie got crushed. No one ever mucks out the goat shed. And we were supposed to dig out a new latrine last spring, but Percy only ended up digging a hole that flooded out when it rained."

Wenna wanted to say that she wouldn't be here long enough for peat-cutting or the cranberry harvest or any of the rest of it, but she'd told Nora already that she couldn't stay and she knew that Nora hadn't forgotten. She remembered, now, her sister's habit of speaking in incantations, as if saying something enough times in a sure-enough way could make it true. The workings of the household were such that sometimes Nora was right.

"You must feel very busy," she said, pleased by how much she sounded like Alyson the therapist when she said those words: empathetic and yet implacably neutral, neither promising nor refusing anything to her sister.

"Sometimes," Nora agreed, distracted now, kicking her feet restlessly behind her. "Wenna," she said, her voice lowered, her gaze stuck to the quilt beneath her. "What do you think it's going to be like, when the bog-wife comes?"

"I don't know," Wenna said, because she didn't know the answer but also because she didn't want to think long on the Haddesley household's future. When she did, the urge to intervene harassed her like an itch, like a pain, and she could no longer sustain her hard-won fragile belief that she was not complicit in whatever her family did, whether or not she was there to see them do it.

"I just keep thinking," said Nora, "will she be like Mom? Or different?"

"Like Mom how?"

"I mean," Nora said, with half-concealed exasperation, "you know what I mean." But she didn't seem to know exactly what she meant. "Sad," she said, at last.

Sad was a hopelessly inadequate word for what their mother had been, but Wenna wondered if that was the way the family thought of her now—if sometime in the past ten years they had all concluded that what had been wrong with their mother had been something internal to her and not something inflicted upon her by anyone else. How could any of them bear to live with their father, otherwise? How could any of them bear to live in the bog's sight?

"It probably depends," said Wenna, carefully, "on how Charlie treats her."

"It's strange, but I can't really imagine Charlie getting married. Can you? He's always just been *Charlie.*"

"Well," Wenna said, "getting married to a bog-wife isn't really getting married."

"Why?"

Wenna didn't know how to explain in terms that her sister would understand. She herself had only become dimly aware of the bleak emptiness of her parents' marriage after hours of exposure to sitcoms, insurance ads, reality shows where women shopped for wedding dresses. She had really *understood* only when she'd already destroyed her own marriage. Their father had treated their mother with an unpredictable mix of shy reverence and visceral unrestrained loathing. Their mother had treated their father like a dangerous animal that she half tamed and that half tamed her. And Wenna, child of their union, had tried to do neither of these things in her marriage but had apparently done some muted version of both. Even Alyson, who was Wenna's therapist and had no loyalties to Michael, could not deny it. *It's very hard*, she'd said, face scrunched up sympathetically, *to trust people. Or to be trusted.*

"Haddesley marriages aren't for love," Wenna said, at last, feeling that this still did not really cut to the heart of it. "They're just for the compact."

"It's still love," Nora said.

"But it's not," Wenna said. Even as she spoke, she knew that she was getting too involved; she wouldn't change Nora's mind, and her sister's probable last memory of her shouldn't be some pointless argument about whether their brother would love his vegetable-wife. "Bog-wives don't even choose to be with Haddesleys. Do you think Mom *wanted* to marry Dad? Truly, do you?"

"I don't know," Nora said, quietly. "I didn't want to have a fight, anyway."

Wenna felt like she'd felt when she dropped Nora's pet mouse on the floor, the same guilt laced with irritation, the same sense that she'd been led into a trap but was nonetheless responsible for ending up there. Feeling that there was nothing else to be said, she began unravelling the sleeping bag that Nora retrieved from the closet. She knew better than to think she was sleeping in the bed. The quilted fabric exuded a musty scent, one that almost obscured the putrefied odor underneath, that hostile smell that clung to everything now. She thought it would linger in her clothes after she had gone.

"Wenna," Nora said, after a while, with a tremor in her voice as though she'd been nervous to speak, "did you ever fall in love? When you were out there?"

For a second, Wenna wanted to tell her sister everything. But she had already decided that Michael was not something her siblings could handle knowing about. Eda, in particular, would be thrown into an unnecessary and exhausting panic. She would say Wenna had violated the Haddesley compact, although really, as Wenna understood it, she had not. After all, the interdiction on the marriage of Haddesley sisters was not an interdiction on marriage so much as an interdiction on children. And Wenna had stood so firm on not having children with Michael that now she was no longer even married to him.

She peeled back the sleeping bag's dark mouth and crawled inside, rolling onto her back so that she did not have to look Nora in the eye. "No," she said. "I never did."

Nora didn't speak for a long time after that. Wenna succumbed to temptation and glanced sideways at her sister. Nora was lying on her side, her unconquerable tangle of hair splayed on the pillow, her spine curled. She'd slept like that as a child. Thumb in her mouth until she was ten or so. Blanket to her chin even in midsummer. Wenna used to find it maddening when they shared a bed. She'd stick one leg out of the side of the bed to cool herself, turn her pillow over again and again. But for some reason she'd never considered sleeping somewhere else.

Outside, rain began to fall, at first in a hushed whisper and then in a full-bodied hammering swell. Nora sighed content- edly. "I really am so glad that you came back, Wenna. We so needed you."

CHARLIE

Charlie did not sleep the night after his father was buried. He lay on his mattress in the study with the sheets wadded in a ball on the floor beside him listening to rain pour out of the gutters, his eyes fixed on the oak-paneled ceiling. If he allowed his gaze to drop, he would see the faces of his predecessors in the portraits that lined the walls of the study—the early oil paintings professionally done in muddy, visceral hues; the more recent ones unmistakably the work of Haddesley younger brothers or aunts, done in quick-fading watercolors, smudgy amateurish bundles of teeth and waistcoats and noses. Lying beneath those portraits was like submitting himself to a monstrous tribunal that found him guilty of everything.

Whenever drowsiness pushed on his eyelids, the same thought jolted him awake: in the morning, the bog-wife would be there waiting for him. She was, even now, being hewn from algae and sphagnum, millions upon millions of vegetable cells undergoing transformation. Slime and mire coalescing into a head, neck, breasts, hips, calves. The thought made him nauseous. His father had never gone into particulars about the way the bog-wife was born, and he could think only about the agonized efforts of the nanny goat in the yard when he tried to imagine. He had been kept out of the room when his mother gave birth to his younger siblings, but he had been exposed many times to the sight of poor Mathilde with her rolling white eyes, valiantly pushing until a pulpy purplish-red sack containing an inert bundle of limbs slid out from a hole in her body that never seemed large enough to have opened to the thing it had opened to. Her cries afterward were always hoarse and grief-stricken, mourning the horrors of the birth itself or the thing that came from it. What if his bog-wife was born like one of her kids: no eyes or twisted feet or teeth sprouting from her back or two heads? Two heads meant it was supposed to be two kids, his father had said. And what if there were two of them, out there in the bog, right at this moment taking form? The only certain difference was that the bog-wife always survived being born, and Mathilde's kids never did. Whatever happened, some creature would be there lying in the sedge, waiting for him.

Charlie spent the rest of that night falling through half-lucid dreams, cascades of images half-realized and dissociated from one another. The goats rutting in the yard, Claude's hooves hooked into Mathilde's back; eight-year-old Wenna throwing her dessert down into the bog pool in case the bog-wives were hungry down there, the unfrosted spice cake breaking apart into heavy orange clumps before it vanished; his mother sitting upright in bed, baby Nora at her breast, silently weeping. In the blackest part of the night, he dreamed he saw the study door open and Percy standing in the doorway with a cup like the cup that Eda had given their father before his burial. Charlie said his brother's name and Percy startled. "I'm supposed to," Percy said, despairingly. "Just let me." When Charlie opened his eyes again, his brother was not there. The study door was closed. The sun had already risen, though the day was pale and bleak-looking, rain still falling heavily. He had overslept his initiation into patriarchy.

Charlie pushed himself up from the mattress, cringing through the pain that radiated down his groin. He lifted the shirt he slept in over his head, then slowly and reluctantly removed his underwear. The sensation of air on his bare skin was discomfiting, but he had to go to the bog-wife completely naked, without even the ritual sheaths worn for the burial. He took the dowsing stick from the wall, held it in both hands, and walked forward, stopping to scrutinize his face in the small gilt-leaf mirror that hung by the door. He slicked his palm with spit to flatten the stray tendrils of hair that rose stubbornly from the crown of his head. With a sense of estrangement, he registered his own features: his bloodshot eyes with their brown irises, his unkempt and loosely woven eyebrows, the sharp and pronounced point of his chin. Sleep crusted around the corners of his mouth. He saw himself as he thought the bog-wife would see him, a hunched-over miserable-looking boy of thirty, and he realized he did not want to face her. He shut his eyes so he would not have to look at himself and then made for the back door.

He knew his siblings were watching as he walked through the yard, although they had thoughtfully absented themselves from the kitchen and the hallway so he would not see them or they would not see him as he walked naked through the fragile and fraught moments before the marriage rites transformed him. Undoubtedly they were upstairs now, gathered in the room that Nora and Wenna were sharing, Eda sipping the disgusting weedy-scented tea that she loved, Nora feeding the last of the week's groceries to her pet possum. He had a strange and disorienting recollection of the dream he'd dreamed of Percy coming into the study with a cowbane tincture, and for a second he thought it must have been real before he decided that it hadn't been, it couldn't be. He tried to think of nothing besides the sensation of the rain-saturated earth beneath his bare feet, cakey and soft, but then he considered that he was practically walking on his wife's flesh, so he did not let himself think anything as he made his way through the thicket of alder toward the bog's mouth.

The bog had been flooded out until it resembled its old self, strange and lush and boundaryless, the bog of Charlie's forefathers. Dry-appearing land was revealed to be suffused with water as soon as you stepped down onto it. The ground sank underneath Charlie's feet as he waded deep. He felt loose fibers of moss swirling in the floodwater around his ankles and then his calves. At last, he came to the bog's swollen mouth, where the water deepened to his thighs, seeping between his legs, chilling his crumpled testicles. Before him lay the half-sunk body of his father: crownless and unceremonious, tangled in moss, slightly bloated. In death, Charles Haddesley's face assumed a horrifying kind of smug complacence, as if he were on the cusp of saying, *My troubles are over, so what if yours aren't?*

Charlie looked and could not stop looking. He should have known that his father would not have gone under yet. He wondered if this was how every Haddesley eldest son last saw his father, and he was surprised to feel a throb of sympathy with his many predecessors—the smushed-looking figures in the paintings and even the father that was now, still, after death, tormenting him. Four decades ago, his indomitable father had been a young man stripped naked and shivering, compelled to wash himself with mud and usurp his own father's place, to spit on the mouth of a bog-hewn woman. *Someday, it will be my son,*

Charlie thought, and then he remembered that probably he could not have one.

Slowly, he reached into the water and came up with a handful of earth that he ground into his skin, taking care to coat everything. In the rain, the mud slathered easily, forming a loose paste that clung to him. When only his eyes and mouth and genitals were still bare, he closed his eyes and held the dowsing stick in two hands and waited for it to lead him.

But the dowsing stick did not lead him. He felt no pull, no inclination. In all his most anxious imaginings, he'd never considered such a possibility. His fingers shook around the narrow rod, willing it to work. How could the dowsing stick not pull him? He held the stick in one hand; he held it facing downward. He squeezed open one eye and examined it, but the dowsing stick looked unrepentantly normal. He closed his eyes again. "Please," he said aloud, to the bog or to the stick or to his dead father. None of them capitulated.

After a few minutes of waiting, a strange calm overcame him. He opened both eyes and understood that he would not be able to do the rite as he was supposed to. But if he could not be led to his wife, he would find her himself. He glanced over his shoulder, warily, at the dead body of his father. Beneath Charles Haddesley the Eleventh's contemptuous gaze, Charlie held the dowsing stick at his side and began hacking through the sphagnum, his eyes struggling through the mist. He did not think he could miss the figure of a woman. He became coldly determined, his focus blindered and defiant; he did not even think of anything that was to come after the moment of discovery. If he found the bog-wife, the rest would follow naturally, he told himself. *If* he found her.

For hours, he searched the bog meadow, seeing phantom wives in every raised hummock of earth and rotted log. Hurriedly, with his heart in his throat, he'd run toward them until he could no longer see the contours of the woman-body where he'd imagined it. He permitted himself only two or three seconds of despair with his hands on his knees, his breath coming in labored puffs, before he began again to search. Sore already from yesterday's labors, the usual dull ache in his hips and pelvis had become a sharp and insistent burn that snatched at Charlie's focus, made him careless. He didn't see the branch that caught his foot and brought him down. The earth beneath him was soft, but not soft enough. Searing pain tore into his groin and settled there; for a moment, Charlie couldn't move, couldn't even breathe for how it hurt. He sat in the mud and stared across the pitiless gray-washed landscape. She was not there. The exchange had failed, or he had. He had no wife. The bog had not made him one.

NORA

hey knew something was wrong as soon as Charlie came stumbling back through the yard alone. Eda, sitting at the windowsill with a book in her lap that she hadn't even opened during the hours he'd been gone, was the first to see him. "He didn't get her," she said, speaking just above a whisper.

Nora went with Percy to the window, Buz Lukens clinging with his long possum toenails to her shoulder. Wenna hung back, muttering something about not seeing your brother naked. They watched as Charlie progressed slowly through the yard. In the downpour, stripped of his clothes, he had the look of a drowned creature washed to shore. *Could he still be only* that? Nora wondered. A slumped pale figure whose feet stuck in the mud. A patriarch was supposed to be something else, something more. She had imagined him coming back from the bog transformed: bigger somehow, no longer hesitant or stiff or fumbling like the old, non-patriarchal Charlie she had grown up with.

Beside her, Percy worked his hands into fists and then unfisted them and flexed his fingers out as long as they could go.

"So he couldn't even do this part," he said.

Eda turned only for a second to look at him before she resumed staring out at Charlie. "Maybe the bog-wife is still back there somewhere," she said, seeming not to believe herself. "We don't really know what he's supposed to do with her, at first."

"He's supposed to bring her back!" Percy said. "He's supposed to rut with her in the bog where she was born and then

78

lead her home and wash the mud from her in a bath of boiling water. We *do* know."

Only then did Eda's attention really turn from the window. A look of alarm crossed her face. "No one told me there was supposed to be a bath of boiling water. Do you know how long that would take? Are you sure it *has* to be boiling? It can't only be warm?"

"Well," said Percy, doubting himself now, or merely realizing that he had miscalculated by revealing anything to Eda when she was already upset, "I mean, it doesn't matter now, does it? Because she's not with him. There's no one to bathe."

"I wonder what happened," said Wenna, half-audibly. "Or, didn't happen."

Eda opened her mouth to answer—probably, Nora thought, to say that it was somehow Wenna's fault—but she was interrupted by the slam of the back door.

"He's mad," Nora whispered. Charlie never slammed doors.

They went downstairs in a clump, the weight of their steps straining the staircase. Charlie stood in the kitchen, his hair rain-slicked to his head, his eyes pinned to the floor. Mud cut dark streaks across his face and legs and stomach. Nora concentrated on not looking at his crumpled-up testicles and still ended up looking at them. They all waited, no one seeming to know how to approach the feral creature that had come back to them. Then Wenna said, "You want to get dressed, Charlie?"

"Get him a towel," Eda ordered no one in particular. Nora looked at Percy, but he looked back so fiercely, with such loathing, that she relented at once and went to the linen closet. Charlie held the towel as if he did not know what to do with it until Eda stepped in and, with a sigh, pulled it from his grasp, shook it out, and wrapped it around his shoulders like a cape. Nora remembered, with a vague pang of some feeling she could not name, how Eda used to do the same thing when she and Percy had their baths as children, shaking out one towel and then the other, kissing them on their foreheads as she drew them out of the enormous old basin in the sunroom.

"So . . . what happened?" Eda asked, using a tone of voice that she seemed to think sounded gentle but, really, to Nora at least, sounded like she had a mouthful of nails. She was somehow managing to lean down into his face even though he was several inches taller than she was.

"She didn't come," Charlie whispered.

"Obviously," said Percy.

Eda looked over her shoulder at him. "Percy, make coffee. Make a lot of it."

Percy's face twisted in fury; for a second, Nora thought he was gearing himself up to say something terrible to her. But then, as if something had occurred to him that changed his calculations, his mouth slackened. His hands dropped to his sides. "Fine," he said, and he retreated to the stove.

"Okay." Eda pushed out a chair across from Charlie. "What happened?"

Charlie said nothing for an endlessly, torturously long time.

"Maybe we should just let him get some rest," Wenna said.

"Now?" Eda whirled to face her. "You want him to rest now, when the bog-wife could still be out there somewhere, dying or being born? I know the compact means nothing to you, Wenna, but for the rest of us—"

"She's not out there," said Charlie, and he looked surprised, almost betrayed, by the sound of his own voice. "The exchange didn't work."

"But," Eda said, slowly, trying and failing to disguise that she was on the edge of complete panic, "*how* can you know that? It's just hard for me to believe that you looked everywhere. Don't you think you could have missed something? I mean, it's acres and acres of land out there. And it's not easy to find someone."

"That's what the dowsing stick is for," said Percy from across the room. "Did you use the dowsing stick?"

"Yes," said Charlie, miserably, "I used the dowsing stick."

Everyone was, for a moment, silenced. There seemed to be nothing more to say. The failure of the ritual was stupefying. The scream of the kettle startled all of them. Percy took it from the heat and loudly, pointedly, removed the four passably un-cracked teacups from the cabinet one by one, setting them on the counter with pronounced clunks.

"There's not enough for everyone," he informed them.

"I don't need one," said Nora, although she knew this was the quickest way to ensure that she would, in the end, get one.

"You have yours, Nor," said Eda. "I'm going out to look for the bog-wife myself."

*

They passed a boring, shivery day positioning buckets and jars to capture the rain that came through the holes in the roof and the cracks in the walls. Late in the afternoon, Eda came through the back door mud-soaked to the waist, her eyes red and her cheeks tellingly puffy. She answered Wenna's questioning look with a single shake of her head as she extricated herself from their father's old waders.

No one seemed to want to have dinner, but after dark they

all became hungry at roughly the same time and they ended up huddled around the kitchen table, their father's old seat dragged out of retirement to accommodate the five of them. They were only eating motley scrounged-up combinations of leftovers and canned soup and sardines on toast, but there was a strangely formal feeling to the gathering. As if they had all been ordered, separately, to appear there. Charlie was the last to come into the room, probably hoping to avoid them, and they all sat waiting as he heated a can of SpaghettiOs without any pretense of urgency, no one saying a word. Outside, rain hammered, punctuated occasionally by murmurs of far-off thunder.

The quiet in the room felt to Nora like a precarious kind of quiet that might at any second be shattered by an outburst of unbearable emotion and violence. They needed conversation; to be specific, they needed a conversation that wouldn't end with someone storming off. What she did not want, above all, was for Wenna to get up from the table and pack her things and leave them in the horrible confusion of an exchange half-done. "Do you know," she said, brightly, "I read that a woman in Arkansas found the Holy Grail?"

"It's Arkan*saw*," said Wenna. "Not Ar-kansas."

Embarrassment coursed through Nora—how had she not known, and how was she even supposed to know, when she had never heard the word spoken aloud before?—but she persisted. "Also, a kitten, in Texas, was born with three heads. And *lived*."

"That wouldn't happen," said Percy.

"It *did* happen," Nora said.

Charlie sat down with his bowl of SpaghettiOs steaming before him and began scooping large spoonfuls into his mouth, wearing a tortured expression.

"I think we should do the ritual again," Eda said.

Charlie held very still, his spoon suspended. Wenna made a soft but conspicuous little huff of disbelief.

"What?" Eda asked. "You think this is funny?"

"No," Wenna said. "I just don't know what you think *we* can do. Are you capable of forcing the bog to spit up a woman for Charlie?"

"Don't make it sound so . . . vulgar," Eda said. "We're the bog's custodians. It is, strictly speaking, our job to make it spit up things when we need them."

"Charlie's job," Percy pointed out.

"Charlie's job," Eda conceded. Her eyes darted to Charlie, then back to her empty plate. "At any rate, it's supposed to know what we need, and give it to us."

"Well, we don't have anyone else to exchange," said Wenna. "Unless you're volunteering."

"I don't mean that part. We did that part right." Eda paused, as if waiting for someone to argue otherwise. "I mean the second part. Charlie's part." She looked at him. "I think you should go back out there. Tomorrow morning. Make sure you didn't forget anything. There's a book, isn't there, Percy? Go get the book."

Percy gave Eda a withering look. "You get the book," he said. "It's none of my business. *I'm* not the patriarch."

Eda's eyes widened. She had not anticipated his resistance. "Nora?" she said, her voice a note higher than normal.

Nora's first instinct was to protest. It set a bad precedent for everyone to think she would simply do anything that Percy didn't feel like doing. As it was, she had already gotten the towel for Charlie when Percy didn't want to. Besides which, Wenna was here, and Nora did not want Wenna to think that she was always blindly obedient to Eda, that she was always on Eda's side. But protesting would have meant a fight, probably a fight between Wenna and Eda, and Nora didn't want that either.

"I'll get the book," she said.

The book was the Borradh book, a fragile-looking manuscript that their father kept in a small chest to protect it from the assaults of sunlight and moisture. Nora had never been permitted to touch the book herself, but she had seen it on a few occasions when her father took it out and laid it reverently on his desk and let them watch as he gently thumbed through the pages with their cheerful, demented illustrations and their dense rows of handwritten script. Only the boys knew how to read the old French of the book. The Haddesley girls had not been made to learn it, for which Nora was mostly grateful—Percy always used to look hollow-eyed and exhausted when he finished his old French copy-work, as if the life had been drained out of him—but which she occasionally resented, because it felt like a door shut in her face to see an illustration of a woman with a scythe harvesting fur from a half-wolf, half-tree creature, and to have no way of knowing for herself what it meant or why it was there.

She held the book on two flat palms, as if it were the Holy Grail that the woman in Arkansas found, and carried it to the kitchen. She'd expected her siblings to prepare the table for it, but they hadn't, so she set it right in the middle between Charlie's half-eaten bowl of SpaghettiOs, the breadcrumbs from Eda's toast, and Percy's sweating glass of goat's milk. For a second, they all sat motionless before it.

"Charlie?" Eda prompted, not willing to commit the transgression of trying to read the Borradh book herself.

Charlie grunted as he hitched his body forward. He opened

the book and paged through, with none of the caution or delicacy of their father. "Here," he said, when he came to a page decorated with green braids of moss. The bottom margin showed an illustration of a gray woman lying flat in a brackish gray-green horizon of water, then rising as if lifted by wires.

"The bog-woman is raised from the heath by this practice," he said slowly. He paused every few words, so he could translate the language on the page into the language of their kitchen table. "The sacrifice of the father is necessary first. Let the body be prepared for burial while the father is still living. Let all the offspring of the father join together and lower the father into the bog's mouth."

"The *lip* of the bog," Percy muttered. "Not the mouth."

"Does it matter?" Eda asked.

"Something must have mattered," Percy said, and with this no one could argue.

"One day after the burial, the supplicant must bathe in the mud of the ancestral burial ground. Then the supplicant is led by the instrument—"

"The wand," Percy corrected.

Charlie began to get flustered. "We know it means the dowsing stick," he said.

"*Do* we know that?" Eda asked.

"Dad told us," Percy admitted.

"—to the place of the bog-woman's hewing," Charlie went on, doggedly. "The bog-woman will there have been formed. The supplicant must clean the bog-woman's mouth."

"It says wet her mouth," said Percy, with pleasure.

"It says *water* her mouth," said Charlie, "technically." Nora could see his anger in the set of his shoulders, the way he bore himself down onto his ribcage.

"Whatever it says," Eda interrupted. "Did you do that? Whatever . . . that is?"

"There wasn't a wife to do it to," said Charlie.

"So something must have gone wrong before that."

Everyone fell quiet, waiting for Charlie to answer her. He did not answer her. Outside, visible through the window, a fork of lightning knifed into the earth. The succeeding thunder made the house shudder.

"Are we really all pretending we don't know what went wrong before that?" Wenna asked.

"What are you saying?" Eda sounded not at all like she really wanted to know the answer. She watched Wenna with her chin jutted out, daring her.

"You know," said Wenna.

Nora's chest tightened. For ten years, they had not spoken of their mother. She felt as if Wenna had betrayed a confidence. It was one thing to talk about their mother in the soft, protected dim of a shared bedroom, another to do it out here at the kitchen table, and to invoke her in *that way*. She almost could not believe that Wenna would come so close to the subject.

"Don't," said Eda, jabbing a finger at her. "You are," and she fumbled then, as if she hadn't prepared for the sentence to have an ending, then concluded, with dissatisfaction, "a guest in this house."

"She is not," Nora said, although she couldn't help but feel that Wenna had committed a kind of violation for which she deserved not punishment, exactly, but a reminder of what was permitted. "She's our *sister*."

Wenna reached for Nora's hand underneath the table and squeezed it. Then she let go. "You're right," she said to Eda.

"This really isn't any of my business. I said I'd stay for the burial. And I did. So I can go." But she stayed where she was.

"Go ahead," said Eda.

"Please, Wenna, don't leave," said Nora. "Eda, please don't let her leave."

"You can't leave tonight," said Charlie. "It's flooded out. Wouldn't be able to get the car out of the driveway."

Wenna's gaze fell to the lightning-splattered horizon out the window. "I'm not going to stay here," she said, to no one in particular. "I don't live here anymore."

Above them, with spontaneous vigor, an old and familiar crack in the ceiling began to leak, spilling fat drops of dirty water onto the table. Wenna flinched back, looking distrustfully at the jagged path worn through the plaster, but the rest of them met the new hole in the house with resignation. It was only coming from Charlie's room upstairs. Charlie moved the manuscript out of the way, though not before a water stain sank blackly into the middle of the parchment. Percy relocated a mixing bowl from one of the kitchen's less urgent cracks to the new one.

"If anyone wants to see the article," Nora resumed, "I can show you a picture. Of the woman with the Holy Grail in Arkansas." She realized she'd said it wrong again.

"We're going to be the last ones," said Eda, despairingly. "The last Haddesleys."

Fall

WENNA

very second Wenna stayed at the house was a capitulation. She had said that she would stay only for the burial. Staying the night afterward had been a compromise, but it had not seemed dangerous because the bog-wife's appearance in the morning would have marked a clear and well-defined end to the ritual moment. Now there was no end. The unfinished work of succession unspooled around them. They lived inside it, their bodies inclined very slightly at all times toward the windows as if at any second the bog-wife might appear in the yard, naked and mud-slathered and panting to marry Charlie.

What everyone seemed to know but no one wanted to say aloud was that the bog-wife was not ever going to come. The exchange was over, if incomplete, and Wenna had made her contribution. She was no longer ritually necessary. But she stayed, not because the family needed her and certainly not because she needed them but because she could not at any moment decisively choose the formless horror of *out there alone* over the familiar horror of *back here with them*. She no longer possessed the brazen, desperate courage of herself at seventeen. She could not regain that version of herself who had crossed the property-line for the first time in her life without any certainty that she would even survive the crossing; who had blundered along the state road in the dark, searching for a town she had never seen; who had gotten a ride from a perfect stranger and then relied on a man sleeping on a bench at the Greyhound station to feed her small pile of stolen bills into a machine and purchase a ticket, because she could not work out how to do it herself.

Twenty-seven-year-old Wenna found the entire thing insane, the dangers that seventeen-year-old Wenna had opened herself up to. But seventeen-year-old Wenna had not been naïve—or if she had been, that didn't account for why she'd gone through with it. Rather, she had understood that staying was a kind of annihilation worse than what any man at a bus station could have done to her. At some point, Wenna thought, she would feel that way again. In those first weeks, she kept thinking the moment had come: when Eda caught her and Nora in the kitchen rolling cookie dough into balls and descended into an afternoon-long fit of agony over the butter she said they had wasted; when Nora and Percy involved everyone in a violent dispute over some mushrooms that Nora apparently saw but did not uproot, or didn't see but should have, or—*something.* Or when the steady leak from the kitchen ceiling finally drove Wenna to see for herself Charlie's old bedroom, and she found the walls coated in a skin of moss, the furniture dirt-blasted and crumpling, the bed *still* nine months later pinned beneath the hemlock tree's enormous weight, the roof split by a long gash that had never been closed so that even now the room was open to the cloud-mottled sky. In that moment, she was face-to-face with the bleak reality of the situation. A household that left a tree embedded in a roof for most of a year was not a sane or healthy household. She felt certain that even Alyson the therapist would have suspended her "no judgments" philosophy to draw this distinction. But when she thought, *And where will I go, when I leave?* she still had no answer.

The simplest thing would have been to return to Illinois, where she knew the layout of the grocery store and the freeway exits and the vicissitudes of the weather. But the only thing she really had to go back to was Michael, whom she could not go back to. She had never really lived there without him, although technically she lived there for four years before they ever met, renting rooms in extended-stay hotels and dubious shared apartments where her name was never on the lease, working a sequence of jobs chosen purely because they paid under the table and the employers did not care that she had no social security number, no real work history, no driver's license. She had slipped anonymously in and out of half a dozen transient existences, a stable hand at an exotic-animal petting zoo and a housekeeper at a motel off the freeway and a dishwasher at a failing Polish restaurant, all in two- or three-month stints that ended when she could bear the work no longer or she was no longer needed. Always supplying a false last name out of the misguided and almost quaint fear that people in the suburbs of Chicago had any idea who the Haddesleys of West Virginia were.

She met Michael a few weeks before she might have begun to carve out a real life for herself. She was in night school taking a GED prep course, which she'd signed up for because one of her roommates suggested that she might make more money if she had a degree. Michael was there for a pottery class offered by the parks department, which he had taken because he read online that it was a good way to meet women. He struck up a conversation at the water fountain during an overlapping break. He wore a blue dress shirt and a clay-smudged canvas apron. There was a soft, dusty quality in his voice that reminded her somehow of Charlie. In his presence, she felt visible but safe, a conjunction of things that Wenna previously thought impossible. When he asked if she wanted to get a cup of coffee after their classes, she said yes. A year later, they were married. Wenna presented a four-month-old social security card secured with Michael's assistance at the marriage-license office and eagerly assented to have her last name changed. The last trace of her Haddesleyness vanished.

But then, even with a GED, she kept losing jobs almost as soon as she acquired them. Without the threats of starvation and homelessness hanging directly over her head, she could no longer put up with the indignities of minimum-wage work. Or else there was some truth in what her father had always said, that Haddesleys had too much bog in their blood to live in the world beyond the property-line. Once, at a waitressing job that Michael's friend arranged as a favor, Wenna came out of the kitchen with a tray balanced on her arm and was suddenly overcome by the terrible ugliness of the faces of the diners, the monstrosity of other people. She left the tray on an empty table and walked out of the restaurant and ran until she came to a mud-sodden patch of grass in a city park, where she lay face down with her limbs outstretched until Michael found her. After that, he said she didn't have to work anymore if she didn't want to, that she could take a break, return to the workforce when she felt ready. She never felt ready. She lived a closely bounded life, leaving the house only for errands and to visit the drainage pond at the other end of the neighborhood, which she stared into as if its bleak rain-fed surface could absorb her. She understood how completely she had failed to make a life for herself, but she did not really feel it until the moment her husband said that she could stay on the couch for a few weeks, if she wanted, but not forever.

So Wenna could not go back to Illinois. And she did not know where else to go. With a nagging sensation that she was slowly sinking down into depths from which she would not rise again, she stayed through the last rainstorms of the summer, through the first cranberry harvest of autumn (meager and too early, a shadow of the harvests she remembered in childhood, producing only a few buckets of wizened dark berries that were too sour for raw consumption), and finally even through peat-cutting at the end of September.

Peat-cutting was a ritual basically indistinguishable from a chore, except that you had to feign solemnity while you did it and at the end you got to drink cranberry wine. Even their father, whose main pleasures in life were upholding Haddesley traditions and getting his children to do manual labor, could summon no great enthusiasm for the work of carving bricks of soil out of the bog's margins and stacking them to dry in the goat shed. But peat-cutting meant the beginning of the end of the year. It was the hinge between the languorous sun-warmed part of the harvest season and the chill dying-away final days. It meant Wenna had stayed too long, more than a month, far more than the handful of days she had promised. When she woke to Eda's too-bright pronouncement that *we have to cut peat today!*, spoken through Nora's bedroom door, she fumbled for her phone and looked in disbelief at the date that appeared on the screen, even though it was no surprise; she had chosen consciously every day to stay one day longer.

"Come on," Nora said, awake for hours by now probably, swinging her feet on the side of the bed. "Come on, Wenna, come on."

There was nothing to do but come on. Useless to say that she did not want to cut fuel to see them through a winter that she did not intend to stay for. Wenna began rifling through her suitcase, which she had still stubbornly not unpacked, even though she had done laundry in the bathtub twice. She decided on running tights with the cotton sweater she had taken from Michael's dresser on her way out the door. It was the warmest thing she'd brought. She had been holding out on wearing it, knowing her scent would eclipse his as soon as she did and then she would have lost the last trace of him. But it was getting cold. If she stayed much longer, she would have to borrow clothes from one of her siblings or dig her old wardrobe out of the attic and hope that her body had not changed too dramatically since she was seventeen and accustomed to hard work and fed on forage.

"We could," Nora said, "dress up." From the tone of her voice, it was plain that this suggestion for *we* was really for Wenna, that Wenna's outfit did not pass muster.

Wenna noticed only then that her sister was wearing a funereal dress of velvet, itchy-looking and completely impractical for a six-hour jaunt of cutting and hauling bricks of soil out of the mire.

"Why?" They had never dressed up for peat-cutting before.

"It's a ritual," Nora said, tugging at her dress's shoulder. It was slightly too small for her, fitted to some long-dead great aunt. "It's . . . special."

It wasn't special, Wenna wanted to say, but she didn't. In the last weeks, she had seen the essential featurelessness of her sister's existence, an unending run of days distinguishable from one another only by the color of the leaves on the swamp maples or the depth of flooding in the yard. If Nora lived as other Haddesley sisters had lived, she would pass from childhood to death without encountering any of the milestones that gave form to a life besides the ones her own body thrust upon her. Peat-cutting was what Nora had.

"You look pretty, Nor," she said, finally. "You look grown-up."

Everyone besides Charlie went out to the bog meadow in a loose clump, Wenna and Percy carrying the iron spades that innumerable generations of Haddesleys had used to cut peat before them, Eda and Nora pushing wheelbarrows that had come from the tractor-supply store twenty years ago. The day was cold but dry. They passed the line of birches, moving away from the path that would have carried them to the bog's mouth, and walked through new-growth forest: slim stands of tamarack and black spruce interrupted by rangy heads of pine and even big-bodied young hemlocks. None were higher yet than Wenna's head, but the new trees were jarringly solid-looking in that place where all the vegetation used to be fine and wispy and low to the earth, their broad gray roots spreading in muscular knots across the ground. There were, she thought, too many of them, extending too far out, depriving all the smaller vegetation of sun. Where those trees grew, the sedge thinned out and lines of orange mushrooms threaded incautiously across the ground.

Percy, seeing the mushrooms, swung his spade with vengeful uncoordinated force. "You see?" He glanced indignantly over his shoulder at Nora, still chopping. "You see what happens?"

"It's not my *fault*," Nora said.

"Later," Eda said. "Not now." But Percy finished tearing out the mushrooms before he listened to her, his fear of the trespassers greater than his fear of his sister.

In years past, before Wenna left home, they had cut peat from the edge of the bog meadow, ripping into the oldest and sturdiest ground they could find. Easier, for drier earth to become so dry that it would burn. But there was no old or sturdy ground without trees now. The bog meadow had contracted, the lip between dry and wet narrower than before. On the border between the two, they stood in a row, no one wanting to be the first to begin. It had always been their father before.

"There's no way to start but to start," said Eda, firmly, and she thrust her spade into the earth.

Wenna found something perversely admirable in her sister's refusal to be stymied by reality. It did not seem to matter to Eda that she was not the patriarch, that they were basically without one, that the ritual rhythms of their life lacked meaning if the bog was dying or had rejected them. Eda watched the phases of the moon and remembered that a full moon at the hinge of autumn meant they were supposed to do peat-cutting, and so she made it happen. Now, she was singing one of the old folk ballads that their father used to sing to them, rife with filicide and live burial as the ballads all were, categorically inappropriate for children and yet soothing if only you didn't pay attention to the words. After a moment, Nora began to sing too, in her high, thin, lilting voice that wavered on any held note, then Percy in his lower scratch of a baritone, and at last even Wenna grudgingly found herself murmuring the words, which she could not help but remember, the song giving rhythm and form to the work.

Through the morning they labored, Wenna and Percy ripping up foot-long and four-inch-deep bricks of peat with hard motions of their spades, Eda and Nora gathering them into loose sooty piles in wheelbarrows and driving them back to the goat shed, Charlie stacking them in rows so they could dry into fuel for the winter's fires. These were not their usual roles. Their father and Charlie did the cutting before while the rest of them ran wheelbarrows. But today they took up their new positions without discussion. They all knew, too, that they would work continuously until they were finished, as if the work could not be set aside and picked back up, although any uninitiated stranger would have said that of course it could.

There was calm monotony to be found in the digging-up of peat, the four cuts of the spade into the earth, the hooking of the spade onto the newly defined brick, and the dredging-up motion that tore the brick loose. Yet, if she hesitated for even a second as she lifted the mounds of earth and flung them away, Wenna felt the basic and unassailable truth that they were mutilating the bog when they cut peat, as surely as their father had mutilated the bog when he cut the swale into it. Those glistening black cavities left in the earth were like open wounds, and their practice had always been to *leave* them open, to let time and water and the sphagnum's hunger for conquest suture them. She thought, then, *We have* never *taken care of it.* Always they had been portioning out fragments of the bog's life in exchange for fragments of their own.

"It's not healthy," she said aloud, and Percy—several feet away, hacking furiously at the peat—tore up a fresh brick that scattered dark sweet-smelling dust into the wind and looked at her.

"What's not?"

"This," Wenna said. "What we're doing."

"Why?"

She was surprised to find that he sincerely seemed to be asking.

"It won't regrow," she said. "The bog is shrinking."

Percy leaned on his spade and looked across the bald expanse of the land. "It's our bog," he said. "It's always done this for us."

"We do this *to* it," Wenna said.

He stiffened, very slightly. "But we have to heat the house," he said. "Don't we?" And he went back to cutting peat.

It was late in the afternoon when they finished, Charlie sending the message back through Nora that the goat shed was full. Wenna stood back, letting Percy gather the last crumbly bricks that only half filled the wheelbarrow. She thought of the year she turned twelve, how, after peat-cutting, after they had scrubbed the dirt out from underneath their nails and sipped their allotted sips of cranberry wine and gone to bed, their mother had come to Wenna and Nora's bedroom and gently nudged Wenna awake. "Come on," she'd whispered, the look on her face conspiratorial and almost girlish. Wenna moved to wake Nora, but her mother shook her head. "Only you," she mouthed, and so Wenna crawled across her sister and tiptoed into the hallway, down the staircase, through the kitchen, out to the yard. "What are we doing?" she whispered, once they were safely outside the house. "Taking care of it," her mother said. She went to a maple tree and gathered up an armful of leaves. "Come on," she said to Wenna. "You too." Together, they carried their wet bundles through the sparse conifers to the riven place where the peat had been cut. "Spread them here," her mother instructed. "Press them gently down, so they don't blow away." Slowly, they dispersed leaves in all the wounded places, working until the fibrous nerves of the cut peat were hidden, until the gash in the land looked sutured.

"I want you to know how to do this," her mother said

afterward, grasping Wenna's shoulders, her look intent. "Tell me you could do this again." But she never asked Wenna to do it again. The next year, her mother was there for peat-cutting but she was not really *there*; she stood at a distance, she observed but did not speak. Afterward, late into the night, Wenna lay awake waiting for her mother to come and get her, but her mother did not come and the next morning she saw that the wound in the peat had been left open.

Now, as dusk fell and the air chilled, they concluded the ritual like they had always done before. Eda opened a bottle of cranberry wine with the year 1976 written on the cork and they congregated on the porch, sipping from crystal glasses, the smell of peat on their skin.

"We did it," said Eda, resting her feet on the arm of Charlie's chair. "Our first peat-cutting without Dad here."

"One down, the rest of our lives to go," Charlie muttered.

They were all silent for a while, contemplating the years that threatened to unfurl before them, each one just like the one before. Except, thought Wenna, that every year the bog would quietly recede another few inches, the trees pressing in a little closer, the mouth closing a little more, until there was no bog left. *It will not survive them*, she thought. *It will not survive us. If we go on.* And she felt an obligation in that *if*, in the possibility that the Haddesleys could do something other than persist now that the bog had refused them a wife and in so doing also refused them a patriarch.

In therapy, Alyson always said that you couldn't be responsible for other people's choices, that we are all independent, singular beings. Alyson didn't, Wenna thought, really know anything.

That night, lying on the floor in their shared bedroom, Wenna whispered to Nora, "Do you ever think about leaving this place? All of us, together?" But her sister was asleep, or pretended she was.

EDA

da waited until after peat-cutting before she went to Charlie, hoping though never expecting that the bog might eventually fulfill its obligations. As the leaves on the maples shriveled and browned, as the air chilled, she woke in the mornings and tugged aside the heavy old velvet curtains in her bedroom and stared out into the waterlogged yard, her eyes gathering one clump of sodden foliage or another into the figure of a woman for a heart-pounding second before she realized there was no woman there, the bog-wife had not and would not come.

Charlie and the rest of them accepted this, in their own ways. Charlie confined himself to the study day and night except for furtive expeditions to the kitchen when he thought no one else was awake; Wenna supported Nora in her ongoing project of pretending they were still children and the land still loved them and there had been no violation of the ancient compact; Percy became sulky and reclusive, stalking the bog's margins with a scythe on his shoulder at all hours.

Eda learned their new rhythms by listening through the floor from her bed as Charlie prepared his secret feasts in the nighttime's darkest hours, as Percy snuck down the staircase and closed the back door and then around sunrise came back, his boots heavy and unsubtle on the threshold, as half an hour later Nora and Wenna began their irritating daily routine of making an extremely elaborate breakfast that no one besides

Nora wanted to eat. Only when they were all finished did she open her bedroom door and admit that she was awake. This was her new rhythm. In the months of their father's illness, Eda had always been the first one out of bed. Her father had been an early riser. Eda insisted she was getting up for his sake, but it wasn't entirely true. She had come to relish the purity and the silence of early morning, the clean, pale way that dawn broke between the trees before it washed the yard and house in daylight, the expectant quiet of the kitchen that was broken only by her noises, her motions. But now that her father was gone and her siblings had adopted new patterns of behavior, Eda could not preempt them and she had no reason to try. She presented herself downstairs in the midmorning when the kitchen's silence felt wind-torn and exhausted rather than peaceful and she could expect to find a towering pile of dishes on the counter. It was assumed that she would wash and dry these dishes, and she did, although not without mentally cataloging who had used which dishes and what extravagant quantities of which foods they had eaten.

She could measure out the time they had left in the amount of wasted peanut butter that slicked the edges of plates and the dull blades of butter knives. Store-brand jars were four dollars now, Charlie had said a few months ago; name-brand ones were five fifty. So much? Eda had said with dismay. So much, Charlie said. They should have begun weaning themselves off it, and off of all the other small luxuries that Charlie carried home in plastic bags. Soon they would have to do without. What only Eda and Charlie knew, what the younger ones refused to understand, was that the Haddesley fortune—amassed over so many hundreds of years and responsibly hoarded by so many generations before it was squandered by only a few—was almost depleted.

They should never have needed the money. They should have taken massive and generous yields from the land: wild cranberries and wild ramps and fat-bellied wild pigs, portions of wild things so heaping that the always-struggling garden in the yard hardly mattered. But the land was starving them now, the garden had never stopped struggling, and without Walmart's inexhaustible supply of food from far-away corners of the world, the Haddesleys would already have been starved.

Eda knew their father had lived too long and the land was worse for it. The bog needed the exchange as much as they did. But their father was gone now, they had fulfilled their obligations, and there was no change in the landscape. There should have been a change. Eda couldn't help but see the bog as a wayward and intractable creature, one that could never be spoken to or reasoned with except in the language of ritual, and now not even that. In its failures to provide, in its erratic fits of rainfall and drought and its endless shrinking inward, she saw not the punishing withdrawal of a great force but the stubborn infant-like passivity of her own mother wrapped in a wad of blankets with the curtains drawn while Nora screamed outside her door and Percy lay neglected in a bassinet with a full diaper. Eda could not find within herself a scrap of reverence for anything so weak-willed. Nor could she resign herself to thinking that there was nothing she could do about it. Despair did not come naturally to her. Within two days of the exchange's failure, she had decided that if the bog would not perform its obligations, that did not mean the Haddesleys could not still perform *their* obligations. There were, she reasoned, other ways to force the Haddesley life cycle forward. Other ways of getting a wife for Charlie without depending on the bog to make one. If they could show the bog they did not need it, maybe the bog would again fruit and flower and flush with life, trying to appease the Haddesleys as the Haddesleys had for so many years tried to appease the bog.

When Eda opened the study door sometime after midnight, her brother was not in bed as she expected but seated at the immense mahogany desk that still felt like their father's exclusive possession, candlelight chasing jagged shadows up the wall behind him. He was looking at a book, his body bent uncomfortably in the wingback armchair that had been their father's preferred seat.

"Nothing useful in here." He closed the book as she approached, and Eda saw that it was their father's memoirs.

"It was noble of him," Eda said meaninglessly, "to write it."

"He was never worried about getting a bog-wife," said Charlie. "At least, not that he wrote."

"He wouldn't have *written* about it," said Eda, getting impatient. "Listen, Charlie—"

Startlingly, in a way that was unlike him, he interrupted her. "It's never happened," he said. "Not to anyone, in one thousand years."

"I know," Eda said, and before he could say anything else, she went on. "Charlie, you have to do something."

Charlie looked wounded. "There's nothing," he said. "That's what I'm telling you. It's always just worked."

"Maybe you can't get a bog-wife, but you can still get a wife."

"No," said Charlie. "Not possible."

"It is possible. Just go out to town and find some woman, and take her back here, and she can be your wife."

Charlie blinked stupidly. "No," he said, "it's supposed to be the bog-wife, it's . . ."

Eda closed her eyes. "Obviously," she said patiently, "it's *supposed* to be the bog-wife. But it's not going to be. So you have to find another way. You're part Mom. Your baby would be part Mom. It's still going to be a Haddesley, no matter who the mother is."

"So, what, I'm supposed to just kidnap some woman?" Charlie asked.

"You don't have to make it sound so violent."

"But it would be violent. No stranger from Marlinton is going to come with me willingly to our house."

Eda really hadn't considered the wife's opinion on marrying into their family, and she was perturbed that it had occurred to Charlie immediately. "How do other people get wives?" she said. "Do whatever they do."

"It wouldn't matter anyway. I couldn't. Even if I had a wife. We wouldn't have a baby." Charlie worked his mouth in his uneasy way and drew his body back into the rigid embrace of the wingback chair with a pained, cautious motion. "I know why the exchange didn't work," he went on. "The bog didn't want me. It never did, probably. And the tree falling was . . . a communication. But the way it hurt me, I don't think that I could father children now."

So horrific was this possibility that Eda refused even to consider it. "You don't *know* that," she said. "How many babies have you tried to have?"

Charlie looked at her with an outrage that was almost awe, his mouth slightly open.

"I know it doesn't . . . look right down there," Eda said. She had seen for herself the shriveled and wrung-out-looking flesh, in the first days after the hemlock tree fell and Charlie couldn't yet get up to use a chamber pot by himself. "But I don't think it always matters, how it looks. You just have to be able to . . . you know. Finish."

He wouldn't look at her, but she could see that he was furious from the set of his shoulders, the way his whole body tensed. She had gone too far. "Even if I could," he said. "Even then."

"So you won't try?"

For a long moment, Charlie said nothing. He shut the memoirs with a decisive thud. "*You* could have a baby," he said.

Eda stared at her brother in disbelief. Even after the innumerable times he had foisted his obligations onto her, she still was unprepared for him to expect that she would step into his place for *this*, this obligation that was so basic and essential that it lived in his body, or should have lived there. She was too stunned to speak. Angrily, she made for the door.

"All I'm saying," Charlie said, "is that it'd be easier for you than for me. You'd just have to find a man who would . . . you know. Once."

Eda froze and turned back, squinting to read the expression on her brother's face. Across the room, his features were a blur. She should probably have been wearing glasses for years now, but none of the pairs in the house made things any better and some of them made things worse.

"You're a coward," she said to him. But after that, she couldn't stop thinking of it.

There was something that she, Eda Haddesley, eldest daughter, could do on her own. An answering violation of the already-violated compact. A reclamation of authority.

Charlie

He was reluctant, at first, to take anything out of the house, but it had to be done; as it was, Charlie was afraid that he wouldn't have enough to pay for his appointment at the clinic in Charleston. He didn't really know what it cost to see a doctor, but once at 7-Eleven he'd stood in line behind a man talking on the phone who said that only the rich could afford to be sick nowadays, and if the Haddesleys were a noble and ancient family, they could no longer be described as a rich one. Besides, Charlie did not want anyone to find out what he was doing, not while he was still afraid it wouldn't work.

It should have been easy to dismiss everything that had come out of Eda's mouth after she'd announced that the solution to their crisis was kidnapping some unsuspecting stranger from Marlinton. But Charlie couldn't stop thinking about what she'd said afterward: that it didn't matter how he looked *down there*, that he didn't know *for certain* that he couldn't conceive a child. Before, it had seemed obvious to him that he couldn't. Why else would the bog have withheld from him a wife? But Eda had made him wonder.

He would never have been so defiant or idiotic as to see a doctor while his father was still alive. Charles Haddesley had assured his children that to the trained eye they were in a hundred ways identifiable as the descendants of bog-women: in the thin bands of flesh beneath their tongues, in the shapes of their pupils, in their unnatural aptitude for holding their breath. If they presented themselves at an emergency room or a clinic, they would be found out. The state might involve itself. Centuries of falsehoods had tarred the Haddesley name unfairly. Charlie had no reason to think any of this was untrue, but he felt he had to take the chance. If he could not rebecome the kind of man that the bog would furnish with a wife, then all their secrecy and their broken fingers that stayed forever twisted and their pneumonias that left coughs rumbling in their chests and his own father's untreated life-ending illness—cancer of the stomach, Eda had decided, after consulting a yellowed book of physick in the study—would be for nothing, because there would be no more Haddesleys to carry on the compact.

It was difficult to decide what to pillage from the house. Before Charlie began to look at their possessions as a form of currency, the masses of objects in the house had been individually invisible to him; he had regarded them almost as parts of the house's architecture. Now, as his eyes swept across piles of books and sheet music and broken furniture and old linens, he understood why Wenna kept saying they were burying themselves alive. There was so much, and none of it was useful. He knew, from driving past the antique mall on the state highway, that some people were willing to pay money for old things simply because they were old, but he could not really make himself believe that anyone could want their tarnished silverware or bedraggled taxidermy. He contemplated selling the Borradh book—certainly the oldest thing they owned, and in better condition than many of the newer volumes in the study—but there was a part of him that believed he could not commit a violation so enormous without his father rising out of death and the bog pool to punish him.

After days of deliberation, he settled at last on the filigreed globe and accompanying magnifying glass that had come down to his father from the first American Haddesley, the first of the eleven Charleses, who had—his father said—carried these small monuments of masculine gentility along with the Borradh book and the wooden shield bearing the Haddesley coat of arms across the Atlantic. The glass and the globe were older than anything else in the house besides the Borradh book, and not so badly worn that they were useless, and, if Charlie was honest with himself, it gave him a vicious twinge of pleasure to think that he was getting rid of them, the instruments of his childhood harassment. The globe had been a prop for innumerable lectures about the oneness of the Scottish Highlands and the Appalachians, while the magnifying glass was used to answer any excuse that a column of old French was too small to read. Charlie and Percy had spent hundreds of hours submitting to their education, and for a second, only a second, Charlie thought to ask his younger brother to go with him so they would be together in this betrayal that was really an act of devotion. But they had never been friends. Percy held nothing but contempt for him, and Charlie could not forget the dream that had not been a dream of Percy standing in the study doorway with a tincture of poison.

He wrapped the magnifying glass and globe in a blanket and loaded them into the trunk of the station wagon, then drove two hours to Charleston, as far from home as he had ever gone before. He could not be sure what inherited superstitions a Marlinton antiques dealer might harbor about a Haddesley artifact, should the objects somehow be traced back to them. The parking lot of the shop he'd found during his research at the public library—*buying, selling, appraisal; specializing in early colonial handicrafts and artwork*—was empty. In the front window was a crumbling bronze plough. He stepped inside to the dusty glue-tinged odor of old things and was greeted only by a tortoiseshell cat, who climbed across stacks of books and heaps of porcelain dolls to sniff at the bundle in his arms as if assessing its worth. No human shop-minder materialized for so long that he began to develop a creeping worry the cat *was* the owner until at last a woman with her hair in a gray braid emerged from aisles of kitchenware, carrying over her shoulder a wooden rocking horse. She set the rocking horse down and squinted at him, as suspicious as the cat. "Buying or selling?" she asked.

Charlie unwrapped the globe and the magnifying glass and laid them out on the counter. "Selling," he said, feigning confidence, as he so often did when he ventured past the property-line. "How much would you give me for it?"

The woman was silent for a moment longer than the forced politeness of cashiers normally allowed, and Charlie was afraid he'd done something wrong. "They're very old," he assured her. "Sixteenth century, at least."

"Well," the woman said, halfway under her breath, "shit." She ducked underneath the counter and came around to examine the objects, wrestling the cord of a lamp until it twitched hesitantly on and illuminated the gold-filigreed frame of the globe, the ornately decorated handle of the magnifying glass. She inspected the globe first, her gloved fingertips tracing the continents and oceans. After a long moment, she huffed out an exhalation that was almost a laugh and lifted her eyes to look at him.

"Son," she said, "these aren't sixteenth century."

"I thought they might be older—"

"No," she interrupted. "Newer. Much."

Charlie felt accused, and vaguely indignant, as if the

Haddesley name itself had been insulted. "But they've been in my family—"

"I'm sure they have," the woman said, almost gently. "But that globe's got Austria-Hungary on it. I'd date this little set around the 1890s."

Charlie had never even heard the words *Austria-Hungary*. Blankly, he followed the woman's pointing finger to the words scrawled across one quadrant of a continent, words that had never once featured in his father's historical lectures.

"The 1890s," he repeated. The Haddesleys had been settled two hundred years in West Virginia by then; Charles Haddesley the Eighth had, if he was remembering correctly, been early in his manhood, probably the father of infants. Certainly not running around Europe collecting newly made globes.

"Maybe as late as 1910."

"How do you know?" But he didn't really listen to the answer; something about empires and the First World War and paint technology *back then*, the wrong *back then*. He felt adrift, his mouth felt as if it were filled with wool, until it occurred to him that a woman in a Charleston antiques shop might certainly be less knowledgeable about history than his father. He began to steel himself to gather up his belongings and take them somewhere else. Then the woman said, "Still good finds, though. Collectors go mad for this kind of thing. Victoriana masquerading as Renaissance craftsmanship. Looks to be real gold on that frame and the magnifying glass handle too. I'll give you four hundred for the set."

Charlie hesitated. It was far less than he had hoped for, far less than he feared he needed. The whole transaction so far had been a humiliation that no Haddesley patriarch should have tolerated. But the idea of starting over in another shop and subjecting himself to another set of critical eyes filled him with such dread that he knew if he didn't sell the objects now, he probably wouldn't sell them at all.

She paid him in cash, fifties and hundreds from the till.

"Are you sure that it's so . . . new?" he managed to say with the bills already in his hands, as if it still mattered.

"Listen," the woman said, "I understand if you want to shop around. Take the piece to someone else, see what they say. I'll still be here. But it's a simple fact that you've got a late-nineteenth-century world on that globe, and factory crafts-manship, besides. Don't feel too bad about it. I can't count the number of times someone's come in here, sure they've got something absolutely invaluable because some great-aunt treated it like a priceless antiquity, and it's really just a nice old keepsake, you know? Meaningful to your family, to you, but not worth as much to someone who didn't grow up with it, at the end of the day."

Charlie thought of his father standing over him as he dragged the magnifying glass across a heavy vellum page, reading slowly and falteringly aloud. "It's not such a nice keepsake," he said. He took the four hundred dollars and drove three blocks to the Charleston Low-Cost Urgent-Care and Medical Clinic with the unquiet sensation that secret and deformed parts of himself had already been laid bare for examination.

❧

Charlie didn't know to make an appointment, so he sat in the waiting room of the clinic for hours as the sky darkened. His eyes strayed to the brochures on the wall, their covers bearing photos of smiling or distraught-looking people, all of them dark-skinned, most of them younger than himself. *HPV and you. Get the facts on HIV! What to know about contraception.* When he'd entered the room, the woman at the front desk had scrutinized him through the bifocals propped on the end of her nose and written down the assumed name he'd given and asked doubtfully if he had insurance. He showed her the bills from the antiques shop, and she sighed.

"What are you here for?" she asked, and Charlie found again that he couldn't breathe. He was not prepared to reveal himself, at least not to a gum-chewing nondoctor in front of an audience of strangers waiting to be seen for mysterious three-letter diseases.

"A tree fell on me," he said, inadequately.

"A tree fell on you," she repeated.

Charlie nodded. He could not say more. After a prolonged, weighted silence, the woman told him he could sit down.

For hours people streamed in and out, their infirmities ranging from invisible to staggering, most of them stopping on their way out to argue in low, urgent voices with the woman at the desk about cost. Charlie sat across from a thin woman of about Nora's age who wore an unseasonably thick coat and a man who came in holding his arm with an expression of quiet, focused agony on his face. They did not speak to one another, but the presence of the man and the woman somehow anchored him. The three of them had been there for close to the same amount of time, so when one was called, the others might reasonably expect to be called soon after. The longer they stayed in that room waiting, the less real everything felt to Charlie, the more absurd became the notion of the hemlock tree falling directly across his pelvis and the notion of the bog-wife appearing fully formed in the mire and the notion that a doctor in a low-cost clinic could possibly cure one by curing the other. Charlie began to doubt his own story.

He wished for not the first time that he and Eda had cell phones, so he could tell her some reassuring story of why he had been gone for six hours now and would not be home for several more. He had never been gone for so long. He would have to grovel and lie when he came home, but he could at least be comforted by the knowledge that Eda would never cross the property-line herself and therefore depended on these excursions of his. She had looked at him with an indignation that was almost terror when he spitefully suggested that *she* go out and get pregnant.

At last, when he was beginning to fear that the clinic would close before they called his assumed name, the nurse in the doorway said, "Charlie Hanesley?" And he was ushered through the doors to a small room with a raised chair coated in paper. Charlie sat down, cringing against the familiar pain in his pelvis, to wait again. At last a brown-skinned man in a white coat entered. Charlie watched warily as the man crossed the room and entered something inscrutably into the computer. His tongue already felt heavy in his mouth as he tried to think of how he would explain his affliction.

"What brings you here?" the doctor asked, which made his earlier humiliation at the front desk feel suddenly pointless.

"A tree fell on me," said Charlie, again. "I want to know . . ." He hesitated now, gathering the courage to say the terrible thing. He had been so composed when he'd left home hours ago, but he was always easily intimidated and worn-out by the transactions of the world beyond the property-line. It had been, he knew now, a grievous error to combine the errand of selling the globe and glass with the errand of the doctor appointment.

"Yes?" the doctor said, impatiently. Charlie thought of the

people left in the waiting room: the emaciated woman shivering beneath her coat, the man with his right arm cradled in his left elbow like a half-drowned animal, the others who came in after them.

"I want to know if I can still have children," he burst out. "My—well, what's *down there*, it was injured."

"Your penis or your testicles?"

Charlie felt his face become hot, unused to speaking of himself in terms that he normally reserved for livestock. "Testicles," he answered, his voice barely creeping above a whisper.

The doctor's face was impassive. "What treatment did you receive at the time?"

It was difficult, still, to remember those first days. Charlie thought there might have been ice packs to bring the swelling down, but he could not really remember any individual time when there had been an ice pack. He closed his eyes and an image of the hemlock tree plummeted toward him. "I don't know," he said.

"Did you go to an emergency room?"

"No."

"Any other kind of medical treatment?"

"No," Charlie said again, his voice like a husk. He was afraid the next question would be *why* and he wouldn't be able to answer without revealing everything.

"All right," the doctor said. "Well. Let's take a look." He made Charlie lie back on the wax paper and wrestle his pants down his legs and answer a new series of questions. *Have you found blood in your urine? In your semen? Are you still able to ejaculate? Do you become erect? Do you feel any pain when you masturbate?* Charlie didn't know what the words *ejaculate* or *masturbate* meant, and he was afraid to admit his ignorance while the doctor's gloved hand progressed methodically across his pelvis, fingers pressing down wherever the flesh yielded. *Does this hurt? How about this?* It all hurt, Charlie wanted to say. It hurt merely to lie down flat on his back. But he didn't care if it hurt; he only cared if he could lie down in the mire with the bog-wife and make a son for his dead father.

At last, the doctor told him he could sit up again. "You've experienced testicular rupture," he said as Charlie squirmed frantically back into his pants, yanking tight the length of rope that he used as a belt because none of the belts in the house fit around his belly. "That's what we call an acute condition. Needs treatment right away. The best chance of effective intervention is within twenty-four, forty-eight hours."

The words blurred chaotically, meaninglessly into one another. It had been nine months now. "Oh," said Charlie.

"With immediate treatment, usually there's a full recovery. If you had come in right away after it happened . . ." The doctor let the words trail elliptically into silence.

"So, there's nothing," Charlie said, feeling the same terrible smallness that he felt at the counter in the antiques shop with his valueless and most valuable possessions laid out in front of him. "Nothing I can do now."

"There are a few diagnostic procedures," the doctor said. "Ultrasounds. Blood tests. But they would only show us the extent of the damage, not resolve it. I'm sorry to be the one to tell you." He met Charlie's eyes too easily as he said it—sorry to tell him, thought Charlie, but not sorry that he could father no children. "Down the road," he went on, "you could explore other options. Adoption. In vitro fertilization. A sperm donor." He turned and consulted the wall of pamphlets, as comprehensive as the rack in the waiting room, then produced a glossy blue one and handed it to Charlie.

Navigating Infertility, said the pamphlet, the words overlaying a photograph of a man with his arms around a blond woman, his expression stricken, her hand covering her eyes.

"I don't need it," said Charlie.

"Just in case," said the doctor. "You might change your mind."

❧

The night was black and the fog closely gathered by the time Charlie came home. Light still glistened faintly through Eda's curtained window, which meant she'd waited up for him, but the light flicked off before he even went around the house to the back door. Was she not going to demand to know where he'd been? He had concocted a lie about the car breaking down that he thought she would not be able to contest.

Charlie opened the back door and only the light-scared nocturnal gaze of Nora's pet possum met him. For a few minutes, he stood in the warm, familiar darkness of the kitchen, inhaling the musty half-rotted odor that was noticeable to him only in the first moments after he returned home, getting comfortable inside the noose that had tightened on him in the hours since he last was here.

When he was very young, four or five years old, Wenna only a baby and the youngest two Haddesleys not yet born, his mother used to lift him with her into her bog-water baths. He would sit snugly in the warm, pliant basin of her lap and run clots of sphagnum through his fingers, and she would say, *You are his son but my child*, and he didn't know what she meant by it, but he felt the force in the words as if she were performing some quiet one-step rite of her own in the bathwater, remaking him.

By then, his father was already dismayed by the kind of child he was; Wenna was supposed to be a second son, a backup, and because she had not been a son, their mother would have to produce another. "How many times?" he overheard her cry once, through the bedroom door. He didn't hear his father's answer. But he knew now: until they were insulated against the possibility of extinction, until Charles Haddesley the Eleventh could feel secure that no freak accident or inborn weakness should deprive him of a viable heir.

When he struggled up the stairs, it was to Percy's room that he went. His brother lay asleep in the dark, the covers to his chin, serene. Charlie crept close to his bedside. He stood rapt, his eyes mapping the features of Percy's face that was so like his own face but in small and almost undetectable ways stronger, leaner, more vibrant; and tenderness and hatred choked each other inside of him.

"Percy," he whispered, and his brother came suddenly awake.

"Charlie?" Percy rubbed his eyes as if he thought Charlie was an apparition that would disappear.

"Did Dad tell you to kill me?"

Charlie knew, immediately, from the expression on Percy's face that the answer was yes. Percy pushed himself upright and sat there for a minute with the covers wadded in his fists, saying nothing, not looking at him. "I couldn't do it," he said.

Charlie wished his brother would meet his eyes. Percy never would meet his eyes. "I think," he said, "that maybe you should do it now."

PERCY

After he failed to end his brother's life, Percy dreamed of Charlie every night. Charlie was never the point of the dreams, in which Percy was usually engaged in some menial and never-complete task that he couldn't remember upon waking, but always his brother was there, sitting in the corner to be noticed an improbably long time after Percy entered a room or standing at the top of the staircase when Percy came up. Sometimes he was wasting away, getting paler and more deflated every time Percy saw him, at last ending up gray and worm-eaten. Sometimes he was healthy, and threateningly more confident than he ever was in real life, his arm slung around the figure of a woman who Percy thought at first was the bog-wife but who always transmogrified blurrily into their mother by the time he got a good look at her.

He was almost unsurprised when Charlie appeared to him in the middle of the night, neither hale nor dead but certainly on the dying end of the spectrum, his forehead slick and the sour smell of terror on him. When he asked if Percy had been told to kill him, it felt like the conclusion that never came in his dreams, the thing that the lurking Charlie of his nightmares wanted to say but couldn't. Percy couldn't lie, but he was frustrated by Charlie's self-pitying pathetic suggestion that Percy kill him now, when the exchange had already failed and there could be no bog-wife.

"It's too late," Percy said. "We would only confuse the bog now."

Charlie blinked at him in that dumb, gentle way of his. Like a deer, or some other herbivorous, perpetually startled creature. "How do you know?" he asked.

"Dad told me."

Charlie's face darkened then, and Percy found in his face strange echoes, faint ones, of the way their father used to set his jaw and tense his forehead when he got angry. "Well, Dad isn't honest about everything," Charlie said. "Doesn't know everything."

It was not obvious to Percy that their father did *not* know everything, although undeniably he had not prepared them for the absence of the bog-wife.

"He said he was sorry to kill you," Percy said, inadequately.

Charlie sat with this dubious comfort for a minute, then said, "I wish he just had done it before. When I was still young enough to not know. Drowned me in the bathwater or put poison in my food. It would have been better."

Percy was unsettled by this confession, laid at his feet like a slightly grotesque and too-large offering that he did not want. In his experience, Charlie confided things to Eda if he confided them to anyone, and mostly he just bore everything heaped on him in silence, with a resigned little frown, as if he'd expected as much and never hoped for better. Hearing yearning in Charlie's voice was even worse than seeing him naked with his testicles shriveled and dark. "Well," Percy said, awkwardly, "I guess he didn't know, what would happen." He couldn't say: *I hadn't been born yet; he didn't know if he'd have a second chance.*

They both entertained the fantasy of Charlie's childhood death for a moment, and then Charlie grasped the footboard and pushed himself up onto his feet with a wince that Percy almost didn't see. "Sorry to wake you up," he said.

"It's okay," said Percy. But he felt hot and strangled with frustration. He could not possibly sleep. He went out to hunt for trespassers and stayed out for hours. When he came back to the house, it was midday, the sun full and warm, and Nora was standing out on the porch waiting to tell him that Charlie had swallowed a whole bottle of cough syrup.

❧

Charlie survived through the sheer force of Eda's will. She made him vomit until his stomach was empty before dosing him with charcoal for good measure. He had been returned to his old posture of convalescence on the mattress in the study, and Eda said he could not be left alone, so she and Wenna were taking turns sitting with him until he was, Wenna said indefinitely, "better."

"You should both sit with him too," Wenna said to Percy and Nora. The three of them were eating bowls of reheated stew, the least-suspect thing they'd found in the refrigerator.

The demand sounded awkward coming from her, as if she wasn't sure she commanded the authority to tell them rather than ask. Percy wasn't sure that she did either. Nora's eyes darted over to him in the old familiar invitation to collusion—it was much easier to resist if they resisted together—but then she lowered her gaze as if it had only been a reflex, an accident. "I know," she said. "Poor Charlie."

"Percy?" Wenna said.

It would have been easier for everyone, including probably

himself, if Percy just agreed to sit in the study for three hours while Charlie snored, but he hadn't rid himself of the smothered feeling from that morning, in fact it had only gotten stronger since learning that Charlie had tried to die, and he needed to *do* something with the feeling, and at the moment the only thing he could do was resist Wenna. "I don't really see how sitting with him will help," he said. "If he wants to do it, he will."

Wenna only looked at him, nowhere near as easy to rile as Eda was. "God, Percy," she said, "he's your *brother.*"

Percy felt chastened and then resentful. He was not going to let Wenna, who had stayed away for ten years and returned only because ritual required it, tell him that he was being disloyal. "I know," he said. "I *know* that."

"Poor Charlie," said Nora, pointlessly, again. "I think I'll read to him from *Yvain, Knight of the Lion.*"

"Good," said Wenna, with forced warmth. "Why don't the two of you do it together?"

"It's not our fault," Percy said, "if he dies. Or yours or Eda's or anyone's."

What he wanted was for Wenna to look at him and say that he was right, and that he could not have made Charlie swallow that bottle by anything he said or didn't say or didn't do. That Charlie would die or he would live, and Percy should never have been made to determine which one happened in the first place. But Wenna only scrunched up her face as if he'd said something incomprehensible. "It was everyone's fault, before," she said.

He understood she meant their mother.

❦

In the small hours of night, Eda came and got them from their bedrooms as if the house were on fire. They went to the study, where candlelight threw weird shadows on the paneled walls, illuminating only the too-pronounced chins in the Haddesley portraits. Charlie was, to Percy's dismay, still awake. They had been alone with him for no more than fifteen seconds when Nora gathered her quilt around her shoulders and opened her love-beaten paperback translation of *Yvain, Knight of the Lion* and said, with no preamble, "Once, as solitary as a peasant, I went adventuring."

"He might rather sleep, you know," said Percy. He himself had lain down in bed a few hours ago feeling certain that his eyes would not be able to close, only to find himself inside yet another Charlie dream, one of the Charlie's-dying variety, an emaciated and grimacing version of his brother drooped on the stair banister and then melting into the seat of the wingback chair where Percy sat now. Percy's eyes strayed to the mattress on the floor before he could stop himself, and it was as if he were still in a Charlie dream. The hollows underneath his brother's eyes, the waxen look of his face, the already-dead look of his hands clasped on his chest. He shuddered.

"No," Charlie protested, pronouncing the word like a grunt. "You can read."

Nora, vindicated, continued. She loved *Yvain*, whose hero promised his lady that he would come home after a year of knight errantry and then forgot, waylaid by adventure, and spent seven punishing years and eighty pages of translated verse atoning for that single moment of neglect—and not only that, but passed a whole season wandering mad in the forest before he regained himself enough to suffer in the right direction. Percy once thought, unkindly, that Nora liked *Yvain* because it was a story about a seven-year-long apology, featuring the kind of groveling that Nora could only dream of receiving for what minor slights were ever committed accidentally or not against her. But now, today, he felt the force of the knight Yvain's despair, the backward-looking frustrated urgency of having needed to do something that you could have done for only a moment in time, that you could never do now. An urgency that came late and felt not like regret but like a fist pumping your heart in your chest.

"A whirlwind broke loose in his brain," said Nora, her voice lapsing into a yawn at *broke loose*. "So violent that he went insane."

In the romance, the madness of Yvain was short-lived or at least politely abridged, so that his days of eating raw meat and sleeping on the forest floor elapsed in only a page and a half. Yvain could, it turned out, still do something. He had a long list of ways to redeem himself. His condition was not really Percy's. "Charlie," said Nora, dreamily, when a noblewoman had come across the knight's huddled form and decided to rescue it, "would you read to me?"

Ridiculous of Nora, thought Percy, to think that their brother, six hours out from having tried to refuse life, cough syrup stains still on his lips, would read her a bedtime story. But he did, sitting up and taking the paperback, his soft voice bearing Yvain to the field where the knight rescued the talking lion that was to become his companion. Nora lay down beside Charlie's mattress, the side of her face pressed into the rough mat of dried rushes that covered the floor, clearly intending to fall asleep. Percy realized this and said, "Let me read," hoping that at least Charlie might fall asleep too, because he did not want to be alone with his brother, but Charlie only said, "I can," as if anyone thought he couldn't, and persisted.

Percy considered feigning sleep, but he was too restless now, too awake, and he couldn't hold still enough. Instead, he rose, half listening as Charlie steadily carried Yvain through his seven years of atonement, through battles with snakes and ogres and the knight's own longing to die, and began to turn through the pages of the Borradh book, which had been irreverently left open on the desk, exposed to the perils of sunlight and moisture. He thumbed past the crucial, useless page with the picture of the bog-wife rising from the mire and the many pages afterward, with their marginal illustrations of scarcity and harvest. In the Borradh book, there was a rhythm to things and the world followed it. Trees leafed and then bloomed and then fruited and then dropped their fruit and stood formidable and bare and then leafed again. Calves frolicked alongside their heavy-uttered dams and then became bulls yoked to ploughs and then became sides of beef. The sun sank and the moon lifted and the moon sank and the sun lifted.

The Borradh book did not know where they were, thought Percy. It had not foreseen the place they lived now. Percy closed the book and paced his father's shelves. Charlie was reading a challenge between Yvain and a knight with ill intentions. "One of us will be brought low," he was saying, "who it will be, I do not know." Beside him, Nora was snoring gently, resting on the thin frame of her own arms. Percy took down his father's memoirs and flipped through them, searching for anything that might guide him home. *Slow down, slow down,* he said to himself, but he couldn't. He almost missed the line, handwritten on a fleshy old sheet of vellum that his father had tucked between two unremarkable diary entries from 1993, that said, in old French, *to hew a wife from naught.*

"Oh," Percy said aloud, without meaning to.

Across the room, Charlie stopped reading. "What is it?" Charlie asked, his voice tight as though he did not want to breathe too deeply until he got an answer.

Percy read the French more closely.

"It's telling how to get a wife."

Charlie hardly let him finish before he said, "How?"

"Make a form of sticks and humus and still water."

"A form?"

"And feed it on your own blood."

"And then . . . ?"

"Bury it for a hundred nights and a hundred days, and let nothing interfere with its grave."

"Okay," whispered Charlie.

"And when you dig it up, it's a wife."

"A bog-wife?"

"It doesn't say that."

"Do you think . . . it would be . . . ?"

A violation of the compact, he meant, Percy knew. To raise a wife when none had been raised for them, to refuse their line's extinction.

"She'd still be made from the bog." What he didn't say was that clearly their father had left the recipe there for them to find, anticipating that the exchange might fail, that they would need an alternative.

"It should be you," Charlie said, "who does it."

"But you're the custodian," Percy protested, although he could not compel himself to argue too fiercely.

Charlie craned his neck and faced him. "It should be you," he said again, firmly, a plea buried one inch beneath the demand. Then, as if Percy didn't already understand: "I don't want to botch it again."

Percy already knew he was going to be the one to do it, and some part of him had known as soon as he had read those words—*to hew a wife from naught*—but he felt he had to do it out of obligation and out of fealty and not out of the frustrated desire that had for years now been rising like a waterline inside him until he could feel it in the back of his throat, until he was almost drowned from the inside out.

"Eda won't like it," he said.

"It's not Eda's choice," said Charlie, with surprising force.

Percy wondered how many times their father said those words to him before he said them to Percy, *don't tell me you won't be able to manage your household*; how many times Charlie sat downwind of those words and tried to figure out what it would even mean, *managing* the rest of them.

"But Eda won't think it's not her choice."

"Eda doesn't have to know," said Charlie. "No one has to know."

This might be the first secret he and Charlie had ever shared, Percy realized. "It might not work," he said.

"It will," said Charlie. "You're not like me. It will work."

Percy felt an unexpected swell of affection for his brother. If the roles were reversed, he thought, Charlie would have existed contentedly as a younger brother for his whole life without ever once begrudging Percy the simple and unasked-for thing that Percy had always been unable not to hate Charlie for. He wanted to tell Charlie that he was glad Charlie was still alive, but he and Charlie didn't say things like that to each other and he thought he wouldn't have known what to do with his face while he formed the words.

"I'm sorry," he said, instead, and what he really meant was *thank you*.

After Charlie swallowed the bottle of cough syrup—clearly on purpose, although Eda insisted it must have been an accident, that he'd never dosed himself before, that he merely didn't know how much to take—Wenna's resolve to separate the Haddesleys from the boglands hardened. Seeing Charlie pale and slumped over, she had seen her mother. *He's not like that*, Eda had said as they dragged him to the chamber pot and got him to throw up. *Well, no*, Wenna had answered, *he only wants to die because he can't fuck a bog-wife, not because he has to be one*, which she was not proud of now, especially because she thought it was distinctly possible that Charlie had heard her.

But Eda was wrong: he was *like that*, and the rest of them were too. The life of their forebearers was killing them. Once she saw this, Wenna could not stop seeing it: in Eda's obsession with grocery receipts and her look of almost-frantic despair when Charlie came home with something he had not been instructed to buy; in Percy's jabs of violent, babyish fury that emerged seemingly out of nowhere when he stubbed his toe or couldn't find something or had to wait his turn; in Nora's cloying pleas for everyone to *get along* and compulsive pulling out of her own eyebrows, which she denied even as her dark eyes stood out from beneath only a faint dusting of wispy dark-blond remains. Her siblings were not, as Wenna initially thought, just the same as they had been ten years ago. They were worse. They had spent the decade of her absence growing around one another like roots in the same crowded patch of earth, contorting themselves so everyone could fit.

Yet she thought she could see traces of the people they still could be beyond the property-line, where all their impulses that were now only destructive and impotent might be otherwise directed, might even be useful. She imagined Eda in a tailored suit, sitting at the head of a long table (never mind that her education had centered mostly on the genealogy of the Haddesley family); Charlie amid the serene quiet of library stacks, advising patrons on how to find the books they might like (never mind that she had only ever seen him reading under coercion and had never seen him advising people); Nora in a college dorm, telling her innocuous secrets to other girls beneath strings of Christmas lights (never mind that she was too old, at twenty-four, to live in a dorm, and the secrets she knew were not innocuous); Percy driving a flatbed truck with a landscaping company's logo printed sharply on the side, leaves swirling in the air behind him (never mind that Percy had never been taught to drive). She began to fantasize about the lives they would lead, the home they would initially share—modest and unpretentious yet somehow spacious enough that no one had to share a bedroom—and the separate homes they would occupy later, their lives not so much entangled as interwoven, as siblings' lives should be.

Some part of her knew that it would not happen. She couldn't not know. But she wanted to think that the reason she failed when she went beyond the property-line was because she had been alone. If she went again—with them, now—they would collectively possess the strength and canniness and resolve and charm that Wenna did not have enough of, on her own, to live as other people did. She knew Alyson the therapist would disapprove of these thoughts. *You are your own person*, she was always saying, a refrain that Wenna learned to agree with but still did not really believe. On the checks she wrote Alyson for her copay, hadn't she signed with Michael's last name?

What she could not resolve, at first, was how they would fund their departure. Fifty years of monthly bank statements, piled carelessly together in their father's desk drawer, revealed to Wenna the diminishment to extinction of the Haddesley fortune. Twenty-one thousand dollars was the sole remainder of the ancestral wealth. Wenna knew how far that money wouldn't go across the property-line, where rent had to be paid and lights kept on and clothes purchased and transportation taken. She was not so naïve as to think that any of them would be well-employed, at least not right away. And so she could think of no way forward but to sell the house—and with the house, the bog.

It was unthinkable as taboo, the notion of letting someone else live on their land. At first Wenna almost could not let herself imagine it. But there was nothing else to be done. She told herself that there must be some way to ensure that it was protected, and that anyway anyone else could hurt the bog only physically. They could not commit the kinds of violations that for the Haddesleys were inborn and hereditary.

Eda, she had no doubt, would respond to the idea of selling the house the way she responded to any breech of the rules Wenna ever suggested, with a virtuous horror that was stagey and high-pitched, as if directed at one or both of their parents who might even now overhear from the grave. She would have to be introduced to the idea slowly, brought to believe that it was her own, given mastery over some meaningless but labor-intensive part of it. Wenna thought the others would be suggestible, but only if Eda was brought to agreement. And she was not ready yet, to bring Eda to agreement. She had to know first what the sale of their inheritance could buy.

When she asked Charlie for the keys to the station wagon, she told him only that she had an errand. He looked at her, his expression unreadable. She was still relearning the language of his silences, the hints of fear or anger in the barely perceptible twist of his lips or the lift of his eyebrows. He pressed his lips together until they whitened, then dug in his pocket and set the keys in her hand. "Okay," he said.

"You all right?" she asked, as she always did now, even though she knew he wouldn't admit it if he wasn't. Even in childhood he had been guarded, an inert observer of their rowdy thoughtless affection and their tantrums, always on the periphery of the piles they heaped themselves into, distancing himself from their mess and their noises. He was only three years older than her but had felt much older. Now Wenna felt like the older sister, scrutinizing the grimy cuffs of his hand-me-down sweater and wondering if he'd eaten anything that day.

"I'm okay," he said. "I'm not going to . . . you know."

"I know," she said, embarrassed that she'd been so transparent. "I didn't mean . . ."

"Have a good drive," he said.

It had not rained in two weeks, but Percy had been flooding the bog every other day with river water, and the station wagon struggled through four inches of wet mud as Wenna pulled out of the driveway. She felt the property-line pass with a little thrill in her stomach as if she were descending a large hill, a second of dizzying suspension before she was in the world again, roaring forward, buoyed on by terror and inertia.

She was a mile or two from town still when her phone lit

up. The road was narrow and winding, and even five years after learning Wenna was still neither a good nor a confident driver, but she could not resist glancing sideways at the passenger seat to see the voicemails stack up. There were six, seven, eight messages from Michael. Wenna forced her eyes back to the road, already imagining what Michael would have said, the *ehh* sound he made at the beginnings of his sentences when he was nervous, the midwestern flatness that lengthened his vowels; in that moment, she could not and did not try to square her certainty that she no longer wanted to be married to him with her desperate, frantic hope that he had called to say that he still wanted to be married to her.

She pulled into the parking lot of a gas station, maneuvering the station wagon into something that might not have been a real parking spot. But as soon as she had the phone in her hands, her eagerness recoiled. Listening to the voicemails felt impossible. She was afraid of what he wanted, or what he had wanted at one moment but might not want anymore now that she had been gone so long. After a long moment of hesitation, she slipped her phone into her back pocket, pulled out of the parking lot, and drove through Marlinton to the next town over.

The real estate office on the main drag had a door painted mustard yellow, window boxes of rain-muddled pansies, a welcome mat with something written on it in cursive that Wenna did not read as she stepped across the threshold. The walls of the foyer were a tidy grid of real estate listings, well-maintained and manageably small houses reduced to a list of desirable parts: en suite, half bath, kitchen for entertaining, stainless steel fixtures, craftsman style. Impossible to envision describing the Haddesley house in any of these terms.

Wenna could hear someone on the phone in one of the back

offices, but no one was at the desk in the front, and she was afraid that she was supposed to have made an appointment, done something online. She felt the disorienting but familiar beginnings of the realization that she was unprepared to do something that was simple and obvious for everyone else, so obvious that no one would imagine they needed to explain it, so obvious that she would not be able to disguise what she didn't know once she started. Wenna had not been prepared for how often she would encounter this feeling—not only during the first few turbulent years that she was on her own but for a long time, maybe even forever, because as she got older it seemed that there were always more things that she was supposed to know how to do.

For a long moment, Wenna stood in the foyer of the real estate office, envisioning what would happen if she stepped forward and got someone's attention—she was always too quiet and then suddenly far too loud—and said to them, firmly, *I want to sell my house.* And then, with the horseshoe thuds of someone walking in pumps, a woman stepped out of an adjoining room and asked if she needed help. The woman was Wenna's nightmare of a real estate broker, young, wolfish, and somehow comfortable in a turquoise skirt suit, but it was too late to turn back now. She did need help and said as much, fighting down the urge to glance over her shoulder as if Eda or Charlie or Nora might be standing there.

The woman introduced herself, but as Wenna followed the scent of hair product and the thud-thud of the woman's pumps into an office, she realized she had not absorbed the real estate agent's name. She began the usual visual scrambling for clues as she lowered herself into a chair, realizing only belatedly that she had not introduced herself.

"I'm Wenna Haddesley," she said, abruptly. She had decided there was no point in lying about her name or even using
her married one. The realtor would find out the truth at some
point. "I'm looking to sell my family's home. It's a big old house.
A fixer-upper." She had once heard this phrase on TV and had
the suspicion that it was too generous a descriptor for a struc-
ture with a fifty-foot length of hemlock tree jammed into it, but
she thought she was at least gesturing at the kind of thing that
the house was.

"Do you have a picture?" the woman asked, only half-attentive,
entering things into a form on her computer.

Wenna dug her phone out of her pocket, wincing past the
voicemails banner, and reluctantly presented the realtor with
the photo she had taken a few days before. Even crowned by
sunlight, reduced to the size of her palm, the house was a bleak
figure, ravaged-looking, a warped and evil cousin to the pleasant
ranches on the bulletin board out front.

The realtor glanced, and then her eyes widened; she scrutinized the photo, leaning forward on her elbows to squint at
the details the phone's camera resolved into shadowy blurs,
and then she drew back with the look of someone reawakening.
"This is the Maturin folly," she said. "You're the owner?"

Wenna hesitated, uncertain whether she was being insulted
or only misrecognized; she did not know what the Maturin folly
was. "My brother owns the house," she said. "Technically. But
I'm helping him." She did not feel *helping* was too generous a
term. Charlie could not, it was clear, survive the inheritance that
had been left to him.

The woman became uneasy, sitting back as if another
inch of distance between them would protect her from being

implicated. "Do you have power of attorney?" she said. "Is he . . .
aware? That you're selling? If it's his name on the deed . . ."

Wenna realized that she had no idea whose name was on
the deed for the house or even if a deed existed. Her father had
made no attempt to settle such urgent questions, at least not
within her earshot. "I don't know where it is," she confessed,
watching the real estate agent's eyebrows lift, her lacquered lips
twist in a polite, uneasy smile.

"Well," said the realtor, her voice wavering slightly, "you'll
need to show me the deed, before we can go any further. And if
your brother would like to be involved . . . ?"

"He's very depressed," said Wenna. And then, already deep
in the mire of humiliation, she confessed, "We really have to get
out of there. But we need the money to relaunch." She could
not meet the woman's eyes after that. She stuck her gaze to her
lap and heard the real estate agent pondering an appropriate
response.

"I understand," she said at last, gentler than Wenna had expected, and Wenna had the mortifying thought that the woman
felt obliged to soothe her because she was acting unstable, or
unsafe, but she saw no fear on the realtor's face when she looked
up, only a vague pity. "I can give you this much for free," the realtor said, her voice lowered to emphasize the gravity of this favor:
"There are two ways you can bring a house like this to market.
As is, you won't get much. Someone might buy it as a project, to
restore. Probably not much tear-down value. If I remember, it's
on marshlands . . . ?"

"A bog," said Wenna, and she felt a passing glimmer of unease at the thought of other people tromping across the delicate
thatch of sphagnum in boot-clad feet. "I could only sell to someone who would take care of it," she said.

"Of course," said the realtor, too warmly to mean it. "Depending on the number you're hoping to arrive at," she went on, Wenna realizing belatedly that she meant *money*, "you might consider doing some of the major repairs yourself, first. The tree in the roof, you know. If you can describe it as move-in ready, you might have a much larger pool of interested buyers."

"Move-in ready," Wenna repeated. It felt absurd to imagine any normal set of people unpacking the boxes of their lives into that house—*their* house: shouldering a TV and sofa into the forbidden parlor, filling the many bedrooms of the Haddesley dead with the *Star Wars* bedsheets and clock radios of the living.

"Or closer, at least. You know, habitable." The realtor slid a card out of the holder on her desk and held it out for Wenna to take. "If you ever sort things out with the deed, please do give me a call. I think there could be a lot of excitement, a historic house like that. The Maturin folly, up for sale! After such a long time. It must be a hundred years since it was occupied. Honestly, I think most folks have forgotten it is still there. I know I did."

She was still confused about the house, Wenna realized. She had mistaken it for some other old residence out in the boglands. Except . . . what other house was there? What other house could there be, when the Haddesleys had owned all the surrounding land for four centuries? When they were bound to the land and the land bound to them by the monogamous ties of ancient compact? Wenna had walked every walkable acre of their property, and she had seen no trace of a house that was not their own. They did not have neighbors.

The realtor was already getting to her feet, standing at the door, smiling expectantly. It didn't matter, Wenna decided. She would come back with the deed and the realtor would sell the house and the strangers who lived there next could call it anything they wanted.

※

Wenna sat in the station wagon outside the real estate office as the sky darkened, paralyzed by the enormity and complication of making the house habitable for other people. Obviously, the tree had to be taken out of the roof. The water damage and mold problem created by the tree's persistence had to be dealt with. Centuries of antique clutter carted out to the dump, anything of worth sold. And the entire house needed to be repainted, scrubbed clean, the cobwebs lifted.

She knew she should have begun with removing the tree, but the prospect of finding and hiring someone, dealing with the suspicion and outright terror that such a person's presence would probably arouse among her siblings, was so overwhelming that she could not yet face it. The tree would have to come later. Tidying first, she decided. Tidying would make the house habitable now, so she could stop waiting for food poisoning to succeed every meal.

Resolved, Wenna turned the key in the ignition and drove to the new Walmart her Greyhound seatmate had mentioned, following the sallow neon glow of the marquee sign up a long hillside. She recited to herself like a charm the chemicals she would apply to the house to scrub decades of neglect out of it. She had barely any cash left, but she told herself as she approached the automatic doors that the cleaning supplies would pay for themselves many times over if the house sold.

There was something both comforting and unmooring to

Wenna in the featurelessness of a Walmart: that she could be anywhere and it always appeared the same, identical gumball machines and limp gray entrance mats and pendulous fluorescents, even though everything inside was arranged differently. In an unfamiliar Walmart Wenna had no instincts but she was supposed to have no instincts. At any given moment ten or twelve other unfortunates would be wandering as lost as she was. She was in a kind of not-unpleasant stupor between shoes and lawn care when her phone rang. She answered it unthinkingly, forgetting that she was no longer a housewife in Illinois.

Michael's voice on the line was strained, quiet, a little incredulous. He did not seem to have expected her to answer. She would not have answered, if she had remembered. "Wenna?" he said, into her silence. "Are you there?"

Wenna turned hurriedly down an aisle as if she could somehow evade him. "Yes," she said under her breath. She was in laundry, which was empty save for one woman pondering fabric softeners. The woman was kneeling and rising, extending to her tiptoes and then flattening her feet, every few seconds glancing askance at Wenna. "Why are you calling?" It came out harsher than she meant, not what she would have rehearsed if she had thought to rehearse.

"Well . . . I was worried about you," said Michael. He sounded careful, deliberate. He had, Wenna thought, probably rehearsed their conversation. And that was obviously not the reason he was calling.

"Why?" It came out hostile and half-desperate, and she thought that he would know now that she wanted him to say he still loved her. She rounded the corner and found herself abruptly in the cleaning-supplies aisle.

"It's been a month and a half," he said. "I haven't heard from you. Where did you go?"

Wenna deliberated between name-brand and store-brand bleach powder for a vertiginous moment. "West Virginia," she said reluctantly. She could not remember what she had wanted to buy, so she filled her basket with heavy-duty sponges, hydrogen peroxide, and glass cleaner, and she felt for a second the comfort of amassing things just to have a great number of them.

"You went to them? Wenna." Michael sounded tired, as if he were the one who had ridden across state lines into the fog of the Alleghenies and buried his still-living father in peat. "I wanted to let you stay at the house while you looked for work, you know."

"I had to go quickly. My dad was dying."

Michael was quiet for so long that Wenna pulled the phone away from her ear to see if he'd hung up. He hadn't. "Has he . . . passed?" he said, at last.

"Yes," said Wenna. "As soon as I got there."

"Oh," he said. "I didn't know." He hesitated. "How is everyone doing?"

The whole conversation suddenly felt perfunctory and obvious, Michael too far behind to possibly catch up to where Wenna was now and disinclined to go there anyway. But she wanted him to be with her; the sound of his voice made her feel bereft and far away, as if she were a lost child, so she said, fixing her gaze on the gritty linoleum at her feet, "I'm going to try to sell the house. Get everyone out. It's gotten bad there."

"*Gotten* bad?" he said, with the doubt that the words deserved.

"Gotten worse."

"What do your siblings intend to do after the house is sold?

Don't they all still live at home? I don't think you know what you're signing yourself up for."

Her fantasies of Boardroom Eda and Librarian Charlie immediately became so flimsy as to be unmentionable. "They'll figure it out," she said, angrily. "Like I did." Although of course she never really had.

"Sure," said Michael, almost with amusement. "That's what they'd do."

"You don't know them," Wenna said, because he didn't. She had managed to mention her siblings by name only a handful of times in the years that she and Michael were together. She was not even sure that Michael could say with certainty how many there were, where Wenna fell in the birth order. She'd always felt that she was protecting him from the horrors of her family, but she understood now that she had also been protecting them—soft-bellied, light-shy creatures—from his scrutiny. In the Marlinton Walmart, before an endcap display of dish detergent that looked identical to the endcap display of dish detergent at Wenna's usual Walmart back in Illinois, Michael and the Haddesleys became threateningly close to one another, to her, and Wenna did not know who to be with them both so close at the same time.

"Okay," said Michael. "Well, I need an address from you."

"Why?"

He went silent again for a minute. "I need to send you some papers. From my lawyer."

She understood, then. He was not going to say he still loved her. "Oh," she said, and she cupped the phone protectively to her ear as if someone would overhear him.

"It's really simple stuff," he said. "A clean break, right?"

"Yes," said Wenna, although she didn't know what that could possibly mean, and then she surrendered to him the street address that had been her precious and shameful possession, secreted close, never given up to anyone, in all the years she had been away.

"Thank you," he said. "Wenna, I . . . you haven't changed your mind."

"No," she said, although a hundred times she had, for only a few seconds, thinking not only of the baby that would be his and hers and only faintly a Haddesley but also of all the many other things she was surrendering by refusing Michael the only thing he wanted. If he had called during one of those fragile and precarious intervals, he would have gotten a different answer. "I have to go," she said, before he could say anything else, and she hung up the phone. At the checkout, in an arbitrary stab of loyalty she seized a copy of *National Enquirer* for Nora and had to relinquish a bottle of grout cleaner so that she could pay for it. She drove back reciting to herself the chain of events that would lead to selling the house. Michael did not try to call back before she lost signal.

EDA

s soon as Charlie swallowed the cough syrup, Eda made her decision. A week later, she asked her brother if he would drive her to Marlinton.

"You don't have to," he said.

She looked at him doubtfully. Despite what she told the others, she knew he'd swallowed the cough syrup on purpose. It was only natural for him to feel hopeless. "I'm doing this for you," she said. "And for all of us."

Charlie contemplated his response for a long time, but at last he sighed with a kind of sputtering sound and said only, "You might ask Wenna. If you could borrow something to wear. Just because . . ." His voice trailed off.

Eda glanced down at her ankle-length shift, pale pink once but a dingy gray now, dappled with faded stains of bleach and mud and cranberry juice. She could admit that it was the wrong outfit for rutting with a stranger from Marlinton, but there were few things she wanted to do less than ask Wenna for a favor, and nothing she wanted less than for Wenna to know what she was doing. Still, from a cursory examination of her wardrobe, Eda concluded that she had nothing like what she gathered women must wear to bars in Marlinton. Newspaper ads and food packaging led Eda to conclude that skirts were short and pants were tight beyond the property-line, especially when women were trying to get the attention of men. Her only choices were the long and formless dresses that had passed from one Haddesley sister to another for untold decades, and the cavernously big men's overalls from the tractor-supply store, six identical pairs originally intended for Charlie and Percy to wear after they grew out of the longest trousers in the household but very soon shared among all five—and then four—of them. There was nothing alluring in the whole pile.

With great reluctance, Eda crept down the hallway to the room that Wenna and Nora were sharing. She stood at the door and listened. They were both inside, speaking to each other in the soft, confidential timbre of nighttime, although it was midmorning.

"Isn't she so beautiful?"

"That haircut, though."

"You don't like it?"

"No, it just feels like it came out of a movie from the 1970s. You couldn't know, I guess."

Eda stiffened, arrested by the unreasonable fear that they were talking about her. She stood fidgeting with the ends of her hair in the hallway for a minute, nauseatingly jealous of the casual intimacy between her sisters. For ten years it had been only her and Nora and the boys, and she had probably never had such a long conversation with Nora that wasn't an argument. Certainly, Nora never let Eda into her room, correctly fearing that Eda would not be able to see or smell so many animals without intervening.

Eda drew in a breath, she set her hand on the doorknob, and then a peal of laughter broke out and she edged back. *Never mind,* she thought. She stood at the top of the staircase for a while, deliberating between the two least objectionable dresses in her wardrobe, and then it occurred to her to look in her mother's closet.

After what happened to their mother, their father had officially retreated to a room farther down the hallway from the spacious master bedroom where the Haddesley patriarch traditionally slept, although in reality the spare bedroom had already been his for a few years by then; their mother was always sleeping through the morning and waking erratically at night, sometimes crying, and no one else could be expected to sleep in those conditions, although Percy valiantly tried to sleep at the end of their mother's bed until he was five or so, old enough that he should have known better, old enough to be told to his face that he wasn't wanted in her bedroom. By the time of her death, their father only needed to gather the clothes he wore least often and carry them to another closet for the room to appear as if he had never occupied it. The door had been shut, the room abandoned. Eda thought no one had gone in that room for ten years. They had not even counted it among the possibilities when deciding where Wenna would stay. Eda hesitated before the door, then, steeling herself with a breath, she stepped across the threshold.

The room had the faded, close odor and ropey cobwebs of a place neglected. The bedcovers, Eda saw, were still strewn wildly across the mattress, dumping in a dark pile onto the dust-glossed hardwood floor. A few knobbly candles sat clumped together on the bedside table. Her mother's bathtub, which everyone else had always been forbidden to use, stood across from the bed in the shaft of light that escaped the curtains. Eda saw the tub and at once knew that she was going to bathe in it. Who would forbid her now? She would have to evict a few dead spiders, a skin of dust, inexplicably a curled old leaf, but she felt firmly that the bathtub was a privilege she must exercise before she went to Marlinton.

She progressed to the closet, as shy and uneasy as if she were going to see her mother alive again and not only the clothes, which were probably mostly Haddesley hand-me-downs anyway. What Eda mostly remembered her mother wearing were white cotton nightgowns that bared her shoulders and her upper back, fragile-looking semi-translucent clothes, at once too sensual and too geriatric, and so often far too light for the weather. In the closet, there were many of these: Eda flicked through lace-edged sheath after sheath, starting to suspect that she would be thrown back on her own wardrobe again. She rejected a number of cotton shifts no better than the one she was wearing, and then she was startled by the appearance of an almost grotesquely vibrant magenta dress with a print of reddish tigers.

Eda held the dress in her fingertips as if she might contaminate it or be contaminated by it. She couldn't recall having ever seen her mother wear anything like it. She wondered if it had been a gift, intended for some occasion. She wondered if her mother had liked it, if she had chosen it herself from a catalog, if she had somehow dreamed it into existence. It was a hideous dress. A stranger as invasive and unnatural as the orange mushrooms that Percy was bent on eradicating. It was the kind of thing that she could wear to a bar in Marlinton.

Eda glanced over her shoulder, to be sure that no one was there, and then slipped her shift over her head. She did not pause long enough to scrutinize herself before she changed into the magenta dress. As she tugged it down her neck, her hips, she caught—only for a second—her mother's deep oaken scent that was so like the smell of the mud in the bog's mouth after rain.

Always, since she was eleven or twelve, Eda had found something fascinating and repulsive in her mother, something she could not bear to look at directly. Even when dressed, her mother was somehow more naked than anyone should ever be, her insides out, the pulpy heart of what she really was still visible even though Eda could not have said exactly what about her appeared less human than the rest of them.

She stood before the full-length mirror and found, to her pleasure and dismay, that the dress fit her perfectly.

❧

After the sun went down, they drove across the property-line, Eda for the first time in her life. She knew or almost knew that nothing would happen to her once they crossed over, for nothing had happened to Wenna, and she had heard her father make vague muttered allusions to wayward Haddesley sisters who fled home and fled their name and became like other people. Still, approaching the row of birches that demarcated the line between Haddesley and un-Haddesley land, she was so anxious that she could hardly breathe. She closed her eyes and sat on her hands as they passed over and opened her eyes only when Charlie said, minutes later, "You look down the hill, you might see Marlinton, for a second."

It felt traitorous and indulgent to look, as the journey was supposed to be ceremonial and single-minded, but Eda did. She was awestruck and vaguely appalled by the town: the clear-cut lots and squat formless buildings; the purplish glow of the intermittent streetlights. As they came closer, she could distinguish the houses from the storefronts, most of which were shuttered or at least dark but a few of which announced themselves with brash neon lights. There was a gas station, a burger joint whose name and logo Eda recognized from the detritus on the floor of the passenger seat. With a sudden lurch of longing, she imagined running errands in Marlinton, compelling the car into fast and effortless motion, making illicit and unbudgeted excursions to fast-food drive-throughs. Charlie was the only one of the five of them who had ever been taught to drive, the only one authorized to leave home.

"It's not much," Charlie said, of the town, but it was *so* much; he didn't even know.

"Where is the place?" Eda asked.

Charlie nodded indistinctly toward the street ahead of them. They drove past a library and a post office, past the feed-supply store, and here the road picked up speed again and Eda was briefly, glancingly afraid of where he was taking her, but then she saw the huddled shadow of a building on the side of the road. He parked abruptly.

The bar was a small, discouraged-looking cabin with a wide front porch, on which a few men sat smoking and drinking from glass bottles, their bottles but not their faces bathed in the flickering glow of a neon sign that read COLD BEER. One of them swatted away a moth; they laughed at something, and Eda was so startled by the sound, the largeness and vigor of it, the sheer number of people in one place, that she almost lost her nerve and asked Charlie to take her home. But she felt she had gone too far to retreat now, so she steeled herself and stepped out of the car, pinching her magenta skirt between two fingers, her feet in their mud-slicked work boots large and conspicuous beneath her. She'd had no shoes more appropriate for the occasion, and no one else in the house did either.

She stood at the passenger door for a minute, waiting for

Charlie to get out of the car, then remembered that he was not coming inside with her and felt her heart rush into her throat. She bent to glance once more at him through the window, hoping that he would meet her eye, wanting him to feel the gravity of what she was doing in his stead. But he was reading a book, a pocket flashlight illuminating the page.

Vengefully, Eda stalked away from the car to the front porch. The men said nothing to her as she passed them, which was both a relief and a disappointment. She did not want to stay long, but she could not see herself letting any one of them go with her into the trees. She had been strict with herself as she bathed and dressed that afternoon, not letting herself wonder what it would be like or how it would feel. It was only another ritual, and invariably rituals were in some way strange and naked and painful, and if they were not, then they were ecstatic in a way that could not be acknowledged after they were over; and sometimes they were painful and ecstatic both, like lowering your father into a bog after helping him drink poison. Eda did not doubt she could endure whatever happened. But she thought it was not unreasonable to be a little particular about a man whose penis was going to be inside of her, whose semen was going to water the seed of her first and only child.

The bar was disconcertingly bright, as if night everywhere else were day here. The log walls were decorated with taxidermized elk heads and moose antlers and the full form of a single coyote, set on a stubby platform of fake grass. Eda stood stunned in the doorway until someone cried, *Shut the door!* She absorbed the words a second late, tracing them only another second later to a man of her father's age who stood behind the bar, squinting through his glasses at her. Eda let the door shut, shivering belatedly at the chill in the night air. She went and sat at the bar, as Charlie had said that she should do.

She understood by the time she sat down that she was overdressed. Everyone else wore denim and flannel or T-shirts that bore names and images incomprehensible to Eda. The man sitting nearest to her had paint stains on his clothes, stark and fresh enough that she caught a hint of acerbic paint scent when he lifted an arm to get the bartender's attention. She dismissed him as unsuitable when she realized he too was near her father's age. A man of that age might not even be able to father a child. Her eyes swept across the room for a prospect, and they had not yet landed on one when the bartender's voice broke again into her consciousness.

"You gonna drink anything?"

"I'll have a beer," Eda said, overwhelmed by the closeness of the stranger to her: the unfamiliar planes and ridges of his wrinkled face beneath his ball cap, the sagging flesh on his sunworn arms, the wiry spines of his mustache. Her sense of how a human could look was so particular that everyone in the bar felt vaguely monstrous. She had only ever known people who she knew so intimately that she was incapable of really seeing them.

"What kind of a beer?" the bartender asked, a laugh in his voice, and Eda realized that strange voices were monstrous to her too. She did not know how other tongues formed words.

"I don't know," she confessed, after a protracted silence. "What should I drink?"

She was afraid when she admitted her ignorance that he might ask to see her ID, which Charlie warned could possibly happen, but he didn't. "Can't go wrong with an old classic," he said, and he withdrew an amber bottle from the fridge at his back.

Eda took the bottle, glancing sideways at the man on the

barstool beside her to see what he was drinking. He noticed, to her horror, and lifted his bottle and said, "Cheers." She had a vague sense that she was supposed to return this gesture, and when she did, clacking her bottle heavily against his, he seemed satisfied. She released the breath she'd been holding.

He asked, then, "You from around here?"

Eda hesitated, wary of entering into any kind of intimacy with a man whom she did not intend to father her child. "Yes, but I'm looking for someone."

"Oh yeah? And who's that?" He too seemed to be laughing at her without laughing. She was doing something wrong, but she didn't know what it was, and she had no way of learning.

"I don't know yet."

"Mr. Right? Well, I'll tell you, free piece of advice, you're in the wrong place for that. If I were a nice young lady like you, I'd make the effort to go as far as Summersville."

Eda absorbed no more than half of the words he said. Her eyes drifted across the bar again, and again she found no prospects. "I have to get pregnant," she clarified, for the man sitting beside her.

The man choked on his beer, spraying droplets onto the bar in front of him. When he finished coughing, he looked at her with an incredulity that reminded her of Wenna. "Well, I wouldn't go around advertising *that*, miss," he said; then he got up and put his coat on.

Eda stayed where she was, too afraid to chance another seat at the bar or anywhere else. She sat there feeling but not letting herself watch the movements of the people surrounding her, taking small and measured sips of the beer, which she initially found repulsive but which became endurable when she got used to it. The entire time, she feared Charlie would get impatient and come into the bar and say they had to go, although he'd promised he wouldn't. She drank two beers, then started on a third. The bartender loudly announced *last call!* And she felt the men in the leather booths behind her rise to pay their checks.

"Do I have to pay now?" she asked, seeing the bartender as a kind of unknowing and conditional ally in her ritual work; he had let her stay there untroubled for two or three hours after his initial demands of door-closing and beer-ordering were satisfied.

"One more drink, if you like," the bartender said. "But," and he looked now at her half-emptied bottle, "you might not. It'll be twelve seventy-five, when you're ready."

Eda dug in her pocket for the money that Charlie had given her. Enough for six or eight beers, he'd guessed, based on the cost of beers he'd seen at gas stations and Walmart, but she saw now that it was only a ten. "You said twelve?"

"Twelve seventy-five," the bartender said.

"I can't pay it," said Eda, her hands shaking. She did not know what happened to someone who stole beer; she could not even bring herself to imagine an encounter with police, a nightmarish ending to a luckless and unproductive night. The first thing they would do was ask her name, first and last. Everyone in Marlinton lived still in terror of the Haddesleys, telling improbable and half-true stories of them, assigning blame to them for all afflictions and maladies otherwise unexplainable. Anything might happen to her if she fell into their hands. Her hands began to shake. Then, beside her, she felt a body close to her hip.

"Let me buy your drinks," said a man she hadn't seen before: young or at least youngish, red-faced, his scalp glistening where his hair ended above his forehead.

"Nathan," he said.

"Eda," she responded, in a haze of startlement and thankfulness. She could hardly believe how easily he had come to her. "Do you want to go outside?" she asked, and it was so simple, so ordered, that it *was* truly like a ritual. He said yes, and he paid for her drinks, and Eda forgot the ten-dollar bill on the counter as she followed him out the door.

The air outside had grown sharply cold, and Eda hugged her arms to her chest as they stepped down from the empty porch. In the red glow of the COLD BEER sign, the man had a strange, craggy look, as if he were a mountainside instead of a living creature, the jut of his nose and the pucker of his lips like unmovable and ancient formations. Eda sucked air into her lungs and stepped close to him. She thought she would kiss him. This seemed a good way to signal what she wanted, but she could not cross the small distance between them to do it; she did not know how.

"You want to go back to my place?" the man asked.

Eda was hesitant to go anywhere with a stranger. The station wagon was still parked in the gravel lot, the feeble glow of Charlie's flashlight in the front seat. Charlie had said they could do it in the woods behind the bar.

"Here," said Eda. "Let's do it here." She gestured broadly to the clump of trees behind them, birches and bare maples mostly, sparse and inadequate cover, except that already almost no one else was still here and she did not care if Charlie saw her.

"You're wild," the man said, laughing, but a little uneasy now. "Wild woman." He was unsteady on his feet. Eda thought he must be drunk. "Right here?"

"Yes, here," Eda said, and, understanding that he needed

encouragement, she reached gracelessly out to the crotch of his pants and rested her hand there.

The man kissed her then. It was not like what she had imagined. She knew from books and magazines that men and women kissed before they copulated, but she had never seen anyone do it in real life and she had intuited wrongly that it must really *feel* like something. But this felt like pressure and wet, and like nothing. Eda grew impatient after only a few seconds, then pulled away and led the man behind the bar. There, in the starved-out fading undergrowth, he thrust his hand into her dress and grasped her breast, hard enough that she almost winced, and began to kiss her again. Eda got the man's penis out of his pants, her focus unwavering. She did not know what to do with it once it was out, so she contented herself with kissing the man back and grasping his penis in her loose fist until he lowered them both to the ground and yanked her dress above her hips and shoved aside her underwear.

The whole time they copulated, Eda thought of the bog-wife rising from the mire, primal and fearless and freshly born. When the ritual was finished, she lay with her legs in the air so none of the seed would come out of her. The man, meanwhile, staggered away, disgusted, asking how she could lie like that on the ground, calling her names, not knowing the power she held now.

PERCY

At the end of October, Percy went to the bog's mouth, bearing with him the slip of paper that told in his father's handwriting how *to hew a wife from naught*, shedding his clothes as he stepped across the peat. He hung his jacket and trousers and socks and shirt on the branches of the tamaracks. Before the bog's slit of a mouth, he stood reverently naked and surveyed the devastation of his kingdom. He had not been here since his father's burial. Everywhere, he found the diminishment of life. A dried-out worm on a bed of dried-out lichen, an abandoned bird's nest, a dead salamander's stiff warped black form lain out on the smooth face of a stone like the bog wanted him to see it. Beaten-down tawny stalks of sedge like thinning hair slicked across the scalp of the earth, sphagnum moss in crumpled lacy piles becoming mulch. The trees were prematurely bare, their shed leaves huddled in colorless piles, having passed from the bright green of spring to the cardboard brown of death without yellowing or reddening first, without waiting for their cues from the sun. He wondered if the desolation was the Haddesleys' fault. First they had starved the bog and then drowned it and then starved it again. For a minute, Percy let grief sink through him. Then he got to work.

It took Percy three nights to gather the bones of his wife, moonlit hours of piling up little stray sticks of maple and birch, the bark splintering wetly off onto his fingers. He dragged himself back to the house before dawn, exhausted, for brief and fitful sleeps in his muddy clothes. On the fourth night, he formed his wife in the cradle of her grave.

The grave needed to be deep. The cavity cut into the peat when he finished digging looked so like an open wound that he wondered if his attempt to heal the bog of its sickness would be more than the bog could bear. Percy whispered pleas as he climbed out of the hole and pasted sticks into a skeletal form, using wet clots of humus to hold the bones together as the book directed, mineral-rich forest soil and bog water mashed into a cakey glue that did not dry but dripped heavily between the delicate architecture of limbs, sternum, ribs, broad-hipped pelvis. The skull, rounded as it had to be, was the most difficult part to form. Twice Percy made a blocky, grotesque head and twice he disassembled it, castigating himself with the words his father would have used.

In a ritual, he knew, any misstep might be the misstep that made the whole thing fail. He feared that she would remember the two malformed heads, his wife. Would she then be insane or cruel or, like his own mother had been, lacking in the will to live? He climbed out of the grave, his bare feet dislodging clods of peat that tumbled down after him onto the unborn skeleton of his wife, and whispered, "Please."

The last thing to be done was to feed the body on his blood. Percy had searched several of the books on his father's shelf for direction on this part and, finding no other reference to the ritual feeding of one's own blood, could conclude only that he should aim for the mouth. Standing at the edge of the grave, he drew the short practical blade that had come down to him from his father and cut a thin slit down the length of his calf.

The sight of his own blood made Percy's head swim; for an

airless second he was eight years old and his sled had gone into a tree with low-hanging branches; he was lying in the snow stunned by pain; Eda crouched above him, saying *show me where it hurts*, rolling his pants up to the knee, and blood bubbled fatly from his white leg like it was bubbling now. Then he came back to himself, a man of twenty-two, a blade in his hand that he threw away so he could hang his leg over the grave and concentrate the flow of blood into his wife's mouth. His aim was imprecise, and the blood dripped down onto all the ridges of her face, her temple and her jaw, her eye sockets that still had a slightly blocky shape despite all his efforts. In the dark, the blood had no color; it only glistened. He felt weak before he felt certain that he'd done enough, and when he sat down it was more of a collapse. He stanched the flow of blood with torn-out fistfuls of undergrowth and sat in the peat, pressing a hunk of sphagnum to the wound on his leg to soak up the blood until he gathered the strength to stand. Then he filled the grave. By the time he finished, Percy did not have the strength to fight his way back through the spongy turf to the house. He lay down beside the filled-in grave and let the earth cradle him as he fell asleep.

※

Percy planned to pass the hundred days of his wife's gestation apart from her, but he soon realized that he couldn't. Once the form was laid in the ground, he could only think of the recipe's interdiction: *let nothing interfere with its grave*. At every moment, a possible disaster occurred to him, and the blurriness of that word *interfere* excluded nothing from consideration. Was he supposed to keep grubs and beetles and spiders from the mound of earth? Was he supposed to keep away the fallen leaves, the wind? He comforted himself by thinking that his wife was buried in the bog and so she could not be eaten as a body lain in fertile earth usually was eaten, by maggots and worms and the hungry roots of vegetation. In the peat, she would be perfectly insulated. Yet still he was nagged by thoughts of bears, coyotes, even weasels or groundhogs or possums pawing at his wife's grave. Crushed-up sticks halfway to becoming bone ground between their teeth, mud halfway to becoming muscle slick on their lips.

He could not know the grave was safe unless he was there, and so it was easiest to stay near the grave as much as he could, in spite of the encroaching cold, the long shadows that fell across the bog's mouth by midafternoon, the frost that silvered the backs of the undergrowth in the mornings. At first he stood vigil in few-hour stretches, trudging doggedly back to the house for meals and baths and chores and fitful sleep, but soon he found even those short intervals of time away unbearable. One night he returned through the darkness from dinner to find a dark figure bent over the mound of earth. He thought at first it was human and became nauseous with panic, imagining Charlie desecrating his wife's unborn carcass, but when he came closer, he saw that the intruder was only a deer, her black eyes wide and vacant in the glare of his camping lantern, her posture stiff with alarm. A wilted cranberry vine hung from her lips. He shouted, "Get on!" and she obeyed, tail lifted. Her furtive pawing at the grave made him fear that all the many trespassers feeding on the bog's sickness would also feed on his wife if they had half a chance. After that, he stayed in the bog through the nights, warmed only by his ceremonial moss sheath, his scythe gathering dew on the ground beside him.

He had been there a few days when Nora came to see him, stepping delicately across the hummocks and hollows of the bog meadow with a plate of dinner and a tin thermos.

"How'd you know where to find me?" Percy felt both kingly and exposed in his ceremonial sheath with its mud-stained tail, its train of dead leaves and twigs.

Nora looked wryly at him and set the plate down on a felled log. "Charlie told on you," she said, crossing her arms before her chest in an overlarge canvas jacket that Percy recognized as his own. "So," she trailed off, waiting for him to answer.

He should have known that Charlie would betray their secret. That no patriarch, even one as discouraged and feckless as Charlie, would ever willingly abdicate his place. But for some reason he had thought his brother believed in him.

"It's not telling," he said. "I'm not doing anything wrong."

"Wenna says it won't work," said Nora. She had been pulling out her eyebrows, Percy noticed. Her face looked stark and doll-like without them.

"What does Wenna know?" Percy stepped closer, asking the question contemptuously and yet meaning it: What *did* Wenna know?

"She said you'll get frostbite," said Nora belligerently, although this was no real answer. "And Eda says that's *if* the bog doesn't do anything worse to you."

"The bog already did the worst thing," Percy said. He resented the insinuation that he could not survive a hundred days on the land when he was going to be the bog's custodian someday soon. He was cold and unbelievably hungry, and he could see a thin veil of steam rising from the food on the plate as the twilight chill ate into its warmness, but he did not want to cede anything to his sister. Obviously, she had come at Eda's behest and she was supposed to get him to come back, like she had gotten Wenna to come back. But he was not going to be gotten to do things anymore.

"I just wish," Nora said, predictably, "that you could come home."

"I can't," said Percy, crossing his arms as she had crossed hers. "I can't let anything to happen to her."

"To who?" Her face was scrunched with confusion.

Percy was not prepared for that response. "What did Charlie tell you?"

"That you were out here hunting trespassers," she said. "Who's *her*?"

Charlie had not betrayed him. Charlie had *lied* for him. Percy felt a rush of affection for his brother, tempered only slightly by contempt. It was one thing for Charlie to step aside and let Percy become custodian, and somehow another for Charlie to actually help Percy usurp his place. "Never mind," he said to Nora. "Just . . . I can't come home yet. You tell Eda—"

"Eda doesn't know I'm here," she said. "I just wanted to talk to you."

He believed her, and he was almost sorry then. The things that Nora wanted were so simple and so easy, yet they were always exactly the things that she couldn't have. "Okay," he said. "What did you want to say?"

"I don't know." He could see that Nora was yanking herself toward some precipice. She had come out to the bog for a reason, just not the reason he'd thought. Her eyes were lowered and her jaw tensed, her arms hugged to her chest in the large sleeves that were his. "That I don't understand," she said. "Why do you have to stay out here all the time to take care of trespass-ers? Is there . . . did something happen?"

"Something?" Percy almost laughed at her. "The compact is broken. The bog is sick. There's no bog-wife. Everything happened."

Nora worried her lip, her jaw ticking back and forth. It made her look strangely like Charlie. "But there's nothing wrong," she said.

"I just *said*—"

"But those aren't things we can do anything about," she in-sisted. "They're not anyone's fault."

Percy looked at her in bewilderment. "I don't know if it's anyone's fault. But we have to do something. We're custodians."

Nora's hand drifted unconsciously to her forehead, her fin-gers searching out the scant line of hair left along her browbone, and then—as if suddenly waking—she flinched, lowered her hand, entwined her fingers. "Wenna said we're all unhealthy." She seemed to test the sound of Wenna's words in her mouth. "She said we should live somewhere else."

Percy was taken aback, but the prospect of the five of them packing their belongings and abandoning the house and the bog and the compact was so absurd that he could not be very af-fronted by it. "Tell her to leave, then," he said. "We don't need her here anymore."

"*I* need her," Nora whispered, her voice almost inaudible among the cries of insects and frogs. "I do." She drew the canvas jacket more closely around herself. "Are you really just going to live out here now?"

"I think so." As he answered her, he decided it was true. She looked so sad then, so wilted, her face like a pale bulb in the purplish half-light, and he wanted to tell her that he would have a wife soon, in only a few months; that everything she had hoped for from the bog-wife could be had in the wife hewn from nothing, whom already he had sometimes begun to call *the bog-wife* in his mind; that he was preserving their family even now. But he didn't.

NORA

The day after Percy went to the bog, an envelope with Wenna's name on it landed in their mailbox: damp and wrinkled from its journey, bearing a return address so smudged that it was illegible, except for the word *Illinois*. At first Nora had the dumb, automatic thought that it was Wenna's yearly Christmas card, and, as she always did when Wenna's card came, Nora felt a kind of satisfaction chased by disappointed longing, and then she thought, *But Wenna's actually here,* and her heart thudded in her chest as she realized that the letter was not from Wenna but *to* her. For too long, she stood in the twilight and studied the handwriting on the envelope, searching it for traces of the stranger who had scratched Wenna's name so fluidly, with such ease and such intimacy, into the envelope. The handwriting was firm and not shaky, the writing of a young person and not an elderly one. The *W* of her sister's name formed an insistent three-prong spike in the middle of the white paper.

Studying that writing, Nora felt a prickle of fear travel down her body, from the hollow of her throat to the soft flighty place between her breastbone and her stomach. She stared out at the slick black line of the country road as if she might catch a glimpse of the sender, the Illinois stranger who felt entitled to pursue Wenna across state lines and trespass on their private property, who thought they had a claim on her sister somehow. She felt suddenly conspicuous and vulnerable underneath the hood of her too-large canvas jacket, able only to see right in front of her. She shrugged the hood off onto her shoulders and let raindrops sink into her hair as she searched the landscape for symptoms of an intruder. As if the letter-writer might be hidden in the branches of the trees, crouching behind a felled log.

She wanted not to be alone with the secret, but she knew Eda would panic if she learned someone was sending letters to them, especially now. Charlie swallowing the cough syrup had made Eda nervous and impatient, frantic about things that weren't frantic and always seeming on the verge of tears but never crying anywhere that Nora could see her. And Charlie would be worse than useless as a confidant. If told, he would only say something dull and indifferent—*Let Wenna get mail, if she wants*—not understanding or at least not caring about the significance of a stranger knowing where to find them. What she really wanted was Percy, who was the one she used to tell everything to, but he felt so far away now.

She knew she had to tell Wenna that the envelope had come for her, yet if she knew, what would she do? What did the letter want from her? Was someone calling her back, away from their home?

It never really occurred to Nora that Wenna had known people during her ten years away from them. Fleetingly, she envisioned an entire second family, a second Charlie and a second Percy and a second Eda and of course a second version of herself, except that they all wore the same sleek and plastic-looking clothes that Wenna wore and they all went to work in the morning and none of them ever asked Wenna to root out bull thistle with them, and they lived in a skyscraper with indoor plumbing. Undoubtedly, Wenna could not love the Haddesleys as much as she would love a family like that, and she remembered Wenna whispering once, when Nora was half-asleep, *Do you ever think about leaving this place?*

Nora decided not to decide yet, and she tucked the letter into the secret inner pocket of her rain jacket as she carried the rest of the mail home. Wenna was in the kitchen when she got back, sitting at the table drinking coffee and reading one of the old spy novels that had been their father's. The tartan blanket from the end of Nora's bed was draped over her shoulders. Nora felt such a rush of love for her sister there, comfortable and warm and as familiar as if she'd never been gone, that she knew then she could never show Wenna the letter.

"Anything good?" Wenna asked as Nora set the limp bundle of wet mail down on the counter. Later Eda would page through it all, cutting out coupons and piling them up for Charlie to use even though he mostly never did, and then she would condemn the remains to the kindling pile.

"Nothing," Nora said, the envelope crunching soundlessly flat against her chest.

❧

Nora tore the seal on the envelope. Though she was not yet prepared to read the letter, she knew she was committing herself to a real lie. She would have to find another envelope that fit the paper, she would have to forge the handwriting on the envelope, which she was not certain she could do, she would have to be careful not to smudge or tear or fold the paper inside. Over and over again, she imagined Wenna finding out and no longer trusting her, and she felt so bereft when she thought of how

Wenna would sound, the expression that would cross her sister's face, that she almost couldn't do it.

But she was more afraid of losing Wenna than of losing Wenna's love, and she decided that she wouldn't get caught. She wormed the letter into an old hiding place that only she and Percy ever used, a notch between the stone of the wall and the floorboards at the end of the west wing's corridor, no wider than her thumb and second finger but deep enough to admit and conceal a sheet of paper—or an envelope.

As she hid the unread letter there, Nora felt a glimmer of the old pleasure of conspiracy with her brother, and she almost hoped that he would find it there, read it himself, come to her with the secret. She imagined him coming out of his bedroom and checking, just in case, as she sometimes still checked the notch when she had no reason to expect to find anything there. But probably he would never see the envelope and step inside the secret with her. All she had now were secrets that no one else could be let into. Later that day, she snuck back to the notch and withdrew the envelope—dusty, and a little crumpled from being tucked into the wall—and went to Percy's bedroom and sat with her back to the door. It brought her some comfort to read the letter there, with the sheets still wrinkled and wadded at the end of the bed as if Percy might at any moment come back, faint traces of her brother's smell lingering in the room still, the half-dusty and half-salty odor so close to the smell of Nora's own body it should have been undetectable to her, yet wasn't.

Delicately, she unfolded the paper, which was written not on the firm cardstock of the bank statements that piled up in their father's desk drawer but on flimsy paper, thin enough that you could see through it. Both sides were covered in the same boxy, assured handwriting as the address on the envelope. As she read, she let her fingers rest on the stubbly ends of her eyebrows, not pulling yet—she kept resolving to stop, Eda always said it was an unpleasant habit—or even grasping at any one hair, but knowing the sensation was there if she needed it.

Wenna (said the letter),

I don't really know how to write this. You won't be surprised that it's my fourth draft. But I'm trying not to be a perfectionist, so I'm telling myself this one is it.

You probably noticed by now that those papers never came. I couldn't sign them. I don't want to sign them now, though I will, if you want me to, and have them sent to you. Obviously, both of us have to agree we still want to be in the marriage.

I keep thinking about that weekend we stayed on Lake Michigan and walked up and down the beach in the freezing cold, too stubborn to change our plans. All that fog was rising from the water, so we could barely see each other if we got more than a few feet apart. You wanted us to take off one glove each so we could still feel each other's hands, and when you said that I loved you so much I thought I would burn up from the inside. That was really the feeling of it. And then you were saying you'd never seen the ocean, and I corrected you like you didn't know the difference between an ocean and a lake even though it was right there in the name, and I saw something in you just—fall and I felt so bad for saying it, but by then it was too late. You'll be thinking right now that this moment wasn't

*important, but it is because I think I was always mak-
ing you feel small like that. I kept thinking I had to
be the one to tell you things, because there were these
things you didn't know, and sometimes it was hard to
tell if you were choosing something because you didn't
know better or because it's really what you wanted.
I didn't always know if you had your reasons. But it
shouldn't have mattered.*

*I never said any of that to you. I don't know if it
changes anything.*

*I do still feel like you were always distant, that you
wouldn't tell me things, so there was a lot of guessing I
had to do. That scared me, it put me on edge, it made
me feel like you had to be decoded because otherwise
how could I know what to do to care for you? How
could I make you stay with me? But I think maybe I
asked for it, because it was thrilling too, especially at
first. It's how you think love will feel, like being asked
an impossible question and miraculously getting it
right. I want you to tell me things. I want to know everything about you. You can trust me with it, I promise you.*

I just want to know why, about the baby.

Let me know what you want to do. I'll be here.

*Love,
Michael*

Nora stared at those last lines for a long time. She felt how
she used to feel after she held her breath underwater: as if her

body were drifting apart from itself, unanchored from whatever held it together. Belatedly, she saw that the paper was littered with slivers of her eyebrow, arced like fingernails or new moons. She blew them onto the floor. Wenna was married. Wenna had married someone. Wenna had betrayed the Haddesley compact more profoundly than anyone knew; she had held ungloved hands with someone named Michael and even now she might return to him. She could have had a baby and she still might have one.

It was obvious that Wenna could never see this letter. Yet Nora understood that the letter also could not go unanswered. If Michael had their address, if he thought Wenna was here with them, he might become concerned when she didn't answer and decide to go after her. He might report her missing and have the police go after her. He might do anything.

Nora sat on the floor, swimming through the lines *it was thrilling too, especially at first. It's how you think love will feel,* imagining Wenna and Michael walking through the mist on the shore of Lake Michigan, both wearing wedding rings, on the cusp of an argument that you could have only with someone who loved you. When she tried to create a picture of Wenna's husband in her head, she could recall only the handsome blond family annihilator whose forced grin appeared on three consecutive covers of *National Enquirer* last year, whose name had also been Michael, who was now sentenced to life in prison. She was angry and disgusted yet somehow also filled with yearning when she thought of the entire life that Wenna had conducted with this dimpled, murderous-looking, un-Haddesley stranger in Illinois. Did he kiss her and not feel on her mouth that she was a bog-wife's descendent? Did he think that she was beautiful, with all her features that were so much like Nora's features (only a little lovelier—maybe a little more capable of being loved)? Did he not know their baby would have Haddesley lungs, Haddesley blood, Haddesley obligations?

That afternoon she went to the bog's mouth, wanting not to be alone in the secret. But when she found Percy stalking through the cold air, his head bent down to scan the half-frozen sphagnum for trespassers, she felt the impossibility of confiding in him. They had barely been alone together since the day she tried to hide the trespassers from him, that day that had been the end of the old days though she hadn't known it yet, and she had the unaccountable feeling that she didn't know Percy anymore. He had always been devoted to the compact, but now he had given his whole life over to the bog and its sickness, and the look in his eyes was glassy and strange when she faced him.

That night, she looked for a sample of Wenna's handwriting, certain what she had to do and that she was alone in it.

Winter

WENNA

ist fell on the cranberry bog, hanging in heavy sheaths beneath the treetops, making everyone nearsighted, insulating them from the world. They harvested the late cranberries and found the fruit rotted from within, frigid little beads of black ice that tasted like how the air smelled. "Not even good enough for pie," Nora lamented. The first snowfall came a few days after, dark and sludgy masses like falling mud, only for a few minutes, distinctly unbeautiful, but the four of them—everyone but Percy—stood before the bay window in the gallery on the third floor of the house and observed the fall of snow where they had always observed the fall of snow, gathered there as if by silent consensus, their bodies lumpy and indistinct in flannel overcoats and wool hats and heavy knit socks. Even inside the house, it was cold. "I hope Percy's all right," Nora whispered, her breath fogging the glass. Eda said, "He won't die. Living out there, it's in our blood."

If there was something in their blood that inured them to the cold, it still did not make them comfortable. At the end of the month, they resumed their childhood habit of sleeping in impromptu nests of comforters and quilts and blankets before the vast gold-lit mouth of the stone hearth. Someone rose every few hours to prod the flames back to life or add another brick of peat, the fire-crackling and the rich scent of burning earth stirring everyone else into a half-lucid, liquid state, only awake enough to appreciate the pleasure of not waking up.

Wenna resisted the communal sleeping at first, fearful of ceding ground not easily won back. Sharing a bedroom with Nora had already been a compromise. Alyson would undoubtedly have been disappointed in her failure to hold even the simplest of lines with her siblings. But she told herself she could afford these kinds of small allowances, because she was spending her days sorting all their heirloom junk into piles of sellable and not sellable, herding the latter into a series of black garbage bags to heap on one end of the house. One day, she would find the fortitude to load them into the back of the station wagon and take them to the dump. While Nora sat reading old *National Enquirers* aloud, legs swinging no matter where she'd perched, Wenna dismantled great heaps of yellowed and sour-smelling linens, broken and frail wooden furniture. In the attic, she found a dried-out palate of watercolors, a bundle of cross-country skis, an English saddle, relics of an era when the Haddesleys still apparently had fun. In the pantry, old wide-mouthed stone vessels and flat-faced ceremonial spoons with nightmarish figures engraved in their soapstone handles. "Like things recovered from an archeological dig in a movie," Wenna murmured. Nora didn't understand the reference. In the forbidden parlor, no longer forbidden, a quantity of books that dwarfed the number of volumes on the bookshelves in the study. They were mostly profoundly out-of-date atlases and leather-bound studies of "primitive" peoples, ruminating on root-gathering and rites of passage. Wenna suspected they would be thrown away immediately if offered to the Marlinton Goodwill. Yet Nora was drawn to them, salvaging a small pile from a black garbage bag, exchanging her dog-eared *Enquirers* for a day or so before she got tired of trying to decipher the purple academic language of the old volumes and returned to UFO sightings, dead-for-months starlets glimpsed on hotel balconies, and disgraced congressmen.

No one protested the removal of the junk. Wenna had thought her sisters would put up a fight, maybe Charlie too. But she was getting closer to Nora's bedroom, where the clutter to be sorted was not objects but a population of half-domesticated amphibians and rodents that she knew Nora would never willingly part with. All her sister's foundlings had to go, Wenna decided, except possibly Buz Lukens the possum, which seemed to have attained the status of a real companion somehow and therefore was probably a nonnegotiable, although she went back and forth on this. A domesticated possum could only bring complications: they would have to convince some especially gullible landlord that it was really no different than a cat, which was not true. Nora didn't know yet that her animals had to be returned to the wild. If she suspected their shared bedroom might be subject to the same treatment as the rest of the house, she gave no indication. Wenna couldn't tell her now, not with the house still half in disarray, the hemlock tree still stuck through the roof, the question of the deed and where it was and whose name was written on it still unsettled. She felt she had to go to Charlie first.

Every day, for weeks, she thought that today she would go to Charlie, and then she did not go. She knew she could not afford to wait. At any time, the driveway might become impassable with snow. For weeks, they would have to subsist on canned goods and cranberry preserves and cellar potatoes, filling the bathtubs with snow, venturing out only to feed the goats. In childhood, she had hated this time of year. Their mother always escaped into her long sleep and their father became a grim, erratic version of himself in her absence, stalking gloomily around the house, startling when he came upon his children. Instinctively, the five of them shrunk inward. They put away their loudest and most joyful games (no more jousting with paper-towel-roll lances on the backs of Eda and Charlie; no more seeing how many stairs in a row they could leap). They settled their disputes in harsh whispers and glares across the table. They developed winter habits, winter voices. They held themselves in a defensive flinch that loosened only in the spring.

Even now, Wenna felt the instinct to hold still. To let the winter pass, to not change anything until the balance in the house did not feel so delicate. But when she went out to the yard and breathed the spoiled air exuded by the bog's slow dying, she became more afraid of staying than of going. While that fear quickened inside her, while the snow had not yet closed in on them, she went to Charlie to ask him for the deed to the house.

❧

It was difficult to get Charlie alone, ever since he'd swallowed the cough syrup. Eda no longer maintained an official policy of supervising him at every moment, but she stuck close, suspicious of any time unaccounted for. Wenna supposed this was probably why Charlie was mucking the goat shed, a chore that was Percy's once and should have been the responsibility of anyone besides Charlie now. It was obvious that the motions of scooping manure and lifting the pitchfork to the waiting wheelbarrow hurt him. He winced every time he bent at the waist. But he got to be alone. The goats stood out in the rain looking bored and disgruntled as he worked. Wenna stepped past them and onto the shed's raised plywood floor. Inside, she huffed the unmistakable odor of goat urine out of her nostrils.

Charlie nodded hello. "Eda looking for me?" he asked.

"No." Wenna took a deep breath and prepared to ask about the deed. "I was wondering," she said instead, "if we could get the hemlock tree cut out of the roof."

"Why?" Charlie sounded genuinely bewildered, as if he could not think of one reason why they should not have a tree embedded in the house.

"Well," said Wenna, slowly, "I think the house would be easier to heat, for one."

Charlie weighed this consideration. The goats, having jointly decided they were tired of waiting in the cold, came clopping up into the shed, where they regarded Charlie and Wenna with twin expressions of glassy-eyed contempt. "I'm not done yet," Charlie said to them, and then, in the same tone, almost in the same breath, so Wenna didn't realize at first he was now speaking to her, "How would we do it?"

"There are services. For tree removal. We pay them, they come out."

Charlie said nothing and then, with a shrug, "If you want."

He spoke in the same downtrodden tone that he used when Eda wanted something unreasonable. Wenna tried not to be irritated.

"It's insane it hasn't been done already. You know that, right?"

Charlie wouldn't look at her. He worked his mouth. "The hemlock tree was the bog's doing. The bog made it happen."

"Is that what you think?"

"I know," Charlie said. Then, with a menace in his voice that might have been anger or only self-loathing, "*Dad* knew."

Wenna did not doubt that their father had spent the last nine months of his life persuading Charlie that the bog had sent a hemlock down onto him as a punishment for . . . something; the particulars of what Charlie had *done* never seemed to matter very much to their father. At once, her irritation subsided. She could only feel sorry for him. "Listen," she said urgently, stepping closer to him. "It doesn't have to be like this. I think we should sell the house. We should leave here."

For a long time, Charlie held perfectly still, as if he thought she wouldn't see him. Wenna tried to be patient, but she was too afraid of the meaning of his silence. "What?" she asked. "Why aren't you saying anything?"

Charlie squeezed the rake handle until his knuckles turned white. "We can't," he said. Then, softly, "Could we?"

"Why not?"

"The compact. And . . . where else would we ever live?"

"Anywhere."

"We *sell* the house?"

"Yes," Wenna said, impatiently. "For the money. It could be worth a lot." This was an exaggeration that was almost a lie— the realtor had only said that it might be worth *more* if there was not a tree inside it—but she doubted that Charlie had even a vague idea of how much money you could get for a house in any kind of condition.

"But . . . it's our house," Charlie said.

"Are you happy here?"

He gave her a look. As if to say, didn't she know that *happy* had never factored into any of it for him? "We're supposed to be the bog's custodians," he said, without conviction.

"Are we?" Wenna asked, her voice coming out too loud and yet harried and thin. "Do you think it's doing well?" She lowered her tone almost to a whisper. What she did not want was for Eda to overhear. "Do you think we've been taking good care of it?"

Charlie's face fell, and Wenna thought he was going to cry, which she had never seen him do, not even when he was fifteen and slipped and sent the blade of a saw into his thumb, not even when he was twenty and their mother disappeared. Then he stiffened; he reverted. "I'm trying," he said. "It doesn't work for me like it did for all them."

"It's not your fault," said Wenna. "It's because of what happened with . . ." But somehow she could not say it aloud here in the yard, without the protective barrier of walls between herself and the bog, so she finished, vaguely, "With what Dad did."

"*Dad* got a wife," said Charlie, like nothing after the wife-getting mattered. He glanced in the direction of the house, though he couldn't see it through the windowless wall of the shed. "You can have the money for the tree," he said. "But I can't let you sell the house."

He almost sounded like a patriarch, thought Wenna. Forbidding and stern, handing down prohibitions. She thought, *What would he have become, if he had gotten a wife?*

"Don't tell anyone about this yet," she said. "Please."

Charlie returned to shoveling. He said nothing for a while, as if holding her in suspense, though Wenna knew he didn't do things like that. "Obviously," he said, at last.

❧

In Wenna's entire childhood, only one stranger ever crossed the property-line. Wenna never even saw the woman, but Charlie said she had dark skin and thick locks of dark hair. She drove a blue sedan. Fearlessly, she approached their front door. In the time it took the stranger to walk from her car to their house, their father gathered the five of them from their disparate corners of the house and shepherded them into the cellar. There they crouched in the shadows behind shelves of cranberry preserves in glass jars, listening with heads tilted, none of them completely certain they would not evaporate if the stranger laid eyes on them. Their mother had not been gathered and shepherded; she still lay in bed far above them, deep in the throes of the long last tiredness that never subsided, although no one knew yet that it was the last, or that it would not subside. Soon came the sounds of knocking. Faintly, they heard, "Mr. Haddesley? Haddesley family?" Terrifying, their name in a stranger's mouth.

Long after the knocks ceased, they stayed hidden. Their backs ached; Nora whispered that she had to pee. At last, they thought they heard the car driving away, and their father crept upstairs to see if it was safe. They spent the afternoon reifying the property-line with lime and salt, their father irritable and tense as they worked, glancing over his shoulder in case the stranger came back. At dusk, their mother came out and stood before the furrows in the earth where the stranger had parked her car and spit into the furrows. And, one after another, the five of them spit too.

They clung to one another then, as if reassuring themselves and one another that they were all still there. Something had gotten in, but nothing had gotten out.

Now, as a team of men in fluorescent vests backed an eighteen-wheeler down their driveway, they found no shelter in one another. Eda stood seething in snow boots and a moldering mink coat; she would not speak to Wenna or even look in her direction. Charlie stood beside her like a bridegroom-sacrifice, his back stiff, face impassive; Nora was on Eda's other side, gnawing on her lower lip, tearing discreetly at her eyebrows. Wenna reached for her hand and pulled Nora's searching fingers away from her face, closing them inside of hers. Nora did not yank her hand loose, but Wenna could tell that she wanted to. Her sister was watching the truck as if she were trying to destroy it with her mind.

Somewhere in the bog, thought Wenna, Percy was hearing the roar of the engine from a distance, like faraway thunder. She hoped he did not come out to see what it was. She could not imagine how he would feel, her brother who was so obsessed with trespassers, who had dedicated himself to hunting down even the smallest and most benign intrusions of the outside world on their property. She had not told him that anyone was coming. Only last night had she gotten the nerve to ambush her sisters with the information. The tree was going to be removed, she announced at the dinner table, with authority. "Why?" Eda asked, eyes narrowed. Wenna listed out the too-many good reasons that Eda could not argue with: They could never warm the house as long as there was a hole in it. The whole east wing was flooded. She and Nora were still sharing a room.

Eda was unmoved. "What does Charlie think?" she asked, as if she already knew the answer. Wenna feared that she did: that Charlie had confessed everything to her. He could never be counted on to go out of his way to keep secrets. But she looked staggered when Wenna said that Charlie had given her the money for the removal of the tree. "Oh," was all she said, eyebrows lifted, mouth puckered into a tiny pale knot. "*Oh.*"

Nora said almost nothing, only looked anxiously between them. But later, in the frozen black of the night, as she and Wenna took their final turns in the outhouse, she had spoken through the door: "Wenna, I don't want strangers to come here."

Wenna did not really want them to come either. "I know," she said. But she could not tell Nora they didn't have to come.

Now Nora's fingers tensed around hers as the truck stuttered through the muck surrounding the house, its white steel body disproportionately large even amid the old thirty-foot-high hemlocks. She could feel Nora's heartbeat in her palm.

In the undergrowth, feet from the wrecked east wing's crumpling wall, the truck's front wheels plunged suddenly down into a weak patch in the peat. The engine groaned; the front wheels spun impotently, the many behind them grinding into the dirt. Mud rose from underneath like dark spit, splattering the body of the truck and the clothes of the man who had waved the truck onward. The man leapt back. The driver, his face drawn as if in pain, threw the truck into reverse. From the cab issued shrieking frightened beeps whose echoes bounced between the trees and the house, getting penetratingly louder. The rear of the truck pressed back into the slender taut bodies of the yearling birches, which gave and then cracked, green wood exposed. Still the driver persisted backward, inching now, the truck's rear wheels churning and mashing the undergrowth. Wenna felt panic rise within her, as if it were her body at stake and not the land. The reality of what could happen to the bog in non-Haddesley hands came suddenly and starkly upon her, and she almost told them to stop, but she told herself that all the destruction would be for nothing if they didn't get the tree out now.

"Hey!" She tugged loose from Nora and crossed half the distance to the men and the truck. "Can you keep it on the driveway?"

The beeping stilled. "It's sinking," the man standing at the side of the truck said to the driver, his voice barely audible above the engine's dull, somnolent roar. He whipped his head around. "You didn't tell us the house was on a swamp," he shouted.

A bog, Wenna thought. "It's just a tree," she said helplessly. "I didn't know it would be so hard."

But it was hard; the two men worked for hours, one standing poised on the twenty-foot-high crane attached to the truck and making delicate, precarious overtures toward binding segments of the hemlock tree's trunk to other trees near the house with lengths of cord while the other stood below, one hand on his hip, murmuring disapprovingly, sometimes running the crane up and down. Eda said she could not bear to watch, and Nora slunk away too. Only Charlie stayed, his hands clasped behind his back, the look on his face wavering between awe and horror.

Because they could not get the crane as near to the house as they wanted, they could not make promises about the cleanness of the extraction, the on-the-ground man warned Wenna, punctuating this disclaimer with wolfish bites into a banana. "Might take out more of that roof on its way out," he said, and he tore the banana peel down in three strips and swallowed the nubby end without chewing. "That all right by you?"

"Whatever you need to do," said Wenna, because she could not say no now; she had gone too far already. She stood a ways back—the man suggesting it would be wise not to get too close—and together she and Charlie watched as the crane man set an electric saw across the hemlock tree's rotted girth, the noise deep and yet shrill. Charlie closed his eyes against it in a way that looked almost worshipful and, abruptly, pained.

"It's really going to be gone," he said, not particularly to her. The end of his sentence was lost to the sound of the hemlock's trunk cratering down to the earth from where it had been suspended, for almost a year now, in the horizon above the roof. Wenna felt the resulting thud as much as she heard it. Above their heads, birds scattered, an angry colorless pack of nonmigratory creatures chased at last from home. *What if they don't come back,* Wenna thought, and she felt sick, she felt panicked.

It was clear from the way the men talked to each other that the end of the tree was not supposed to fall like that. Cords had snapped. Saturated with a year of rot, a whole habitat perched in the mist, the tree's bottom had doubtless been heavier than they'd expected. The crane man swore at the ground man in a resigned, self-soothing way. They glanced in Wenna's direction as if imploring her to ask them to stop, but she didn't. They persisted. She wished Charlie would hold her hand, but he stood with his hands clasped, holding himself in, a vein on his pale neck throbbing.

The portion of the hemlock's trunk still embedded in the house looked bereft, stunted. The crane man reached down and sawed another segment loose; this one swung as intended, hanging from the branches of a spectral old hemlock like a limbless hanged man. After a while, Nora emerged from around the house with sandwiches. She could only have gotten them from the kitchen, and they were not supposed to enter the house while the men were working, but Wenna ate and said nothing. Nora disappeared. The men did not stop to eat. They worked ceaselessly, with grim determination, until they were done and the hemlock tree was only a pile of logs and the hole in the roof looked like an immense window of darkness, so much bigger now that it was empty. They said to Wenna that they'd bill her, and there was a pallor on their faces as if even they understood they had done something irrevocable.

"You oughta get the lot of these cut out," the driver said from the cab of the truck, gesturing broadly at the huddle of trees that surrounded the house. "You see those roots? Buttressed, we call it. All bunched up aboveground. Not stable. You'll end up back where you started, or worse, next time there's a storm." He did not suggest she enlist their services. He backed the truck down the driveway.

Wenna listened to the sound of the engine fade. The silence of the aftermath felt brittle, wounded. She understood, vividly and at once, that the bog would die if they left it to someone else, as certainly as it would die if they stayed.

CHARLIE

Charlie only went to the bank in Marlinton for the cash that Wenna needed to pull the hemlock tree out of the roof, but once he had the money, he found himself turning back to the counter and asking the teller if he could please see his safe-deposit box. He only wanted to verify that the deed was there, he thought, twisting the delicate brass key that he'd brought from home. *In case.* He did not know *in case* of what. There was no circumstance under which he could let Wenna sell their house. It would have been an unforgivable betrayal of the Haddesley compact. Like killing their father—and his father's father, and *his* father, and so on—after he was already dead.

But it was not a betrayal only to look at the deed, to hold the yellowed paper in his hands and assure himself that it had not been lost, it still existed. To read his own name there—*Charles Haddesley*, no mention of *which* Charles Haddesley—and to be steadied by the knowledge that, whatever his defects, his weaknesses, his failures as a patriarch, the law knew no difference between Charlie and every Charles Haddesley before him. He had practiced enough that his signature was indistinguishable from the signature on the original deed to the house—a signature, Charlie noticed now, that was dated 1897.

Charlie stared at the date on the paper, trying to figure out what it meant. Eventually he folded the deed in half, tucked it inside his pocket, and locked the safe-deposit box back up with nothing inside it. He thought of the antiques dealer in Charleston laughing at him. Her gloved fingers on the marbled surface of the globe that was supposed to be older than the American Haddesleys. *Around the 1890s,* she'd said.

❧

Until the day that the hemlock tree came down from the roof, Charlie refused to face the date on the deed—and the natural following question: Should there even have been a deed, or a date, when his father said they had always been on the land? *Always* not meaning *always,* of course, but a blurrily long time dating back to whenever the first American Haddesley fled persecution in the old country, for the Haddesleys' ways were noble, they were ancient. They—*we,* Charlie kept reminding himself—had come to the cranberry bog when it was still virgin and pristine. All this was true or else his father was a liar.

What, he wondered now, *did the bog do before we were here?* For the Haddesleys were not always *here.* Whatever his father's globe was supposed to show about the same mountains, the same veins of water, Charlie knew the Scottish Highlands were not the Appalachians of West Virginia. And that globe, anyway, was fraudulent. Not as old as it was supposed to be.

No one could deny the agedness of the many books in the study, especially the Borradh book with its violent and badly drawn pictures of people enacting the same rites that the Haddesleys enacted still. Or the house itself, which looked like nothing Charlie had ever seen in Marlinton or Charleston. Or the bog's need for a custodian. The bog was an endlessly needy creature, always in peril, vulnerable to trespassers, to changes in the weather, to its own need for a very particular balance of earth and water. *If we were not here,* Charlie concluded, *it would have succumbed long ago.* It would have become like anywhere else. And a small secret part of him thought—spitefully—that would have been better. *If this place had not been our obligation for as long as we lived and longer. If we could have let it waste away into nothing.*

The night before the men came with their enormous white truck, Charlie dreamed a dream that he had not dreamed since he was fourteen—young enough that he was not yet anticipating his father's death but old enough that the weight of his future had begun to set in. His father had said the word *copulation* and he had understood what it meant to marry the bog-wife. Afterward, he dreamed that *he* was the one incarnated from the mud and the mire, *he* was the one waiting patiently with legs open in the sedge, *he* was the one whose soft earthen mouth was spit upon, and then at last *he* was the one whose body was cleaved open.

Charlie used to wake from that dream shuddering and confused, his heartbeat throbbing all over his body. He'd spend the rest of the night lying as still as a corpse on his back, not letting himself fall asleep in case the dream came back. Eventually he stopped having it. He grew four inches in a year. He began again to sleep through the night. He had almost forgotten that time in his life, which had passed with the blurry formlessness of one long nightmare. But the night after the men cut the hemlock tree out of the roof, he dreamed the dream again, only different than before. On the study floor, surrounded by the portraits of his ancestors, Charlie dreamed that he was lying in the sedge, the undergrowth cold and damp and feathery-soft on his back and haunches, the moon full above him. All at once, the moonlight was blotted out. A dark figure stood above him. He was incapacitated by fear. The figure bore down on him, crushingly near, and Charlie saw it was neither human nor animal but the hemlock tree, thick and unrelenting and magnificently large.

Charlie woke coiled with rage and fear, as if he'd been held back in the middle of a fight. He got up off the mattress, wincing through the pain in his groin, and paced the study's length. From no vantage could he avoid seeing the Haddesley portraits, those impossibly many generations of progenitors, most of them done in oils and signed by artists with discreet right-hand-corner flourishes, only the last few done in a soft and resigned watercolor palette, signed by no one, fitted uneasily into their gilt frames. As if, only a few generations ago, there had been a break. As if something had changed. Charlie looked at his great-great-grandfather and felt nauseous. He thought of the doctor saying, *If you had come in right away.* He thought of the hemlock tree being cut down to manageable segments and torn out of their house so easily. It might never have been there, except for the gouge left in the roof and the gouge left in his pelvis.

In the morning, he got into the station wagon without making any excuse to his sisters and drove to the library in Marlinton.

⚘

The Marlinton Public Library was open only a few hours each week. Charlie made a habit of running errands at times that aligned with those hours. He'd begun his secret trysts with the library a few years before, after an approved visit to find a book on breeding goats. (They were doing everything wrong, he'd learned; shouldn't his father have known?) In the few minutes he'd spent there, he had been enamored by the quiet, gentle orderliness of the place. The outward-facing children's picture books with their sanitary-looking, soft-colored illustrations, the gleaming plastic covers that protected the fiction from the hands of readers, the narrow grid of shelves that barely fit two people between them, even the flat burgundy carpeting that smelled of being vacuumed. He had been, at first, half-afraid of the computer tucked into one corner. But since that day, he'd come back as often as he could and learned, slowly, how to navigate both the card catalog and the internet.

He could tell that the librarian recognized him by the way that the librarian's chin jerked as Charlie came through the door in front of the check-out desk. Charlie ducked past the man with averted eyes, not wanting to be questioned or even to be seen. He did not want to admit aloud what he was doing. He went to the stacks, first to *History*, which was all World War II and the fall of Rome and, tauntingly, one book entitled *Early Human Settlement in Appalachia*, which should have been promising but only described tribes of people that the writer called Native Americans, who resembled the Haddesleys not at all, making arrowheads, wearing unfamiliar clothes, speaking unfamiliar languages, spreading their civilization from New York to Georgia. The last chapter was on European settlement, and here too was disappointment. *The entrance of European settlers into Appalachia occurred late in the colonial period, during the eighteenth century*, the book said. The book described enormous hungry throngs from Ireland and Germany building small cabins in balds, setting up villages, hunting moose and bison to extinction. There were no manors, no families noble and ancient. The Haddesleys were unknown to this history. Charlie shut the book and continued fruitlessly down the row, past *Sciences*, past *Philosophy and Religion*.

Marlinton's collection was small, and Charlie soon resigned himself to the internet. He typed, *Haddesley*. Too much came up. So many hundreds of people with their name who were not them. Charlie wondered if they were relations but decided they could not be, for their family line had never branched: it must be only a coincidence that those other Haddesleys shared their name. Those people were college professors and heads of the garden association and arrested for breaking and entering. They were not truly Haddesleys. Glancing over his shoulder to see if the librarian was watching, Charlie typed *Charles Haddesley*. Still, there were imposters. Strangers wearing the Haddesley name. Charles Haddesley the graduate of Elk River High in 1962. Charles Haddesley the director of finance. Charlie had a strange and momentary fantasy of changing places with one of these other Charles Haddesleys. Living another man's life, heading something called a homeowner's association. He would shake hands firmly in this other existence. He would not even know what a bog was. He would never have been castrated by a hemlock tree. *Charles Haddesley* and *bog*, he tried. Now the search returned nothing.

Charlie sat stiffly upright in the too-small wooden chair before the computer for a long time before he got up the nerve to go to the check-out desk. Once there, he was too afraid to speak. The librarian lowered the book he was reading. He was the age of Charlie's father, his dwindling hair falling in a soft white haze around his ears. He wore a denim shirt and small round glasses.

"What do you need, son?" he asked.

Charlie balled his hands into fists inside his jacket pockets and said, "I am wondering if you know how to look for something." At the librarian's nod, he went on, stumbling on his words, "I'm trying to find the history of my family. It's . . . a very old family."

"And they're from the area?"

"Yes."

The librarian showed him the old newspapers. "Check marriages and obituaries," he suggested. "It goes back to the 1860s."

Charlie thought that wasn't possibly old enough. But he didn't want to seem ungrateful, and he didn't know what else to do, so he sat thumbing through them, pages upon pages of beloved grandmothers and devoted fathers and cherished sons until suddenly, abruptly, he came to a grainy photograph on a human-interest page facing the obituaries that showed their house, still under construction, pristine and young and unbattered. The caption read, *The Maturin folly, under construction.*

Charlie read and reread the words. The paper was dated June 10, 1897. He felt dizzy. Maturin was not their last name. Had the house belonged to someone else, before? He hunched his shoulders to conceal the newspaper and the offending photograph from the librarian, though the librarian had already returned to the check-out desk.

Charlie read the columns of text that wrapped tightly around their house, crushing it inward, confining it. *After four years, construction is nearly complete on the so-called Maturin folly, the seventeenth-century-styled manor built by Charles Maturin, youngest son of coal magnate Pierre Maturin. The manor sits on a four hundred–acre portion of the wilderness that has been in the*

Maturin family's possession since a controversial 1876 deal netted the Maturins more than seven thousand acres of property previously held by over ninety local farmers.

Charlie rose, still holding the brittle sheath of newspaper, and returned to the computer. He searched—typing slowly, feeling himself on a precipice—*Charles Maturin*. Now there were results. There were pictures. Charlie clicked through. A larger portrait of Charles Maturin emerged. The man in the black-and-white photograph possessed the smug and slightly withdrawn look of the man in the last of the oil portraits on the study wall. He had the same dark-blond hair, faint and gray in this photograph, and a mustache that he did not have in his portrait. The pointed Haddesley chin. The pale Haddesley eyes. He wore a wool overcoat, carelessly large, a white button-down underneath. He was slimmer and younger than the man on the study wall but unmistakably the same person. *Charles Maturin, antiquarian and eccentric*, read the caption. Charlie had only a vague idea of what either word meant. The website was filled with photographs of their house from different angles. Charlie felt a visceral and instinctive horror when he thought of a photographer tramping all over the bog, fixing a camera's lens on their home. On the screen, Charlie read on.

Charles Maturin, the youngest of Pierre Maturin's four children, was born in Pittsburgh in 1859, attended the University of Pennsylvania for two semesters, and embarked on several failed business ventures before becoming one of the East Coast's most prolific collectors of occultic objects from Celtic Great Britain and France. Charles possessed a life-long interest in European primitive civilizations, subscribing to the mythic ancient master-race theories popular in his day, and once embarked on a six-month tour of Europe in an unsuccessful effort to trace the Maturin family's origins back to the pre-Roman era.

Relations between Charles and his father were said to be strained throughout their lives. Nonetheless, Pierre Maturin continually financed his son's ventures and, in 1897, gifted him a plot of four hundred acres in northern West Virginia, mostly consisting of wetlands not suitable for coal mining or development. Over the next five years, Charles poured considerable resources into the construction of a rambling manor on that land, loosely styled after the country estates of the seventeenth-century Stuart kings in Scotland. This house, known locally as the Maturin folly, he filled with an extravagant collection of antiques and occult objects.

Charles briefly became the subject of a media spectacle in 1902 following his father's disappearance, as a witness initially told police that Pierre Maturin was going to visit his younger son when he left his Philadelphia home on the night of June 24. The grounds of the West Virginia property were searched, but no body was found. Although Pierre's porter James Lisbon was eventually convicted of his murder, some historians still maintain that Charles was most likely his father's killer, alleging that Pierre's body could easily have been concealed in the wetlands.

In the decades following his father's death, Charles became a recluse, rarely venturing far from home and cutting ties to the rest of the Maturins. He is not buried in the family tomb, and his death date is unknown.

The Maturin folly still stands today as one of the most unusual remnants of Gilded Age excess in Appalachia. Regrettably, the house has never been opened to visitors. It remains in private ownership.

Charlie closed the page. It had been littered with phrases he didn't understand—*occultic objects, master-race theories, Gilded Age*—but what he understood too vividly was that the house was not as old as it was supposed to be, the land was only the site of their house because it had been good for nothing else, the name *Haddesley* was not even their family name.

With a sinking feeling, he searched *Maturin family history.*

A number of websites came up now. He clicked indiscriminately on the first, titled "Robber Barons of the Coal Age," and read.

Pierre Maturin was descended from a line of textile merchants, members of the bourgeoning middle class in early modern France. In 1679, his great-grandfather Christophe Maturin immigrated from the suburbs of Paris to London during the French wars of religion. There, the family business suffered financial setbacks and the Maturins struggled on the margins of the middle class until Matthieu Maturin found success in the New World by liaising between the cotton plantations of Virginia and clothiers in Britain and France. Matthieu's trade in cotton funded his son Pierre's purchase of his first coal mine in 1851 and ultimately enabled Pierre's rise to prominence as a coal-mining magnate and the owner, at one point, of nearly one fifth of the land in West Virginia.

The words blurred before Charlie's eyes. Had his father known that in place of an ancient compact there was only money and cotton and many immigrations? He hoped his father had not known. What were the chances that his father was the first Haddesley patriarch to conceal a secret from his heir? Only, Charlie thought, his hands shaky and hot inside his jacket's pockets, *he* was not really his father's heir. His father had always wanted Percy to inherit. It occurred to him how likely it was that Percy was the one his father would have told this secret to, and he left the library in a hurry, eyes averted because he could not let the librarian see his distress, feeling wounded and murderous.

At home, Charlie parked, got out of the car, and went around the house so he would not face questions from his sisters. He strode past the empty black gouge in the roof where the hemlock tree had been, his body throbbing beneath him. He pressed on with long and purposeful steps through the wet sedge, down into the bog, until the house was only a dark and tree-sheltered pinprick behind him. There, in the sodden pale emptiness of the bog meadow, he found Percy making a meal of rancid cranberries, wearing only a ceremonial moss sheath. Charlie looked at his brother and saw on Percy's face the whole repulsive Haddesley lineage, the sharp narrow nose and quirked mouth and deep-set eyes of five generations of liars. He had the sickening thought that he could drown Percy out here in the peat and end the entire thing now.

Percy stood looking at him big-eyed and frightened, his legs apart, poised like a deer deciding whether to flee. "You shouldn't be here," he said. "You're wearing clothes. You're not consecrated." What he didn't say but clearly thought was, *The bog doesn't want you.*

"Did you know?"

"Know *what*?" said Percy.

"That none of it is true."

Percy shook his head. "You have to leave," he said. "You're not supposed to get so close."

Charlie persisted. "Did he tell you that we only go back five generations? That it was a rich city man's son who bought this land and built this house for . . . fun? There is no compact. There is nothing ancient."

Percy exhaled heavily, his breath fogging the air. Charlie watched him for some indication of guilt, of knowing. But he saw only confusion on his brother's face, and Percy appeared to him now not like a monument of Haddesleyness but merely like Percy, muddy-cheeked and skinny, a child filling out a man's body.

"It doesn't matter," Percy said—trying, Charlie could tell, to sound sure of himself—"how old it is. There is a compact. Otherwise there would never have been a bog-wife."

"Do we even know there was ever a bog-wife?" Charlie

thought of Eda's suggestion that he could simply steal a woman from Marlinton and make her marry him. What if there had never been bog-wives, only wives dragged into the bog and forced to play a role for their children's benefit? But when he thought of his own mother, he knew that wasn't right. There had always been something inhuman in her, a residue left by the bog where she had been formed. A smell, a feeling. A closeness to the land and a distance from all of them. That there had been women, or at least one woman, brought out of the bog, Charlie could not deny. But had those bog-born women always, or ever, been *wives*? "Maybe," he said, "it was never making wives for us. Maybe it would . . . do *that* whether we were here or not. Maybe that's just what it does." He lowered his voice, as if he were talking about someone who might at any moment enter the room. He didn't think the bog listened like that, but he didn't know. The wind in the sedge made the whole meadow seem to whisper and sigh. Sometimes, in those first years after she left them, he used to think their mother was still somewhere in the boglands, returned to her mossen original form but still in some way herself, still sensible of their movements.

"They are for us!" Percy said. "Or . . . this one is. Charlie, I can *feel* it."

Percy's face was strange then, as if his outsides had been wrapped around the insides of something invisible and very large. "You feel the bog?" Charlie said hesitantly, trying and failing not to stare.

"No," said Percy. He clutched at his temples, his fingers threading through his hair. For a dizzying second, Charlie thought he was going to pull his own head off. "Please, you have to leave," he said. "If you ruin this for me . . ." But he trailed off without making a threat.

"It was never not ruined," Charlie said. "That's what I'm saying."

"Please," said Percy.

"Don't you care?" said Charlie. "Does it not matter to you?" But he knew already that it didn't. The whole arrangement of their world had collapsed for Charlie, but nothing would actually be unarranged. There was no freedom in recognizing the lie at the foundation of everything. There were only the same unmet and unmeetable demands as before. What Charlie knew didn't matter as long as he existed in the world that Charles Maturin had made for them.

That night, he left the deed to the house where he knew Wenna would find it.

EDA

Eda copulated with strangers behind the bar in Marlinton four times before her menses stopped. For weeks afterward, in her bedroom at night, she cupped the form of her belly with her hands and tried to feel something. She felt nothing, nothing, and then in November when the trees went bare, she found she was teeming with life.

In those first months, the baby was like a specter that she was pleading to haunt her. It showed itself only in stabs of nausea, uneasy sensations, sleeplessness. Finally, on a January morning, she stood before the full-length mirror whose concave glass always exaggerated her head and shrunk her feet and she saw a new deformity in her proportions. "Oh," she said aloud. She thought: *Our problems are at an end.*

But of course they weren't. At night, Eda's skin felt waxy and tight, as if it did not fit. Her heart palpitated all over her body: in her calves, her pelvis, her fingertips. When she closed her eyes, she felt them itching to open. She felt a gnawing hunger but not for anything that she could think of. She endured the feeling for a month before one night she surrendered to it and went down to the kitchen and dug through the pantry, then the refrigerator, putting into her mouth whatever held appeal for even a second: a stale crouton, a hunk of Swiss cheese, a swallow of orange juice, a dab of mayonnaise, a fingernail scraping of frozen pie crust. Nothing satisfied or came close to satisfying. She only felt hungrier, and full of guilt for wasting so many groceries. She went back upstairs. Somewhere deep in her abdominal cavity, in the small hollow where she thought the baby was growing, she felt a hitch of pain. She was afraid it meant the baby was dying. How many babies had her mother carried partway to term before they fell out of her in bloody, effortful clots, half-formed or not formed at all? Once, only a clump of moss with eyes and teeth. Her mother had developed a sense of when a baby was dying. Eda should have asked her how she'd known. She needed, now, to know.

She was still in the hallway when the hitch blossomed suddenly into a throb so deep that it almost could not be borne. Eda caught herself with her hands on the wall and lowered herself down to the floor before she fell. She could not let anyone else wake up and find her like this, disheveled and panicked and sweaty. Crawling, her lips bit shut so she would not cry out, she made it down the length of the hallway to her bedroom. She crawled through the door and shut it behind her. *Don't you dare let it die*, she thought as she sat on the floor. But it didn't have the same force as when her father used to say it to her mother.

For a long time, she sat against the door holding on to her belly, pleading with the eyeless, nameless creature inside not to die. At last, the cramps passed, gone as if they had never been there. She stood tremulously in the middle of her dark bedroom for a minute, not trusting the pain's sudden absence, and then crossed the room to the bed and lay down on her side, her belly enclosed by her twined fingers. She stayed like that for hours— afraid that any motion, even rolling over, would disturb the creature inside of her. It was beginning to seem to her that carrying a baby to term was as nervous and arcane a rite as anything that the Haddesley patriarchs had ever done in the bog's mouth.

She felt relief when the sun rose, though it meant her night had been sleepless. Night was always the most precarious time, and clouds hung so thick over the boglands that sometimes, in the winter, morning would seem not to come at all. They knew spring was approaching when the sun was able to evaporate the mist. If the baby did not die, Eda thought, he would be like that kind of morning. If the baby did not die, then winter and the cloud cover and the bog-wife's absence were only a four-month-long sleepless night that could be endured. And Eda knew how to endure.

She decided it was time to tell her siblings.

❧

Eda wanted the announcement of her pregnancy to feel momentous. She decided there would be a dinner, arranged and festive. Cooking was supposed to be the work of the patriarch, and her preparation of a real meal, extravagant and indulgent, would send a message. She went again to her mother's closet, although she already knew that her mother had nothing close to right. She was imagining a ball gown with a glistening full skirt that spread across the floor so that she took up half the room. But she had to settle for something from her own closet, a wrinkled ankle-length crepe dress with a washed-out pattern of pink roses and green rosebuds. The dress was a hand-me-down, and Eda's breasts and stomach strained against the fabric. Inside of it, she felt constrained, too big. Her body's proportions were not queenly but awkward and swollen. And nothing could ever be done with her hair, which hung dry and limp and too small down her shoulders. She regarded herself in the mirror with loathing, yanking her hair into braids that she immediately unbraided, wishing she knew how to do that delicate and careless knot that Wenna always did—something she'd obviously learned across the property-line, the secret province of un-Haddesley women.

All the while, she felt the dreadful pull of time passing. She had not yet even begun cooking. If she waited too long, her siblings would begin scavenging for food on their own and then there could be no dinner. She would have to wait another day to tell them. The prospect had become unbearable to her in the three hours since she first conceived of the announcement.

Downstairs, her hair half-subdued by a barrage of pins, Eda was beset by moldy onions and dusty stalks of dried thyme and a freezer that was nearly empty except for half a bag of frozen chicken breasts—perversely inappropriate, she thought, for a dinner celebrating their persistence on the land—and a frost-crusted side of venison, years-old probably, since no one had managed to shoot anything at any point that Eda could remember. It would be hours before the meat reached a workable temperature, but the venison was the only thing close to a presentable main course, so Eda wrestled it out of the freezer and set it on the counter to defrost. She began peeling potatoes, her eyes wandering continually back to the meat, which sat malevolently unchanging before her. It would not be tender when cooked, she thought with dismay. She finished the potatoes and prodded at the meat with her finger and found it as rigid and cold as before. She felt as if she were drowning. She decided to set the table.

Arranging the table in the never-used formal dining room should have been the simplest part of preparing the dinner, but

Wenna had been using it as a place to stockpile things she'd cleared out of the hallways. Piles and piles of things covered the long oak table and the eight oak chairs, looming precariously over Eda in lopsided stacks that went almost to the ceiling. Here were objects she'd never even seen before but also familiar ones that should never have been treated like junk: porcelain dolls, jigsaw puzzles, a wooden rocking horse. Things the baby would play with, Eda thought, and she nearly began rescuing the toys before she remembered that what mattered now was the dinner. She would get her sister to remove everything, she decided, and this small assertion of her will would almost make up for the months of Wenna thinking that she could simply reorder the whole house without so much as asking Eda first.

To her surprise, Wenna agreed to clear out the dining room, though with the sullen begrudging reluctance that was always her response to any request Eda made. "Find candlesticks, if you can," said Eda, over her shoulder, as she returned to the venison; it could not be such a hard task, for someone who had been rifling through the whole house. The venison was still stubbornly frozen, but night was falling and Eda could not afford to wait. She boiled a pot of water and set the venison in a basin and poured hot water over it. Steam rose in sheets from the frozen side of meat, dispersing a sour and blighted odor. She almost abandoned the whole thing, but Nora was standing at the doorway, leaning on the jamb, asking if she could make herself something to eat. "Absolutely *not*," said Eda, with force, and she decided only as she said it that she was going to persist.

"Well, I'm a little hungry," Nora said, with that slight and almost-undetectable curl of slyness in her voice that Eda knew well and hated. Eda stalked across the kitchen to the pantry, dug out the sleeve of crackers that she had secreted among the soup cans for herself, threw it in her sister's direction, said firmly, "Don't come back in here," and returned to raining down shards of dry rosemary onto the venison as if punishing it. She had begun already to realize that her siblings were not going to celebrate the way they were supposed to, because they never did anything the way they were supposed to. Her whole life had been an endless series of plans perfectly made and then hopelessly muddied, complicated, disregarded. She consoled herself by thinking that there was nothing any of them could possibly do to take away the triumph of the child. She did not need their cooperation, although she would admit to herself now, as she emptied cans of cream-of-mushroom soup around the venison in an enormous stoneware platter and shoved it into the hot oven, that she desperately wanted it. She wanted them to look upon her with the love and admiration that they had never shown before, to recognize her as better than a patriarch, as mother and bog-wife and custodian all in one.

But she could not be the thing they would worship in her current state, disheveled and flustered, cutting the black parts out of the cellar potatoes and wondering whether the canned carrots—two years past their expiration date, because no one ever wanted to eat canned carrots—could possibly be dressed up well enough that no one would realize their origins. They had no fresh vegetables. Charlie needed to go to the store. He kept putting it off, saying that a storm was coming. *It's winter,* Eda had said impatiently, *there's always a storm coming.* But she could not prod him any further without reaching the perilous point where he might really refuse her and she might really have to admit that he could say no whenever he wanted to, she was at his mercy and not the other way around, so she let it go. The canned carrots sat limply, putridly sweet-smelling and wet, in the glass baking dish beside the peeled potatoes. Eda doused them in butter and salt and blew the dust off the crumply old strings of thyme hung from the rack on the ceiling and doused them in that too. She knelt to check the venison. She was sweating through the thin crepe of the dress, although the house was not warm.

Eda could tell that it was late, almost the middle of the night, hours after dinner should already have been eaten, before the venison was anywhere near cooked. The middle was still ruddy and liquid, but she thought they could avoid that part. The potatoes and carrots, thrown into one corner of the oven and abandoned there for nearly an hour during the nightmarish middle hours of cooking, were blackened and coarse, beyond salvaging with balsamic vinegar or honey or careful arrangement on the dainty porcelain serving dish that Eda found on the counter, but she applied all three of those things to them anyway. Nora came sliding back into the kitchen on her socked feet as Eda fidgeted with the vegetables; a look of repulsion crossed her face before she resumed her placating little mask and she said, too politely, "Eda, do you . . . need help?"

She didn't mean it, but Eda said, "Go and get Percy and tell him to come to dinner," as if she did.

The dining room had been emptied of boxes, but it was distinctly unfestive, cobweb-threaded and discouraged-looking, a lone box still tucked into the corner as if Eda wouldn't notice. The chandelier hanging from the ceiling had never worked, so the candlesticks that Wenna had not found were their only source of light. Eda did not waste time being disappointed.

She went to the supply in the kitchen and withdrew a dozen unadorned and nubbly candles, lopsidedly burnt, not at all the elegant long-necked tapers she had envisioned. As she laid out plates beneath their shuddering glow, she realized belatedly that there was no dessert. There should have been dessert. But it was too late now. Charlie entered at a shuffle, then Wenna and at last Nora, who came without Percy and only looked blankly at Eda when Eda asked where he was. None of them were dressed up, not even Nora, who loved nothing more than an excuse to wear one of the too-small ancient dresses moldering away in her closet.

"Why isn't Percy here?" Eda asked.

"He wouldn't come," said Nora.

"Why not?"

"He can't leave," said Nora, shrugging. "That's what he said. He was acting like . . . I don't know. He wouldn't really speak to me."

Eda stifled a groan of frustration. It was supposed to be the five of them; Percy was supposed to find out with everyone else. "Go back out there," she said. "Tell him he *has* to." Without waiting to see if Nora obeyed, she returned to the kitchen and brought out the meat and the vegetables.

In the candlelight, the venison was almost beautiful, crispy and glistening, a sprig of rosemary set precisely in the center. But when Eda cut it open, she could see that the meat was nearly all raw inside, and she felt such a rush of despair that she almost threw the whole platter from the table. Everything was wrong. The tablecloth was wrinkled, the flatware tarnished, one of the plates chipped. She felt a rivulet of sweat flow down her side to her hip, sticking where the crepe clung to her skin and evaporating there. She felt a passing urge to fling herself into the snow. Nora had still not returned. The food was getting cold. Eda poured the cranberry wine, administered small portions of meat and vegetables to her siblings, fidgeted listlessly with the candles. Nora came back alone.

"Percy won't come," she reported, and she sat down at her childhood place at the table.

Eda shut her eyes and held them closed until she was certain that she could contain herself. "Fine," she said, at last. "He'll find out later."

She intended for everyone to eat before the announcement, but now they all knew she had something to say. She made it no more than five minutes before she rose, her chair wobbling back, and lifted her wineglass as their father used to do on the anniversary of his wedding. "We have something to celebrate," she said. "I've been wanting to tell you."

Her siblings stared impassively. Wenna's eyebrows were lifted, her arms crossed. She had already abandoned the pretense of eating the food on her plate.

Eda felt heat blossom behind her ears, at the hollow of her throat. But she pressed on. "I'm having a baby," she said. "An heir. We're not going to be the last Haddesleys."

For a moment, no one spoke. Nora's eyes were wide, her mouth dropped slightly open. Charlie, the only one who could already have known, pushed his potatoes around with his fork and wouldn't look at her.

Wenna made a sound that was nearly a laugh. "No, you're not," she said. "You're not pregnant." But she was looking critically at Eda: at her stomach, the small but pronounced bulge where Eda's dress went taut across her belly.

Eda was unprepared for the possibility that Wenna would just *deny* the baby's existence. "Well," she said, "I am, so."

Wenna's lips pressed together. "You know how babies are made, right?"

Eda's fist tightened around her wineglass, but she made herself keep smiling. She did not want to answer questions about the baby's conception. Wenna would only make it sound unmystical and degrading.

"Of course I do," she said, chin lifted.

"So . . . who's the father?"

Eda sat down. No one had toasted to her and the baby. It was clear that no one *would* toast to her and the baby. She drained the rest of her wineglass and breathed through the familiar agony of watching a well-arranged vision unravel into chaos. There was nothing to do but endure it. She never really let her siblings have the punishment they deserved, even when they were children; always, she needed them too much, and what if they no longer loved her afterward? She hated them, she thought. She hated all of them. "It doesn't matter who the father is," she said. "Why should it matter?"

"In *National Enquirer*," Nora suggested, "a Martian flew down to Earth and got a woman pregnant with an alien."

"Listen," Eda said. A thin sheen of sweat had broken out across her entire body. "It doesn't matter where the baby came from. What matters is that our line isn't ending."

"How could you do this?" said Wenna. "*Why* would you do this?"

"Someone had to do something," Eda retorted. No one was disagreeing with Wenna; no one was defending Eda and what she'd done for their family. She felt her defenses falling, the triumph that had carried her through the whole disaster of the dinner evaporated, and panic rose in her lungs like moss-clotted water. "There has to be an heir," she insisted, her voice high and tremulous, not at all commanding.

"There does *not* have to be an heir," said Wenna. "We had a chance. We could have made a clean break."

Eda was almost speechless. "A clean break?" She'd never heard the phrase before and could only think now of the solemn and businesslike incisions that her father used to make across the newborn throats of Mathilde's defective kids, ending their sufferings almost before their sufferings could begin. "What are you talking about?"

Wenna wasn't listening. "What do you think about this?" She gestured to Nora and Charlie with her empty wineglass. "Is this what either of you wanted?"

Charlie stabbed a carrot on the end of his fork, pressing the tines farther and farther through the vegetable flesh, the look on his face intensely concentrated.

Nora sat on her hands, her face scrunched up beneath her cloud of hair. "I don't know," she whispered.

"Charlie, do you have nothing to say? Are you just going to act like you're perfectly happy raising a child here? Making another Haddesley patriarch?"

Charlie's eyes moved to Eda, for only a second, before his gaze became flat and distant again. "No," he said.

"No *what?*" Wenna said. "No, you're not going to act like that, or no, you're not unhappy? I'm so tired of you playing both sides like this. You tell me we can't sell the house and then you leave the deed folded up in my laundry? What am I supposed to think—"

"Sell the house?" Eda interrupted. At once she understood: why Wenna had let strangers come and pull the hemlock tree out of the roof, why she had been sorting all their possessions into piles, why she was so angry now to learn that there were going to be more Haddesleys. And she felt her sister's betrayal like a heavy weight crashing down on her.

Charlie said nothing. Wenna pressed her lips together and looked urgently, angrily, across the table at him.

"How *dare* you?" Eda said. "Do you think this place belongs only to you? Do you think that because you don't care about the compact, the rest of us don't?"

"Don't talk to me about the compact," Wenna said. "After what we let happen to Mom, all of you should be afraid to *look* at the bog, let alone demand things of it."

"And what is it that 'happened to Mom'?" Eda asked. She was not going to let Wenna win another argument by dangling the specter of their mother over them. She could make insinuations, but she had no proof and she knew she had no proof. "Just say it. What do you think *happened* to her?"

Wenna opened her mouth, then closed it. As Eda suspected, she would not actually say the words *I think he killed her.*

"He had dirt on his hands," she stammered. "When he came inside."

Eda's heart thudded in her throat. It was too easy to imagine: their father coming in the back door with his hands soil-caked, the grief on his face so like relief that it might have *been* relief. But there was no reason to think he killed her when it was so probable that she simply left them. What Wenna still refused to accept, what she would not acknowledge even ten years after the fact, was that their mother had left them long before she vanished. Her disappearance from their lives was the work of years and not hours. If Wenna would think back without the filter of desperate all-forgiving orphan-love coloring everything, she would realize their mother had never really been with them at all.

"So he had dirt on his hands," Eda said. "Like every other day of his life?"

Wenna pushed her plate forcefully away. "I can't do this with you," she said. "You're not the bog-wife and you're not the patriarch and you have no *right*, and yet you went and got yourself pregnant so we could do this all over again."

Eda was startled by the terror that this ignited in her; the one thing she could not do, under any circumstances, was *do it all over again*. She had felt certain that it would be different when the baby was her own, but she couldn't really think, now, why she thought that. "There is a compact," she said desperately. "Someone has to keep it."

"There's not," muttered Charlie.

Eda had almost forgotten he was there, and she could tell that Wenna had too.

"What?" she asked.

"There's not a compact," said Charlie.

"You mean because of what happened to Mom," said Wenna.

"No," said Charlie. "There never has been a compact. There aren't even Haddesleys."

"What are you saying?" Eda demanded. The way Charlie was talking, half-mumbly but stern, seeming to enjoy his own ominousness, was unlike him. He looked, she thought, almost like their father.

Charlie set down his fork. "About a hundred years ago," he said, "the son of a coal miner and a steel heiress came from

Pittsburgh and bought this land and cleared other people's houses out of it and pretended no one had ever lived here before him. And then, probably, killed his father and buried him in the bog and started this cycle we can't finish."

A crush of sound filled Eda's ears like a chainsaw roar. "You're making that up," she shouted above the din. "How would you know that?"

Charlie reached into his pocket and withdrew a folded slip of yellowed paper. Slowly, delicately, he unfolded it and handed it across the table to her.

Eda stared at the photograph—grainy, obscured by shadow, but unmistakably their house—captioned *The Maturin folly, under construction*. It was dated 1897. She could not breathe. Twelve generations of American Haddesleys hung on the wall in the study, men in purple waistcoats and lace collars, men in hunting clothes with small-headed dogs, men in chain mail. Who were they; who had mothered their children?

"Let me see," said Wenna.

Eda passed the paper to her. "This doesn't mean anything," she said with a confidence she didn't feel. "One hundred years or four hundred, who cares? We came from the Scottish Highlands, anyway." But it did mean something, because their father had lied to them every time he said, *Always, the bog has belonged to us and us to it.*

"We came," said Charlie, remorselessly, "from the suburbs of Paris."

Wenna held out the paper to Nora, who refused to take it. She held it out for a moment longer, her grasp wavering, then set it down in the center of the table, where it sat beneath the candles like an unwelcome dessert. "Did Dad know?" she asked.

"I'm not sure," said Charlie. "Percy didn't."

"And what about you?" said Eda. "How long have you known?"
She saw with new eyes her brother's indifference to the duties of
the patriarch and custodian, his perpetually shrugged shoulders,
his lack of surprise when he came back from the bog wifeless.
You could have a baby, he'd said in the study, as if it didn't matter who fathered their heir, because—had he known?—it didn't;
there was no ancient and hereditary promise in need of fulfillment. Her stomach roiled.

"I don't care if there's no compact," Nora interrupted, her
voice too loud and tremulous. "We still live here. It's still our
home. Isn't it?"

"It matters because the bog has never wanted us here!" said
Wenna. "Because it was never an exchange; it was only taking.
Why would it want our patriarchs anyway?"

Eda thought of the bodies deposited in the bog's mouth,
their outsides preserved while their insides slowly leaked out. It
was too much. She retched and emptied her stomach onto her
plate, expelling venison, vegetables, cranberry wine.

When she lifted her stinging eyes, her siblings averted their
gazes, fast and polite as if they hadn't all betrayed her in one way
or another.

"How long did you know?" she again asked Charlie.

"Not long," he said. "Not before . . ." And then he stopped,
as if he was too delicate to allude to those nights at the bar in
Marlinton.

"Everything was for nothing," Eda whispered. The whole
project of her life had been empty: every effort she had ever
made since Charlie was born and she became the eldest sibling
but not the heir.

"Edd," said Wenna, almost gently, which made Eda furious.

Wenna had gotten exactly what she'd hoped for: a reason why she'd been right to disappear, a justification for all the selfish things she'd done. Wenna could now feel vindicated in her scheme to sell the house out from under them and righteous in sneering at Eda's efforts to hold things together.

"You can leave," she said to Wenna. "That's what the bog wants, isn't it? For everyone to go? So do it. Go back to wherever you were before."

"I want to help you," Wenna insisted.

Eda's patience was gone. "Get out of my house," she said.

Wenna flinched. Her lips parted and, for a second, Eda thought she was going to protest, but she didn't. "Fine," she said. "I'll leave tomorrow."

NORA

When Nora first wrote to Michael, her letter had been short and cautious; she was not yet very good at imitating either Wenna's handwriting or the kinds of things her sister would say. She had to sound Wenna-like enough that Wenna's husband wouldn't be suspicious, and happy enough that he wouldn't be worried and think of coming to find her, and kind enough that he wouldn't be angry—though not *so* kind that he would think they should be together again. It hadn't been easy, and Nora hoped that she would only have to do it once. *I miss you, and I am glad you wrote*, she had written, consulting one of Wenna's shopping lists for the curls of the *e*'s, the loops of the *l*'s and the *y*'s. *But I am going to stay with my family for a while.* She mailed the letter with a sense of relief, feeling a kind of guilt that was almost pleasure at having gotten away with something. Then, a week later, his reply arrived. Nora had drawn it out of the mailbox with both dismay and a flutter of anticipation that startled her.

The second letter was, if possible, worse than the first. Michael was a stranger writing to another stranger whom he'd shared a whole life with, in a place that Nora had never even visited. *I keep thinking of things I want to tell you about*, he wrote, *and in the moment I always forget that we're not together anymore and that I can't reach you, and then I'm left with this feeling like I'm holding something I can't let go of. So—here is me letting go of them:*

— That four-mile stretch of 322 that we always said they needed

to clean up? Well, they're finally doing construction on the road, but the wrong part of it!! They're doing the perfectly fine part that's just one lane a side, making it wider, I guess.

– That brand of coffee you love, with the lightning bolt across the whole bag, came back to the Albertsons near my work. I bought three bags and then realized obviously I won't drink them. I actually made a cup. Tried to experience it like you would have. Still tastes like gasoline to me. I know, you always say, how I imagine gasoline would taste.

– Claire at work, last week she said she hoped I was doing all right and gave me a tin of flavored popcorn. Is this the new sympathy gesture? It's new to me. I swear I've been changing clothes, showering, smiling at people. I don't know what she thought she knew. Although—I stood over the sink and ate half of the tin for dinner that day, so I guess she was right.

– You were right about that down comforter. November and it's already worth the money. Especially now that I'm in the bed alone. Probably saving me money on heat. I know I used to say I felt alone with just the two of us in the house, and that seems insane to me now. I've never been lonely like this. It's not like before we met, it's much worse, because now it's like losing a limb (he had crossed this out, twice, but twice rewritten it) or something that I used to have. I know that's overwrought. You weren't a limb, you were your own person. But I mean that it felt natural to have you with me. I'm not trying to make you feel guilty. But, please, I want to know how you're really feeling.

It took Nora many hours to write her reply, her first draft done in skittery pencil in the back of a *National Enquirer* because real paper was scarce and she knew it was going to take multiple tries. She thought, *What would Wenna say she was really feeling?* For days she studied her sister, searching for the answer in every small thing Wenna did. Noticing how Wenna sipped her coffee black, without goat's milk or sugar, savoring the rich bitter taste that Nora couldn't ever get used to. How she lingered at the tree line when they did yard chores, as if she longed to go past the line of birches and into the bog's mouth but wouldn't let herself. How she tucked her hair behind her ear with a quick, nervous, familiar gesture that Nora recognized as their mother's, a slightly unnerved expression on her face that was so like their mother's face. As if she hadn't expected to find hair there, as if she were being haunted by her own body.

It was not really good enough to study the Wenna that was here in their house, Nora understood, because it could not reveal the Wenna that had been out there, in Illinois, preferring certain brands of coffee and getting her husband to buy a down comforter. That version of Wenna disappeared in the Haddesley house, for their Wenna seemed to have no history but their shared history; she seemed to love nothing that they did not love too. And Nora realized from Michael's letters that Wenna had been the same way with her husband, hiding the parts of herself that she didn't want him to know. The Haddesleys had been buried in her life with him almost as much as he was buried in her life with them, for he seemed to think something was wrong with their family—which hurt Nora's feelings, so acutely that she almost could not look Wenna in the face for a few days afterward—but not to know what the wrong thing was. *Will you lose yourself if you live how they live again?* Michael asked in his third letter, the *how* sitting emptily in the middle of the sentence because he could only mean the *self* that he knew, not the one that Wenna was here, and he didn't know how that Wenna had ever lived. He knew only that the Haddesleys were far away from other people, not that they were so close to the land and to one another, that their ways were noble and ancient, that in the winter they piled together all their blankets and slept warmly in the glow of the hearth as they had always done before and as their ancestors had done before them, known and safe and lasting.

There was so much about Wenna that Michael could never really know that Nora thought Wenna couldn't truly be in love with him, yet when she read Michael's letters she understood how Wenna could have thought she was. For minutes at a time, as she wrote her replies or plotted them, Nora *was* Michael's Wenna, and she felt the force of his love as if it were directed at her and not her sister. The nakedness of someone getting to know so many things about you when they had known nothing at first, the terror and safety of someone asking you what you felt without demanding any certain answer or thinking they already knew. The thrill of being wanted. *I stood in the shower for half an hour today thinking of how I used to take you in there, your wet back and ass pressed against me, my hands in your wet hair,* he wrote in his fourth letter. Nora felt, when she read that letter, a longing like pain. Afterward, she paced the length of Percy's empty bedroom until her heartbeat throbbed in her throat and she threw herself down on his wrinkled sheets and gasped into the mattress until she was breathless, wanting to get the yearning feeling out.

For three months, Nora lived in a dream of marriage, answering Michael's letters with ever-longer responses, getting more comfortable in her sister's skin, perfecting the arches of Wenna's handwriting and the nervous half-committed things she should say back to Michael when he said that he still loved her. Yet somehow she still did not really know Michael's Wenna, because when Michael's Wenna appeared suddenly, frighteningly at their dining room table and admitted that she was trying to sell their house, Nora felt as though she were looking at a stranger.

❧

After dinner, Wenna left the room while Eda stayed at the table, her face crumpled. Nora sat across from her, sitting on her hands so she would not pull her eyebrows, feeling urgently the need to follow Wenna upstairs yet finding that she was almost afraid to be alone with her sister now.

Eda opened her mouth and screamed a short loud despairing scream that made Nora flinch, then went on sitting as if the scream had not happened. Charlie began clearing away their plates, Eda's plate with vomit on it; the rack of venison that had gone almost uneaten; the charred little vegetables that reminded Nora so much of Buz Lukens's scat that she hadn't been able to eat any of them, even to make Eda feel better.

"Are you really going to let her leave?" she whispered.

"Do you not understand that Wenna doesn't care what happens to us?"

"But . . . we should all be here."

"Why?" said Eda. "There's no compact."

What Nora could not say to Eda was that she had been so hopelessly lonely before Wenna came back, that always there had been an emptiness lodged inside her so big and full she almost choked on it, and now that Percy had left them to live in the bog's mouth and hunt trespassers Nora would have no one if Wenna left; it would be only her and Eda and Charlie and the weird blurry figure of Eda's fatherless baby for the whole rest of their lives. Nora could not find it in herself to care very much whether there was a compact or not. The relations between the Haddesley patriarchs and the bog had never really been any business of hers. They seemed, to Nora, to have nothing really to do with her life other than the occasional ritual interruption. "We're a family," she said. "Aren't we still a family?"

"What do you want me to do?" asked Eda. "Am I supposed to tell her she can stay here and sell the house out from under us? She never listened to me. Why do you think you had to write the letter?"

For only a second, Nora thought Eda meant the letters to Michael, and panic tightened her throat. Then she realized Eda meant the letter to Wenna, the letter ordered by their father, and she could breathe again. Wenna had answered that letter; she loved Nora at least a little. The problem was that Wenna did not love her more than she loved anything else. Wenna could not, Nora understood, ever possibly love Nora as much as she loved Michael and the world where the two of them had lived together. How could she? If it was a choice between them and that other world, she would never choose them, especially now that she knew the bog didn't need her to stay.

"I just need her," Nora whispered, and she went upstairs.

In their shared bedroom where they had gone only to change their clothes for months now, Wenna was packing her belongings, scrounging through the closet that had become again their shared closet and throwing things indiscriminately toward her suitcase: sweaters that were Nora's and not hers, although they had been sharing. They were close enough to the same size. She must have forgotten she hadn't brought them with her; they were only hers as long as she was Nora's Wenna and not Michael's Wenna, the stranger-Wenna, the Wenna that would sell her own family's ancestral home.

"I don't want you to go," Nora said from across the room, thinking: *See, first, if she loves you. If she'll do it without any other reason.*

Wenna looked over her shoulder, then returned to rifling through the closet. "I'm sorry, Nor. I know you don't."

"But . . . you don't care?"

"I'm not going to stay here and watch Eda play out this whole horrifying thing. I said I was only coming back for the burial." She threw a pile of leggings into her suitcase and crossed the room to Nora. "Listen," she said, her voice low now, her eyes darting to the door. "You can come with me, if you want to. I mean it. I'll take care of you."

Nora was, for a second, breathless with possibility. She could become the kind of Nora that fit into stranger-Wenna's Illinois life. She imagined herself as one of the women that she saw on *National Enquirer's CelebWatch!* pages, wearing something with sequins that did not cover her legs. As beautiful as Wenna and as unafraid. She was almost seduced. Then she remembered the fact of Michael, the marriage that was not hers and could not include her. Probably there were so many facts of Wenna's life like that. She bent her focus to Nora here only because there was nothing else to distract her. In the world beyond the property-line, she would rebecome whatever she had been for those ten years that Nora still could not wholly understand even after three months of pretending to have lived them. And

Nora would be even more alone than before. Without Eda or Charlie or Percy, without Buz Lukens and the rest of her animals. When she imagined her foundlings without her, alone in the boglands with their ailments and deformities, their missing limbs, their too-small corn-fed bodies, she felt a guilt as forceful as if she'd really set them loose. That was *her* compact, she thought. Her unbreakable promise.

"No," she said. "Please, Wenna, you have to stay *here*."

Wenna looked fiercely at her. "Do you support this?" she said. "Did you know about the pregnancy already?"

Nora was so bewildered by the question that she almost forgot to take offense at the accusation that she and Eda were conspiring. "Eda never tells me anything," she said. "No one tells me anything."

Wenna lowered her eyes, and Nora thought she was going to say she was sorry. Then she turned around and crouched and began shoving down the things inside her suitcase so they would all fit, as if the conversation were over.

Nora almost couldn't breathe. "You can't go back, you know." She felt the same head-swimming rush of sensation that she always felt when she said something hateful to Percy. Her tongue was forming words and spitting them out as if she meant them even though they were not really coming from her, even though she did not want to be saying them. "Your husband thinks you hate him now," she said, which was not true yet but *could* be true. She would write to him as Wenna one more time and drive him away, tell him that she was copulating with someone else now, that she had laughed at his letters, that she didn't care what happened to him. "I wrote to him as you. Lots of letters, and always he believed it. He doesn't even know what your handwriting looks like. And . . . he said . . . he loves someone else."

Wenna looked up at her, eyes narrowed; she was trying to decide whether she believed Nora. "No you didn't," she said. "How did you know—"

"I *did*," said Nora, triumphantly. She ran across the hall to Percy's bedroom and dug the wad of Michael's letters out of the bedsheets and threw them at her sister.

Wenna stared at her from a snowfall of wrinkled paper. "How long has this been happening?"

Nora began to realize with a plummeting feeling that she had made a mistake. Wenna did not seem to believe that she had lost Michael, and she was much too focused on Nora's violation, which Nora had almost forgotten *was* a violation, although of course she knew she should not have read and responded to letters that were not for her.

"How come you lied about being married?" she asked instead of answering, for hadn't Wenna's violation come first? Haddesley sisters were never supposed to marry; Wenna knew that. Nora's wrongdoing was small and insignificant by comparison.

"I don't have to tell everything to you!" Wenna said. "Do you not get that we are separate people? You don't get to sign my name as if it's yours!"

"Then you don't get to sell our house like it's *yours!*"

Wenna didn't answer. She gathered up the letters into a pile without reading them and got to her feet. Nora could tell she was going to leave the room, and if she left the room she would leave them for good, she would disappear as she had disappeared before and she would never come back and Nora would always be alone. Her heart pounding in her throat, she stood in the way of the door. "Please, Wenna, please," she said. "Just stay here. Please."

Wenna looked at her with such loathing then, such contempt. As if Nora were something disgusting. "I'm sleeping in the parlor," she said. She dragged the suitcase along after her, and Nora listened as it thudded down each one of the stairs, composing a cruel, vicious letter in her head and getting no pleasure from it, understanding that she had never for even a moment understood her sister and what Wenna wanted and what she loved.

$$\ast$$

They all knew without even discussing it that they would not sleep bundled together before the hearth that night, though the air was cold. Nora made it through half the night in her bedroom alone before the loneliness became unbearable, something she could not breathe through. With a feeling of resignation, she got up and wrapped her quilt around herself and crept down the hallway to Eda's room.

She had not gone to Eda since they were children, Nora almost a baby and Eda still a teenager, younger than Nora was now and yet older than Nora thought she would ever feel. Their mother's door was always closed at night, but Eda had left her door cracked open, and while Wenna peacefully snored in the bed beside her, Nora would climb past one sister's sleeping form to disturb the other. Nighttime Eda was not like Daytime Eda, who was forbidding and so impatient. Nighttime Eda was endlessly tolerant of Nora's stumbling half-vanished recollections of her nightmares, she was gentle, and her body felt so soft and warm that Nora could be soothed to sleep by the sheer nearness of it.

She was not sure if Nighttime Eda still existed, but the bedroom door was cracked like it always used to be, and she stood in the doorway for only a moment before she heard Eda say, sleepily, "Come on, Nor, come in."

Nora stepped into Eda's bedroom and closed the door behind her. The curtains were thin enough that she could see the moon through them, high and full and ringed in the way that the moon was always ringed before a storm. From across the room, Eda looked strangely like their mother in the midst of one of her long tirednesses. But when she said, "You can stay in here, if you want," she sounded only like herself and Nora was reassured; she crossed the room, reaching the side of the bed where Eda piled up the pillows that she didn't need, and shoved them aside and hollowed out a burrow for herself in the covers, like she always used to do, and then slid into it and lay down facing her sister.

"Eda?" she whispered, and when her sister didn't answer, Nora squirmed closer to her, laced her arms around Eda's waist like she used to, getting as close as she could. But Eda did not hold her. She flinched away, jerking her body backward, clutching protectively at her belly.

"I'm sorry," she said. "I just . . . have been having dreams. About something bad happening to the baby."

It still did not seem possible to her that Eda was really going to have a baby, right there in their house. Nora had never even met a baby, other than Percy, whose babyhood she had been too young to remember. That Eda of all people was somehow now cultivating one inside her body felt improbable at best. "Oh," Nora said. "Well. I wasn't hurting him."

"I know that," Eda said, and she reached to smooth Nora's hair back from her forehead, her touch gentle but not too light. "I just wanted everyone to be happy," she said. "I thought I was doing what I had to."

"*I'm* happy," Nora said, although she wasn't. She did not especially want Eda to have a baby; already, the small bulge of her sister's belly was hollowing out a place between them. Everyone loved something more than they loved her.

Her sister was silent, her breathing grew long and even, and Nora was almost afraid that Eda had fallen asleep. Nighttime Eda had always dutifully outlasted her before, singing or telling stories until Nora fell back asleep, so Nora said now:

"Can we sing 'Sheath-and-Knife'?"

Eda didn't answer at first. Deciding whether to pretend she was asleep, thought Nora. Then, relenting; "All right," she said.

She turned onto her back, letting Nora's head settle into the crook of her shoulder, and they lay side by side as she softly counted them in. "The broom grows bonnie, the broom grows fair," they sang together, low and solemn as their father had taught them. "And we'll ne'r go down to the broom any mar."

Nora's fingers twined in Eda's and she held their joined hands forcefully while Eda sang the verse on her own, her voice sweet and clear and familiar. Nora mouthed the words that she remembered, her eyes closed, her lips parting to soundlessly pronounce *taen* and *yew-tree* and *lie* in the accent that their father had used, textured and thick. It occurred to her, vaguely, that she did not know what any of the lyrics were supposed to mean. Eda stopped after the third verse, before the fourth and final, and exhaled a gentle sigh as if she was falling back asleep.

Nora could not let go yet, not without an assurance of how things would be when they woke up tomorrow. "Eda?" she asked, with the feeling that she was offering something delicate and precious, something she could not get back, "Did you know that Wenna was married?"

Eda rolled over to face her. "Does she have a baby?"

"No."

"Hm," Eda said.

"But she *could*," Nora said. "She *could* have one."

"Nor," said Eda, "it doesn't matter."

Nora felt as if the floor had fallen out from under her. She understood now that the compact was the only thing that had ever held them. Those thin and ceremonial threads were the only ties that bound their family, and now Charlie had cut them and everyone was relieved because they were no longer obligated to mean anything to one another.

"I just need her to stay," Nora whispered. "We need her to."

Eda didn't answer. She withdrew her hand from Nora's and rolled onto her other side. In the moon-washed dim, Nora lay alone and wished the bog would rise into the house and hold them all inside like it held their patriarchs.

WENNA

For years before their mother disappeared, her long sleeps lengthened every winter. Her body first followed the rhythm of the sphagnum that fell dormant only when snow-buried and then the rhythm of the sundew that curled inward at the first frost and finally the rhythm of the black spruce that dropped its needles after peat-cutting. She was tired, their father said, and offered no further explanation. He closed her bedroom door or their mother closed her own bedroom door and they didn't know which.

In the last spring of her life, she didn't come out of her room until their father went to her on a bright April morning with an ankle-length parka that he'd gotten out of the attic, and afterward she emerged with her entire body except her face packaged warmly away. Their father held her arm gently, as if she would splinter. He brought her downstairs and none of them could tell if she wanted to be there. She sat at the dinner table and picked at her unseasoned venison but did not make any of it disappear. After that, they never saw her without the coat. As the days lengthened and buds sprouted in the old dead undergrowth of the year before, she walked the margins of the bog meadow with everything covered except her ankles and bare feet. She stopped sometimes, dug her toes into the cakey peat that was just dry enough to support rooted vegetation and held herself there as if suspended on the brink of something. One time Nora and Wenna followed her from a distance. *What does she want?* Nora kept asking. *What does she want?* Really asking, *What does she want that isn't here, that isn't us?*

The night their mother disappeared, no one even knew she was gone. Their father came into the yard from the bog's mouth with mire dug into the furrows of the skin on his hands. It was late. Wenna, too hot to sleep, had gone downstairs for a cup of water, and since the basin was empty, she went out to the pump with a glass. Their father looked startled to find her. He approached without speaking, lifted the pump, and washed his hands, rubbing his palms fervently together.

"Where's Mom?" Wenna asked. Somehow, she had known; she had felt it.

"Your mother's tired; she doesn't want to see you," said their father mechanically, the same answer he always gave in the hall outside her bedroom door. Then he seemed to awaken to himself, to the moment. "She's gone," he amended.

"Gone where?"

Her father turned off the pump. His posture stiffened and he stood, reaching his full height that was only a few inches taller than Wenna's height but taller *enough*. "Gone from you," he said. "Gone from us."

Wenna could hear the finality in his tone and knew that she wasn't supposed to ask more. Any one of her siblings would have understood and submitted, but she was neither dutiful eldest nor heir apparent nor obliging spare son nor beloved youngest daughter, and she could still see dark lines on her father's hands where mire was worked into his skin. "But *where?*" she insisted.

"Go back to bed."

"What did you do to her?" Wenna meant not only that night but the years of recession, of long tirednesses, of absence from them.

Her father took a step closer. Wenna felt herself as a creature he was protecting the family *from*, not protecting.

"Go back," her father said, "to bed."

Wenna obeyed. She could never forgive herself, later, for obeying. Alyson the therapist, knowing nothing about the specifics, told her she was not to blame. It was the family system, Alyson said. The ways they had been trained to relate to one another. The roles they learned to assume. But Wenna knew the real reason she had not pushed further was that some part of her did not really want to know what had happened to their mother, because knowing what had happened that night would mean knowing what had been happening to their mother for the whole twenty-four years that she had been their mother, and even at seventeen Wenna understood her childhood would be forever poisoned for her by this knowledge.

Now she knew fully what part of her had known for a long time. There was no longer any illusion that their father had been acting under some ancient hereditary obligation when he extracted their mother from the peat and held her for twenty-four years above the surface. The union of their parents was only tawdry violence, like something from one of Nora's *National Enquirers*. The same as the union of their father's parents, their grandfather's parents, the union of every Haddesley patriarch all the way back to the first imposter who called himself by that name. They were, Wenna thought, unbelievably lucky the bog had been so subdued in its resistance to them, withdrawing rather than lashing out, offering them the chance to walk away. Only, Wenna could tell her siblings weren't going to take it. Despite everything, Eda had never said that she didn't still want to have the baby.

Wenna spent her last night in the Haddesley house on the

sofa in the forbidden parlor, cold beneath the inadequate blankets she gathered from before the hearth, forcing herself not to read the letters Michael had written to Nora. Thinking that she could go back to him when she left tomorrow because he might love her still; thinking, had he ever loved her at all if he couldn't even tell her and Nora apart? She imagined herself turning back up in Illinois, announcing that she could have a baby, actually; it turned out that the ancient compact that had pronounced her a sister and only ever a sister was not an ancient compact, it was barely more than a practical joke, and no one else took it too seriously. Only Wenna had misunderstood.

She dreamed of riding eastbound Greyhounds that went the wrong direction or never got going; she heard rattling like the buses were shaking, the wheels falling off, and when she woke wind was battering the house.

⁘

When storms came to the cranberry bog, they came suddenly but lingered long, emerging violently over the peaks to the west and then hanging over the cold plateau of the boglands for days before they passed. Wenna looked at the swollen white horizon and knew if she did not leave now, she would not leave for a long time. It had not yet begun to snow, but it would. She shoved Michael's letters into her duffel bag and then reconsidered, took them out, smoothed down the corners so Nora wouldn't know she had wanted to take them away with her. They were really her sister's property, weren't they? She left them on the sofa and went out to the kitchen, where Eda was perched on a dining chair nailing blankets to the windows.

Wenna hesitated in the doorway, listening to the steady thud of Eda's hammer. She was furious with her sister; she did not need to be shy, as if she were the one who'd been in the wrong, but Eda was so authoritative in her men's overalls and dressing gown, swinging the hammer at the wall as if she had stormproofed the house a hundred times before.

When Wenna finally spoke, asking where everyone else was, Eda startled at the sound of her voice. She stepped unsteadily down from the dining chair, almost stumbling before she recovered herself with a hand on the chairback. *She shouldn't be doing that four months pregnant*, Wenna thought, and then she thought, *That's exactly why she's doing it*, and she decided not to feel sorry.

"Nora's getting Percy," Eda said. "Charlie's getting peat from the goat shed." Unspoken was the implication that it was a work morning, there was everything to do, and Wenna should already have made herself useful if she was going to be here.

There was, Wenna decided, no point in reminding Eda that she'd ordered Wenna out of the house not twelve hours ago. "I should go," she said. "Can Charlie take me?"

Eda's mouth quirked downward in a polite, irritated frown. "If he has time," she said, and she dragged her chair across the room to the last bare window. She hung a blanket experimentally across it, checking the size, and Wenna had the unsettling sensation that an uncrossable barrier was being mounted.

"There's a storm coming," Wenna persisted.

Eda hammered one corner of the blanket into the wall before she answered, the motions of her hammer slow and deliberate. "Charlie is getting peat," she repeated. "In case we're snowed in."

The wind made the house shudder. Eda nailed down

another corner of the blanket. Before Wenna had the chance to wonder how long getting peat from the goat shed could possibly take, the back door opened and a loose brick of peat was thrown through the threshold to the floor, followed belatedly by a hunched, white-faced Charlie.

"There's more," he said breathlessly. "Couldn't hold them."

With a look of resignation, Eda set down her hammer. She positioned herself in the crook of Charlie's armpit, guided him to the chair, and then gathered up the crumbling brick of peat from the floor. Unhappily she regarded the dark outline of peat dust left behind. "You stay here," she said to him. "I'll get the rest."

Wenna stood in the doorway, feeling the gravitational tug of the household's need, resisting it because she was not supposed to be implicated; she was not even supposed to be here. Charlie had snow in his hair, she noticed, pinprick flakes cold enough not to melt.

"You think you could drive me to the bus station?" she asked, when Eda had left.

Charlie, hunched low in the dining chair, did not lift his head. She couldn't see his face, only the snow not melting in his hair. "I don't know," he muttered. "I don't know."

Eda opened the back door, dumped a pile of peat bricks on the floor, and went back for another load without closing the door. A gust of wind tore into the kitchen, disheveling the peat. Wenna saw vividly the possibility of gathering up the fuel and carrying it to the shelter of the great room before it was shredded. There were a hundred things she could be doing and was not doing. *You are not responsible for them,* she said to herself. Charlie lifted his head enough to glance across the room at the open door, the whirl of snow in the yard, then lowered it again.

"I really do have to go," Wenna attempted. He didn't answer. Eda came back with more peat and kicked the door shut.

"Goats should get brought in," Charlie said to her. "Windchill's bad."

"I can't," Eda said. "I can't do everything." She pushed past Wenna with an armful of peat and stomped down the hall, leaving a trail of odorous dark dust as the bricks loosened.

Charlie braced himself and pushed to his feet, wavering slightly. His jaw was set, his eyes squinted almost shut. Wenna felt a brief flicker of hope before she realized he was only going to the back door. Somewhere, at any moment, a tree would fall across the road and the buses would stop running and Wenna thought she would never go if she didn't go now, when she was still brave with fresh anger.

"If I bring the goats in, will you drive me?" she asked.

Charlie turned his head and looked at her. But then Nora tore through the back door, her nose running profusely, her eyes teary with wind.

"I can't find Percy," she said. "He's not anywhere."

Wenna's stomach dropped. Whatever hardy blood ran through their bog-mothered veins, it was not clear that Percy would survive exposure to a squall; it was not even clear that he had survived exposure to last night.

"When did you last see him?" she asked.

"Last night," said Nora. "Last night he was acting—I don't know. He wouldn't talk to me; he wouldn't even look at me."

Charlie exhaled through his nose. Eda emerged, boots stomping, from the hallway. Instinctively, Wenna stepped aside to let her pass.

"He's somewhere," Eda said firmly. "You didn't look everywhere."

"I did," Nora insisted. "It's *cold*." She began to cry. "You can't even see out there, really."

Eda's hand slipped half-consciously to her stomach. There was panic on her face. Wenna felt her resolve loosen, felt the inevitability of staying through the storm and burning through her anger until she no longer had the will to extricate herself from her family.

"I'll go," she said. "I'll get him."

Eda looked suspiciously at her. "Not by yourself," she said.

Wenna hadn't expected Eda to refuse her. "The whole point is that you don't go," she said, in case Eda somehow didn't understand.

"You'll just get lost," Eda said. "And then someone will have to come after *you*. How long has it been, since you really went out there?"

They both knew Wenna had not been out to the bog since peat-cutting, and before that only to bury their father. Wenna had no retort.

They bundled into layers and trudged through the yard, retracing Nora's fading footprints. The cake of snow on the ground was still thin, pinpricks of grass sticking through, but the horizon was shrunk to nothing. The forest appeared and disappeared in ghostly fragments ahead of them as the wind drove currents of snow through the air. Wenna did not resist when Eda seized her hand and held on to it.

They passed through a copse of birches, walking with their free hands out before them so they would not collide with the trees. Eda knew the way, Wenna realized. Her sister's body remembered what neither of them could see. But they both hesitated as they felt the ground soften beneath their feet, firm earth subsiding into mire. The meadow was unknowable in its changeability. Hollows filled and emptied, flooding rose and receded, plant growth thickened or thinned and disintegrated. Even Eda would not be able to anticipate when they might be stepping down into ice.

For a while they stood calling Percy's name, one after the other. There was no answer. The wind threw their words away. "We have to," Eda said, and so they went.

In snow, the bog meadow was like a dream of itself, half-familiar and disorienting. They seemed to make no progress even as they moved doggedly against the wind, wading through thickets of alder and dense snow-heavy stands of sedge. When Wenna lifted her eyes to search the horizon for Percy, she froze with a sudden visceral terror of going any farther into that vast and white and unreadable landscape. *It could kill us now*, she thought; and she thought of the birds scattering as the hemlock fell out of the roof; she thought of the gouges cut into the peat by Haddesley spades; she thought of the house in the 1897 photograph, hulking and brazen and nearly ready for the coal-mine owner's son to occupy it.

"What are you doing?" Eda shouted. "Do you see him?"

"No," Wenna said. They went on, Eda a step ahead. The vegetation shrank down until it was buried by snow completely. Wenna thought, *We must be close to the mouth, we've gone too far*, and then Eda's foot punched through the earth and she yelped, the sound dissipating so fast into the wind that it seemed vanished before her mouth even closed. Wenna stepped closer, let Eda lean on her and climb out. They stood looking at the dark suppurating hole in the snow left by her descent. Eda had sunk down only to her mid-calf, but she was soaked now. She wouldn't be able to stay warm.

"We should go back," Wenna said.

"No chance," Eda said. "You go back." She set off, not waiting to see if Wenna would follow.

Wenna hesitated for only a second before she hurried to close the distance between them. She was surprised by her sister's resolve, though she shouldn't have been. It was easy to think that Eda's fierce grasp on the household was only about control, and maybe it mostly was, but there was a selflessness to it that showed itself in glances. Eda couldn't be unaware that she or the baby or both of them might die out here, and she truly didn't seem to care.

They trudged forward in silence until Eda stepped through the peat and fell as deep as her shoulders into the half-frozen mire with a terrific echoing crack.

Eda did not flail or struggle, not at first. The cold must have shocked her. Her mouth opened; she gulped impotently at the wind. She looked horribly peaceful, as if already she were dead. She was going to let herself be drowned, Wenna thought. "Eda!" she screamed, and her sister began to thrash as if resurrected. Wenna crouched and grasped her coat in both hands and dragged her upward, staggering backward until they both lay on land solvent enough to hold their weight. For a moment afterward they lay still. Eda shivered violently in occasional heaving jags that subsided into death-stillness. A sob hitched but did not rise from her throat.

"I'm taking you back," Wenna said.

"But Percy—"

"He's been fine out here, he'll be fine," Wenna said, with a confidence she did not feel. She could see that Eda was never going to make the decision to turn back on her own. "Come on, get up," she insisted. "Lean on me."

She had asked Eda to do it, but she was still startled when Eda crumpled into her side, hanging on Wenna with the unself-consciousness of a child. They strode back through the vanishing shelves of their footprints, Wenna keeping her eyes low so she would not become too aware of the vast featureless whorl of snow surrounding them. All the while thinking, *She would have died.* Thinking, *The bog would have killed us.*

NORA

Almost, at first, the storm felt like the fulfillment of Nora's wishes. For at least a few days, she thought, Wenna and Percy would be forced to stay home. The five of them would ride out the storm together, close and warm and reluctant to argue because they couldn't get away from one another if they wanted to. The normal distance between them would be suspended. Wenna would get over her anger about the letters and Percy would see that the bog did not need him and when the storm receded maybe they would stay like they should always have stayed.

"Someone should get Percy, shouldn't they?" she'd said to Eda, trying to sound casual. And when Eda said, "Why don't you go?" Nora was slightly disappointed, because she knew if she was the one to go and get Percy she would seem to be begging out of her own loneliness and need for him to come home. She wanted Eda to *make* him come for his own good. But she told herself that it didn't matter because he couldn't not come. He would know he couldn't weather a storm out there in only his ceremonial moss, and, anyway, the bog couldn't possibly need him to root out trespassers while it was buried under snow.

She thought the trouble would be convincing him to come. She hadn't expected to not find him, but Percy was nowhere in the blinding white. By the time she got out to the bog meadow, the thin coat of snow on the ground was already vanishing the distinction between land and water, between dirt and mire, and Nora had a terrible vision of treading on her brother's body without realizing it, crushing him down into the earth. She screamed his name only once and then retreated, thinking that Eda or Charlie would know what to do. She was not yet dismayed until Eda and Wenna came back from their search mud-soaked and shaken and without Percy after what felt to Nora like an interminable length of time, and yet also not nearly long enough for them to have tried their best, which was what Wenna said they had done—firmly and without sympathy, like it was the end of the conversation.

"How can it be your best," said Nora, "if it didn't work?"

Wenna wrested her foot out of her boot. "Nor," she said, wearily. "Come on."

"I don't want to come on," said Nora, hearing her own voice climb to the trembling heights of a squeak, hating how childish she sounded but powerless to correct course now. "He's out there for *us*. You can't just leave him."

"He's out there satisfying a made-up obligation that he knows is made-up," said Wenna. "It's his choice."

"Well, then . . . I'll go back out," Nora said. It was a desperate measure, and she wasn't sure yet whether she was really willing to take it, but what else did she have besides herself to take away from Wenna? Part of her knew already that it wouldn't work—that she was not enough to send Wenna out into the squall, because Wenna didn't love her like everyone had always thought; Wenna didn't care about any of them—but still, with deliberate slowness, she began to bundle back into her cold-weather clothes, watching her sisters out of the corner of her eye, doggedly waiting to know that neither of them cared enough to get in her way.

Wenna turned her back and crouched, helping Eda with the stuck zipper on her coat, saying that really they should strip everything off and change into dry clothes because they'd never get warm while they were still wet. Beneath her layers and layers of clothes, Nora began to sweat. Her heart pounded in her mouth, in the hollows of her wrists. She stepped into her still-wet boots and stood at the door, grasping the handle but not turning it.

She heard Charlie's shuffling footsteps. "Shouldn't go back out there," he said, not particularly to her or anyone, and then, "Goats are acting hungry."

"There's some old turnips in the fridge," said Eda.

Nora put her hand across her mouth and stifled her scream in her gloved hand. Slowly, she began to strip out of her winter layers.

❧

They spent the rest of the day before the hearth, listening to the wind howl through the hole in the roof. It was all like a warped and impoverished version of what Nora had imagined; no one speaking; no one wanting cocoa; no one suggesting they play cards or read aloud. Claude and Mathilde shuffled loudly around on the old bedsheet that Charlie put down for them and grunted threats in their incomprehensible goatly language at Buz Lukens until the possum fled to Nora's bedroom. When the sky darkened, Eda cooked the last three cans of mushroom soup left in the pantry and they ate at the table beneath flickering lights, watching droplets of water bloom from the crack in the ceiling above them. No one spoke. They were all stiff with one another, angrily polite, still remembering last night's fight.

Nora sat at the table between her sisters, swallowing tasteless custardy hunks of cream-of-mushroom soup around the lump in her throat, hating everyone in the house passionately—including herself for lacking the nerve to go back out into the squall and find Percy. She'd rather die with Percy than live with the rest of them, she thought, except that this apparently wasn't true, because she was right now choosing to live with the rest of them and not die with Percy.

"Think it's settling down," Wenna said, glancing toward the ceiling as if she could see the weather through it.

"Maybe you'll be able to get out tomorrow," said Eda.

"Maybe," Wenna said, but she sounded doubtful and almost sad about it.

Charlie mashed his soup into a flat cake, then raked back through it.

Nora imagined herself saying, *You should at least stay to look for Percy's body.* But she thought Wenna would not feel guilty and Eda would only say she was being inflammatory and nothing would change besides that they would be angrier with her than they were now. She sat and ate as much cream-of-mushroom soup as she could tolerate, and then she bedded down before the hearth, pushing her mound of bedding a defiant foot away from everyone else's. In the dim glow of the burning peat, Nora lay awake, reading the romance of *Yvain*, wishing someone would tell her they were sorry.

$$\text{\symbol}$$

The crash woke them. Eda cried Charlie's name in a stifled voice, as if any tree that fell must naturally fall on him.

"I'm here," said Charlie.

A faint tail of smoke was rising from the ashes in the hearth. The peat had burned to nothing or had been extinguished, and the air was cold.

Another gust hissed down through the chimney, and they heard the distinct cracks of tree limbs yielding to the wind. They rose from their beds and huddled close in the center of the room and held still listening, Wenna gripping Nora's fingers as if they still depended on each other. Eda fumbled for the matches in the dark and lit a candle, and only then could they see the veins of water trickling out from new cracks in the walls and the ceiling, puddling darkly on the floor.

"Oh," said Eda. She stepped back with the candle held aloft, illuminating the bowed-in wrinkled ceiling over their heads. The floor upstairs was not holding, Nora realized. She felt the unaccountable urge to crouch, as if getting low could protect her if the whole house collapsed.

The next crash that came from overhead shook the whole house, as if it were from underneath and not above that the battering had come, as if the tree had erupted from the ground and not fallen. Nora thought then, belatedly—too late—of her animals stuck in jars and cages in her bedroom, Callahan and Sonny and Arlan Strangelands and most especially Buz Lukens, poor three-footed Buz Lukens, who had trusted that the couch cushion in her closet could always be his sanctuary. Nora tore her hand out of Wenna's and ran for the staircase, not thinking of what she would do when she got to her bedroom. There were far too many of them for her to carry, and some of them opposed being carried, but she had to salvage what she could. She climbed the stairs in a harried crouch, not looking ahead. At the top of the staircase, she stopped, stunned. Before her, the east wing-hallway ended in a fountain of broken wood and stone rubble and plaster that flowed out of a cavernous hole in the floor of the attic.

"No," Nora said to the house. It was too much; she refused to accept it. Since she'd realized that Percy was not going to be found, her whole body had felt rigid and tight, as if there were too much of her inside her skin, but now she felt insolvent, full of holes, as if she were dissolving. She yanked at the rubble, searching for a path through the wreckage. The entire floor couldn't be collapsed, or the ceiling would already have gone. There was still a chance.

"Nora!" she heard Eda say—faintly, as if from a mile away. "What are you doing?"

She glanced back only for a second. Eda and Wenna and Charlie stood at the foot of the stairs, shadowed and lit by the moonlight that came through the forbidden parlor's broken windows. "My animals are up here," she said.

"You can't get in there," said Wenna. "Come on, get down before the stairs give out."

The possibility that the stairs might give out beneath her had not occurred to Nora, but she was not going to be discouraged now. Defiantly, almost wanting something cataclysmic to happen, she pried a splintered board out of the rubble and threw it backward over her head. Then another.

"You get down here now," Eda said. "Right now."

Nora ignored her. There was too much material to dig through; she would simply have to climb, she decided, and let her body find a gap. She imagined herself like her salamander or her mice or Buz Lukens, capable of contorting to fit whatever narrow corridor of the world she needed to wedge herself into. She stood back for a moment, then threw herself at the pile.

From above came a wounded architectural groan. Shingles fell like rain down the unsteady hill of the rubble. Teeth-sized chunks of fieldstone followed, broken slivers of joisting. Nora realized, then: the attic was not yet finished crumbling.

"Get down!" Eda screamed, her voice shrill and high like Nora had never heard it.

"But I can't leave them," Nora explained. "They're the only ones—"

The end of her sentence was swallowed by the sound of another hole opening in the ceiling. The attic floor surrendered, collapsing in heaps of plaster dust and broken wood and shards of peat insulation. Nora was thrown down the stairs in a wave of wreckage. For a moment, she was dazed by the sudden loudness and the pain. She could tell she'd hit her head, and she was dizzy. But when she regained focus, Wenna was holding one of her arms and Eda grasping the other. "The hearth," Eda was saying. "The hearth will hold." And then they were crawling into the stone cavity, breathing smoldering ash of peat, retreating from the annihilating openness of their home.

PERCY

ercy had spent the first weeks of his wife's gestation rooting out trespassers, his eyes combing the sphagnum mat for orange stems, his father's scythe always in his hand although, really, it was too large for the work and it cut an unwieldy swath across the vegetation however lightly he swung it, however close to the blade he grasped the handle, always nicking the landscape like an uncareful shave. At night, he shivered and lay close to the raised dimple of earth where his wife was being formed, trying to feel some inkling of her presence underneath, thinking that one hundred days was an unbearable length. He tried to imagine the woman that the form of sticks and humus would become, staving off his loneliness and the cold by dreaming of the wife waiting for him at the end. But always the images were hollow ones, vague.

When his wife's voice first came to him, it came softly, not entering through his ears but seeping into him like water. Percy heard it with his skin, with the hollow between his sternum and his belly, with his closed eyes, with the arches of his feet. He did not know it was coming from her. He could not have repeated or even pronounced what she said to him. But he could translate her utterances into his own language: she said, *Ingest*, she said, *Reach*, she said, *Retreat*, she said, only very rarely, *Rest*. Without his consent, his body answered in strange compulsions. He found himself chewing fistfuls of peat, mashing the soil into the roof of his mouth as if his tongue could parse the weave of dead plant matter for nutrients. He found himself closing his eyes and huddling close and staving his breath as if he wanted a predator not to smell him. He found himself sitting with his neck angled sharply to the horizon, holding his mouth open so rain would land on his tongue.

At first, he had been afraid of these communications, of the things they made him do and especially of the feeling they sometimes left him with—an urgent and yet directionless sensation that was worse for being so easily confused with his own unsated hunger. Nora was not constant in bringing food to him, and what food she did bring was never enough for a body that shivered day and night. But Percy soon learned he could eat himself sick without even making a dent in the hunger, and he realized it was not his hunger but only a hunger shared with him, and then he recognized all the sensations—the hunger and electric fear and curiosity and deep calmness—as intimacy, a closer closeness than any entangling of human limbs could ever have produced. And he understood: even while his wife still lay in the ground, their marriage had already been consummated. She was already here with him. They were honeymooning in her home country.

All through the darkest weeks of winter, he lived halfway inside of her, inhabiting a rich well of sensation. In that time, language and his own body and his selfhood became loose and abstract to him. So much clearer and more meaningful were those needs and impulses and longings that they shared—to *become*, to *survive*, to *endure*. He forgot his questing to annihilate the orange mushrooms, the urgency he had felt to get rid of all the trespassers. He languished in new love.

Then, as the season advanced, his wife's voice multiplied

outward: at first developing a soft echo, then many whispers, and at last a disorderly weave of voices, as if there were thousands of women there below the earth and not just one, all of them wanting and striving and fearing and retreating in their own dialects of the same language. He could barely hold their abundance. In those final weeks of winter, before the storm, his body wanted water then soil then sun. He wanted to twist his limbs out to the side and plunge down underneath the earth and arch his head to the horizon. He felt jealousy like another sense, as primary as sight or hearing. He woke once to himself with a fly in his mouth, the insect twitching frantically behind his slightly parted lips, half-drowned in his saliva.

He began to fear what his wife would be, when she rose from her grave.

❧

His wife felt the storm before Percy would have, long before the winds lifted or the sky darkened. He felt her thousand forms of anticipation: her compulsion to huddle low, to close herself, to warn, to scrape up every remaining nutrient in her reach before it was carried away or pushed underneath the peat. By then, he knew how to interpret everything she said to him, so he huddled low too, secreting himself in a thatch of sedge near the grave and bundling his comforter over his back to brace himself against the coming weather. He, unlike her, could not go under, could not go dormant. They fed off each other's unease as she told him, *Cold*, told him, *Wind*, told him, *Snow*, and then suddenly she was gone.

Percy had never known a loneliness like the loneliness he felt when she left him. It was as if his brain were evacuated and he were now the only inhabitant of a once-crowded household. In his wife's absence, he felt both the smallness and the vastness of his own self, the limitations of what he could perceive and the many things he could think to himself when it was only him. For the first time in weeks, he felt the frozen grit of the soil beneath him, the prickly delicate brush of sedge against his knees and chest, even the light pressure of the moss sheath on his bare back. He waited out the storm in this unnerving bachelordom, alone with himself in the bog's mouth, feeling wind and then frozen rain and then sleet with a strange detachment; he could no longer remember exactly what any of it was supposed to mean to him, and the fear that passed through him when the wind roared through the sedge was distant, as if he were looking through a dirty window at himself and not living inside his body or even his brain. He fell asleep waiting for her to come back to him.

❧

When Percy woke, the storm had receded and a faint wash of light shone through the cloud cover. All around him were broken tree limbs and bowed tree heads, whole thatches of alder and elderberry smashed down as if a crowd of feet had stomped across them. The bog's mouth was clogged, snow and detritus forming a thick paste across the place where the pool should have shone glossy and dark. Percy listened for his wife, waiting for the flood of sensations, the many insistent voices, but he could not feel her. He was alone.

Frantically, he tried to count back the days since he'd buried the form of sticks and humus. He'd stopped keeping track when she began communicating with him. Numbering the days had come to feel like a false and inadequate way of judging time: he would *feel* when the time was right, he had thought. But now he could feel nothing; now he didn't know whether his wife was still months from maturation or if she was overdue. What if he left her in the earth too long? What if she grew past wifeliness into something else?

It was by accident that he found her, his eyes catching on the huddled form sticking out of the bog's mouth. At first, he thought she was a felled tree trunk, then a crumpled-up blanket or tarp, then a drowned animal. But when he came closer, he could not have mistaken her for anything but a woman—face pressed into the earth, body twisted to one side, arms splayed out before her. Her skin and matted long hair were a uniform deep amber. Percy reached greedily toward her, then caught himself just before his fingers landed. His hand hovered in the air for the length of a breath before he lowered his fingertips to brush her shoulder. He was afraid of what he would feel or not feel when he touched her. It did not seem possible to him that anything they did aboveground could be as revelatory as the communion they'd shared with four feet of peat between them.

Under his shaky fingers, his wife's body felt stiff. With a thrust of effort, he pushed her onto her back. She unstuck from the ooze with a visceral sound and then fell flat. Her face was hidden in a batter of mud. Slowly, gently, Percy smoothed it away. He unburied her brow bone, her heavy-lidded eyes, the slope of her nose, her pursed lips. He began to feel that he had always known this face, that somehow it had always been there waiting for him. He swallowed his nausea and persisted. He had gone too far now to stop. Working his tongue in his dry mouth, he produced enough saliva to spit. Beneath him, the woman drew breath. He knew her then. It was not his wife; there had been no wife. He was looking at his mother.

Spring

CHARLIE

In the hearth, everyone else fell asleep, but Charlie stayed awake, listening to far-away crashes and feeling the shudders of close ones. His body regurgitated the memory of the hemlock tree's fall. He hung suspended for hours in the second before his maiming, always on the cusp of being hurt. What he knew now that he hadn't known last year was that he was not being punished for his failures as a custodian but for his birth into a line of custodian-trespassers. The bog was not punishing him but trying to expel a sickness from its diseased pores. But was that any better? He could never not be a sickness. He could never make himself weightless enough to go unfelt.

Even after the wind let up, Charlie held still for a long time, his body tensed as he waited for the crack-smash music of another tree falling. He released a held breath only when a shaft of light moved across the room to light the floorboards in front of the hearth. The light was wan, thin, but it meant the storm had gone.

Slowly, Charlie uncurled his limbs. His groin hurt with fresh force. He felt as sore as he'd felt last spring, when he needed a cane to get anywhere and the stairs were an impossible prospect and he struggled to drive the twelve miles to Walmart because even shifting gears sent spikes of pain up his legs into his pelvis. He didn't know he could go backward like that, months of recovery lost in a single night.

When he crawled out into the great room, he found the

ceiling partly collapsed, broken floorboards sticking out like whiskers from the sunken-in place in the middle. There was a thin layer of snow covering the floor. The house felt force-fully, angrily cold. He glanced back at his sisters, but they were still a sleeping bundle, their limbs braided, their heads on one another's shoulders.

There was icy floodwater in the hallway, which deepened as he got closer to the kitchen. In the kitchen doorway, he stood and stared first at the debris-muddled taupe sea of the kitchen floor, then looked up. There was no ceiling, barely any roof. Sometime in the night, a dead hemlock tree had fallen on the house, sinking right down into the notch in the wall carved by the first hem-lock, as if the hole in the house had cried out to be refilled and the storm or the forest or both of them together had answered. Charlie had not been there to absorb the blow this time, only broken roof and empty bed and weak rotting floorboards, and the second floor had not held. Chunks of wood and stone and peat insulation were strewn like islands across the kitchen floor. The detritus of his bedroom, too, drifted limply through the wa-ter. Charlie recognized the BB gun handed down to him from his grandfather or great-grandfather (perhaps even from the origi-nal fraudulent Charles not-Haddesley), which they had no BBs for and he had never learned to shoot; wool sweaters colonized by thick furs of moss and lichen; a lampshade without a lamp.

Charlie's toes curled in his shoes; his whole body felt throt-tled and tight. He felt a terrible and distinct longing to do something violent, to leave his own redundant mark on the storm-ravaged landscape. But before he could think of what to do, he saw that Percy was standing at the back door.

Charlie opened the door, letting a current of icy water

rush across Percy's calves and down the back stoop into the snow-blanketed yard. As the kitchen slowly drained, they stood across from each other with only the cold air between them. Percy had patches of fresh dark mud on his skin everywhere his sphagnum sheath didn't cover him. He smelled powerfully of the bog: he smelled, Charlie thought, like their mother. His jaw tensed as if he were anticipating a blow to the face.

"I need you to see something," Percy said.

Charlie knew right away, from the edge in his voice, what the *something* was. Naturally, the misbegotten secret rite stuck between the pages of his father's memoirs had worked for his brother. Percy had hewn a wife from naught. He wanted nothing less than to see the bog-wife that his brother made, yet he couldn't not look. He followed Percy out the back door.

They tromped through the icy snow in the yard, Percy walking with determination, not checking to see if Charlie was following; Charlie slower, trepidatious, maneuvering unsteadily across the ice-slicked grid of fallen sticks and branches left by the storm. Everywhere were broken trees, their decapitated heads hanging down at sharp, painful angles or lying balanced in the narrow cradles of their neighbors' branches. He remembered that the tree men said they would be back in the same place they'd started if they didn't clear the hemlocks. He wondered how much of the house would be left when the trees finished falling.

Ahead of him, Percy walked on the bog meadow. His stride lengthened as he crossed the frozen earth, and Charlie hurried to catch up, his pelvis throbbing. When he saw the dark hole of the bog's mouth in the middle of the snowy plain, he stopped. He felt that even now his presence would damage the integrity of the ritual, that somehow Percy's bog-wife would dissolve back into moss as soon as he came near.

"I'm not wearing my sheath," he warned Percy.

"It doesn't matter now," Percy answered.

It couldn't not matter now when it had always mattered before, when Percy himself had been so terrified only weeks ago at the prospect of Charlie getting anywhere near the filled-in grave, but Charlie followed him. In a matted-down thicket of sedge a hundred yards or so from the bog's mouth, he saw the head propped on a flat stone. The rest of the body, a second later. He thought it wasn't alive until he saw the eyes blink like wet holes in the amber-colored face and the leathery chest lift with breathing.

With disgust and a small guilty stab of pleasure, he thought the ritual must have worked but not worked right. Percy had made something but the something was not marriageable, maybe not even fully alive. The body with its head propped on the rock had the parched, shrunken look of something that had been buried in the bog for a hundred years, not days. The limbs were stiff and motionless, the hair slicked to the ridges of the skull, the clothes tannin-dyed to the same burnt color as the flesh.

Charlie thought, *She shouldn't have clothes already.* And he realized then: the body was not a new creation; it was an old one dredged up.

"It's Mom?" he whispered, afraid even to pronounce the word.

"Yes."

"How did you . . ." Charlie began, but the sentence had no ending because he didn't even know what to ask. He felt sick.

Had she always been there, waiting for them to discover her? Had she been there when he came naked to slick himself with mire and marry his own bog-wife? Had she witnessed his humiliation?

"I didn't mean to," Percy said. "She was just *here*."

It was pointless, Charlie decided, to wonder whether he was telling the truth; if the ritual or Percy's performance of the ritual or only the interplay of water with peat had unearthed their mother from wherever she had been for almost eleven years.

"She's still alive?"

"Yes."

"Is she awake?"

"I don't know," said Percy, flinching his eyes shut. "I was supposed to . . ." But he didn't say what he was supposed to do.

Charlie could not go any closer.

"Can she hear us?" he whispered to Percy.

"Yes."

"How do you know?"

Percy wrapped his arms around his head, the flesh of his inner arms pressed to his ears, his fingers threading through his hair. "I think I could hear her," he admitted.

"How?"

He didn't answer. Except her labored breathing, their mother was still. Her mouth was wide open, but her eyes were closed.

"Can you hear her now?" asked Charlie. "What is she saying?"

"I don't know." Percy's chin shuddered as if he was shivering or sobbing. "Charlie," he said, urgently, "from underground, she talked to me. She told me things. I didn't know who it was. I thought she was my *wife*. Have you ever felt like that? That you were in love?"

Charlie didn't know how to answer. All his life he'd bent himself toward wanting something that he suspected could never possibly materialize; and when it didn't materialize, he realized he had never wanted it and he had still been collapsed by disappointment. Realizing your love had no object and never had an object was a feeling *like* the heartbreak that made knights wander madly through forests and wastelands in the romances, but it was not heartbreak.

"You were never in love," he said.

"I didn't know," Percy said. "I promise I didn't know. I would never have . . ."

"Have . . . what?" There was a shattered look on his brother's face, and so much mud on his clothes and on his skin. Charlie thought of the dreams he himself used to dream of the bog-wife, dreams in which gradually and without his notice she always changed into his mother.

"Have . . . answered her," Percy said vaguely. "It only felt like being close, like being part of each other. I just *wanted*."

He looked at Charlie, his eyes beseeching. Charlie could not look back. He was embarrassed by his brother's unrequited passion, naked and demanding, indiscriminate in its hunger. Almost, he was jealous. He kept remembering the glassy carried-away look in Percy's eyes when Charlie had seen him at the bog's mouth before. *They are for us!* he'd said. *I can* feel *it.* What had he felt that deluded him into thinking the bog would make him a wife? And why hadn't Charlie ever been able to feel it?

"She never wanted you," he said viciously. "She begged him not to get her pregnant with you; she cried when she knew you would be born. You had to be nursed on goat's milk. Do you think she wants you now?"

Percy's mouth wobbled. He didn't answer.

Beneath them, the body that was their mother issued a faint sound like a croak. There was a thin remnant of their mother's old voice in that sound, Charlie thought, and her presence became at once horrifically real to him. He had not been speaking to her when he spoke before. He had not really thought what it would be like to face her: the last of the Haddesley bog-wives, risen to avenge herself like a specter from one of their father's old ballads.

During the long embarrassment of his puberty, his mother used to look at him sometimes with an expression he couldn't read. Repulsion or contempt on her face; also what he thought was fear. And Charlie always thought she was seeing his unfitness as an heir but now he thought she had only been seeing that he *was* an heir. He'd inherited everything from his father. The doctor at the clinic in Charleston had checked his eyes and throat and lungs and found nothing in him that was not human.

He wondered if his mother would be glad to see what the hemlock tree did to him. He could almost believe she might even have had some part in it. Lying in the bog, had she sent secret vengeful whispers out through the earth to the shallow-rooted trees?

"Don't let her see me," he said, stepping back.

"Please, Charlie! I don't know what to do," Percy said.

It was too much. Charlie turned around and struggled through the frozen sedge, heading in no direction besides *away*. He heard Percy call his name, but he did not answer to it. He ran until his body refused him and he was forced to slow down, to contract the length of his steps. Then he walked. When he came to the property-line, he stood at the line of stones that marked the edge of their land, his pelvis throbbing like a heartbeat. Everywhere around him were felled hemlocks.

Charlie had an image—vivid and clear—of walking across the property-line, walking down the dirt road that led out to the state highway, walking past the sign that pointed toward Marlinton and down to the interstate. He imagined himself vanishing into the loud fabric of the outside world. Assuming a new name, working for a paycheck, going home to a building with air conditioning, becoming in every way indistinguishable from a person whose mother had not come out of bog mire, gone back into it, then risen again.

The fantasy soothed him; it made him feel as if a heavy weight had been lifted from his chest. For a fleeting moment, breathless and surreal, he really thought he could do it. But then he heard a scream from the house, and the weight came crushingly down on him again. He stood a moment longer at the property-line, then turned back.

WENNA

hen Wenna woke, Charlie was not with them in the hearth. Wenna tried to squirm free from the hunched position she held between her sisters but succeeded only in waking them up.

"Is it gone?" Eda asked drowsily.

"There's sunlight on the floor," said Wenna. There was snow too, but she didn't mention that. Eda would see it soon enough.

Nora pushed her head into the crook of Wenna's shoulder and then stretched, stiffening her legs first and then her torso and then her arms. She woke up enough to realize it was Wenna she had cuddled into and sat up straight, throwing a reproachful look in her direction.

"Where's Charlie?" she asked.

"I guess he got up already," Wenna said. He had been there with them when they crawled into the hearth. He had been there in the night too, his eyes white-rimmed and wet. Wenna had been woken by a crash and seen him awake. Their eyes met for only a second in the darkness before he looked away.

"Maybe he went to find Percy," Nora said.

"I wouldn't count on it," Eda said, and she nudged Wenna with her shoulder. "Come on," she said. "Get up."

"It looks bad out there," Wenna warned her.

"It's ruined," Nora clarified, crawling out onto the floor. "It looks like it's been abandoned for a hundred years."

Wenna watched her sister's expression as Eda crawled out of the hearth, but Eda was stolid, impassive. "Later," she said.

She didn't seem to be looking at any of it: not the wet snow and debris on the ground, not the warped bulge of the ceiling.

They waded through the wreckage of the kitchen and went out the back door. In the snow on the back step they found a swirl of footprints, the gridwork of boot soles mingling with the toed imprints of bare feet.

"Percy and Charlie together," Eda said, surprised.

"Percy!" Nora screamed, and she broke into a run.

With Nora bounding ahead, they followed the prints through the birches into the undergrowth on the fringe of the bog meadow, where the trail became muddled and obscure, visible only as disturbances in the alder. Everywhere the undergrowth had been trampled it was trampled twice, as though Percy and Charlie had not been following each other but walking apart, giving each other a wide berth.

The bog meadow was unhurt by the winds that devastated the house and forest. There were no trees to be felled, no branches to be scattered. Snow and ice formed a dense glistening coat over the vegetation. The hole opened in the peat by Eda's stumble was buried now, along with the lesser gouges dug by Wenna's scrambling feet. Their brother was the only dark thing Wenna could see in that vast whiteness. He was crouching with his back to them near the bog's mouth, scarecrow-thin in his moss sheath, apparently alone. At Nora's shriek, he startled to his feet and turned to face them.

Eda and Wenna watched as their sister crossed the distance to Percy in long, ground-swallowing strides and caught him in a hard embrace, wrapping her arms around his spindly shoulders, rocking both their bodies back and forth.

"He survived the night, at least," Wenna said to Eda.

"But where's Charlie?"

They both looked down. "His footprints are here," said Wenna.

Eda shook her head. "They're going the wrong way."

Wenna considered the boot print on the ground in front of them. "He was here and then left."

Across the meadow, Nora screamed again, not exhilarated now but upset. "What is that?" she was demanding of Percy. "What did you do?"

Eda glanced sideways at Wenna and her look was not fearful but exhausted, as if Nora could only be getting after Percy for some petty, meaningless offense. But they both ran ahead until they could see through the snow-weighted vegetation what Nora had seen, and then they stopped short. Wenna shot an arm out in front of Eda, overtaken by some unconscious impulse to protect. Her first thought, panic-blurred and confused, was that they were seeing Charlie's body, that Percy had done something to him. Then she thought, no, it was a woman, and the hideous possibility occurred to her that somehow Percy had dredged a wife out of the bog's sickly mouth even though he was not an eldest son and even less entitled to the privilege than his ancestors before him. She did not come near the truth before Percy said, "It's Mom."

The body on the ground was small and gnarled and ancient-looking but the face was their mother's face, unaged and unaltered except that it was pressed slightly inward, as if she had been slowly crushed through the whole almost-eleven years of her disappearance. Wenna looked at her and felt a wrenching, hard grief, more solid and clear than anything she had felt in eleven years. She had been *here*? Always?

Wenna crouched in the melting snow and with her eyes absorbed every way the eleven years had bent and warped the body of their mother. *We'll bury her now*, she thought, *respectfully, like she should be buried.* And then her mother's chest lifted as her lungs drew in breath and Wenna realized, heart hammering, that she was not looking at a dead woman. In fact, she thought, the state their mother was in now was not visibly so different from any one of her long tirednesses, except that their mother had always appeared serene and even luminous in her winter torpor, and she appeared now like a half-resurrected corpse, her entire body except her face slicked with mire, her leathery chest beginning to rise and fall in effortful spasms.

"She's alive?" she said.

Percy nodded.

"Where did you find her?" Eda asked. She was standing back a few steps, unsure if it was safe to come any closer. Nora curled into her side, holding her hand.

Percy didn't answer.

"Has she spoken to you?" Wenna asked.

"No," Percy whispered.

"Mama?" Wenna said, too loudly. "Can you hear us?" She felt small and young and self-conscious, like she used to feel when she and Nora stood at their mother's door and squinted through the crack to see if she was awake. Afraid that if she was, she wouldn't want them.

Her mother's mouth opened, dark ooze spilling out and settling on her lower lip. She had no teeth anymore, or at least her teeth were too thickly coated in peat for Wenna to see them. She croaked something indistinct.

They all fell silent, trying to parse the lump of sound that issued from their mother's mouth. For a long time, there was only the hiss of wind through the sedge, and then their mother croaked again.

"Water," Wenna realized. "She's saying she wants water."

They fed their mother on melted ice from the bog's mouth, collected in a cup that Percy produced from the hovel where he'd spent his winter. Wenna held the cup and slowly tipped it toward their mother's lips. At first the water dripped back out as if her mouth was stuffed too full to swallow anything, but then her breathing hitched; violently, she began to cough. Ooze spilled from her mouth, first in heavy lumps and then in thin strings and at last in a watery dribble, until her body loosened and her head eased back into Wenna's hand.

"Mama?" Wenna said.

Weakly, their mother lifted her hand. Her fingers found Wenna's wrist, her thumb landing on the delicate place where Wenna's heart beat. *She's here*, thought Wenna, *she's here and it's her and she's holding on to me.* She was staggered.

"Is he here?" their mother rasped.

"You mean Dad?"

She made a sound like a yes.

"He's . . . gone. Buried." Wenna couldn't guess whether their mother would be relieved or devastated or if this would mean nothing to her.

Their mother said nothing for so long that Wenna was afraid she'd gone back into herself. Her leathery face was impassive. Then she loosened her fingers from around Wenna's wrist and lowered her hand to the earth. She pushed with her fingertips at the icy peat, met resistance, and then withdrew her hand.

"Bad soil," she said. "I need . . . to move."

Wenna glanced over her shoulder at Eda and Nora and Percy, as if they would be any less confused than she was. "What?" Her voice sounded stilted and polite, like her mother was a stranger.

"Move me," their mother said. "To the trees."

They carried their mother out of the bog's mouth like a burial performed backward, bearing her body not on a spruce plank but in the tenuous cradle of their arms. She felt impossibly light, as if there were no bones or muscle or fat inside her; as if she were only skin. Eda held her neck and Wenna supported her torso while Nora and Percy balanced her lower half. Her leathery skin felt slick and cold in their hands. She did not speak as they carried her; she did not even breathe. When they came to the fringes of the bog forest, where thin stubborn tamaracks and black spruce stood in a scraggly line against the alder, she said, "Here."

They set their mother down in the undergrowth. Her withered fingers dug weakly into the snow, searching.

"I can't reach," she murmured.

Wenna glanced at Eda, who appeared as confused as she was.

"Mom, I don't know—"

"The snow. Clear it away."

Wenna dug out a furrow in the crust of snow with her hands, exposing the soil beneath.

Their mother traced her fingers across the earth. They looked like dead things, limp and inert, but Wenna saw them tremble as her mother pushed downward.

"Too hard," she croaked.

"The ground's frozen," Eda said impatiently. "She can't do . . . whatever she's doing."

"I have a spade," said Percy. His voice sounded faint. "I could break it up?" He looked at the rest of them for approval. When Wenna nodded, he disappeared into the trees and returned, several minutes later, bearing a rust-eaten tool over his shoulder. The rest of them stood back. He worked the blade into the frozen earth at their mother's side. It was hard work, Wenna could see, but he didn't stop until he'd exposed the soft loose soil inches beneath the frozen surface.

"Is it good, Mom?" he asked faintly.

Their mother didn't answer, but she found the place he made for her and sank her fingers to the knuckles. They slipped easily and at once into the dirt. Wenna thought the stiffness in her wizened body eased. She seemed, almost imperceptibly, to stretch out.

Percy exhaled as if he'd been holding his breath.

"What is she doing?" Nora whispered.

Wenna shook her head. Their mother's return felt precarious and half-complete. At any second, she could disappear from them if they were undeserving. Asking questions might be undeserving. She knew that wasn't how it worked, but already she felt drawn back into the anxious ritual-logic of her half-mothered adolescence, when she and Nora used to try to do everything *just right*—curtains opened one and then the other so it wasn't too bright; no whispering in the hallway, but a soft and gentle greeting once inside the room—in hopes of getting some response from their mother in the interstices of her long tirednesses.

They stood before their mother for a long time as she lay on the forest floor, her body twitching slightly as if a current were running through it. She did not speak. If she was still aware of them, she did not betray her awareness.

Eda lost patience first, pacing with her hand on her belly. "There are things to *do*," she said.

"Then do them," Wenna snapped, feeling betrayed by her own feelings of restlessness. She was ravenously hungry, and not dressed warmly enough, and she needed to pee. But their *mother* was here, wasn't she?

"Eyes stuck," said their mother, from the ground.

So unready were they for her speech that neither of them understood at first. When she repeated herself, Nora was the first to respond, gathering a small heap of snow into her hands and rubbing her palms together until it was reduced to watery slush.

"Be gentle," Wenna said.

"I *know*," said Nora. Tenderly, with as much care as she touched her mice or turtle, she massaged their mother's closed eyes with her snow-wet fingers, one and then the other.

When their mother opened her eyes, they were incongruously round and white in her crumpled tannin-dyed face, as if they were the only parts of her that were fully alive. At first, she stared at nothing. She did not seem to see them. Then she blinked several fluttering blinks, withdrew her fingers from the earth, and touched Nora's cheek. Nora leaned close, her brow wrinkled and her mouth tight like she wanted to cry. "Mama," she said, almost inaudibly.

"Nora," she answered.

Wenna was overcome by joy and tenderness and relief. Nothing was as wrenching as having reached for her mother and not grasped her; nothing was as gratifying as their mother emerging from her reclusion enough to come within reach.

"We missed you," she said, crouching at her mother's other side.

Her mother looked at her then, as if absorbing every detail of Wenna's face. Wenna imagined what she was seeing. Every way Wenna had changed since age seventeen, every part of her that had lasted.

"Wenna," she said. Her gaze drifted away from Wenna to rest on Eda, then Percy. "Where is Charles?" she said.

Wenna glanced over her shoulder, as if her brother might somehow materialize there. "I don't know," she stammered. "We can get him. Eda, can you—"

"I want to walk," their mother interrupted, as if she'd already forgotten Charlie. And Wenna couldn't forbid the thought, *She's strange now, strange and urgent and unfeeling,* quick enough to not have thought it.

"We can help you," said Nora.

They looped their mother's arms over their shoulders, Wenna on one side and Nora on the other. Slowly, on the count of three, they rose together. Their mother billowed slightly between them, as if they were holding a down comforter. She was taller than they were, by a little, and her feet dragged furrows across the snow as they stepped forward. Percy followed them at a slight distance, afraid to come too close.

"I need to see the mouth," said their mother, so they stepped through the graveyard of felled trees, their mother's big-pupiled eyes roving their surroundings as they maneuvered across narrow pine trunks, through little ravines, between the snarled brown vines of last year's cranberries. Wenna watched her mother out of the corner of her eye, but the leathery face was unreadable as they stepped across the bog meadow, through the snow-coated stands of sedge and alder that subsided at last to a flat carpet of sphagnum. They came as close to the bog's mouth as Wenna dared, thinking of Eda sunken chest-deep in the peat the night before.

Their mother said nothing as they brought her across the boglands. Now, she only said, mournfully, "He held it back."

"He held it back?" Wenna repeated. On her mother's other side, Nora shivered; the feeling passed through their mother to reach her.

"The bog is sick," said Percy, coming closer to them, hungry for the answer. "Isn't it? We tried to take care of it. Dad tried lots of things. But the mouth keeps shrinking."

"We didn't know," Wenna said, "that there was never a compact. No one told us." She hated how implicated she felt they all were by the *lots of things* their father had tried. As if they could possibly have stopped him.

Their mother said nothing for a long moment. Then she rasped a long breath down her throat. "Go back to where the earth is soft," she said to them. "And get Charles. There are things I need to tell all of you. Things you need to know."

At the bog meadow's edge beneath the naked tamaracks, they gathered like they used to gather before the hearth when their father recited their family's history, except now the five of them sat apart before their mother, distrustful of one another, rain falling in a warm vapor around them. The odor of wet moss lifted from the earth.

Their mother said, "Anything that lives and does not live alone makes compacts."

She said, "The first compact made here was made in the melt

of glaciers. No rooted plant could survive in this place, a kettle of a lake—crush of mineral-poor limestone below, pillars of hot steam overhead—but the sphagnum only needed moisture and sun and air to live. The spores, carried by wind, settled on the surface. In time, they soured the water, drove out what other vegetable life might have moved in. They made their compact on terms agreeable to themselves. Of the lake, they asked enough water to fill them in times of dryness; in exchange, the invisibly small whip-tailed creatures of the lake asked only for the bodies of their dead.

"A moss-generation passed. The sphagnum began to bury their elders. Under the surface, whiptails ate dead tissue and released sour emanations. Layers of dead soaked and steeped, formed a weave of plant matter beneath the surface so thick that nothing but the whiptails could breathe there. Open water became dense mire. Then the sphagnum and the whiptails made compacts with shrunken stubborn plants that had nowhere better to go. Leatherleaf, cranberry, orchid, sundew, tamarack, black spruce, Haddesley. The sundew ate flies drawn by the odor of the sphagnum-dead; the sphagnum watered the leatherleaf in times of dryness. The whiptails made wives from dead vegetable matter that Haddesley men had children with. Of the bog, these creatures asked reprieve from competition; the withering deaths of those tall and heavy-leafed intruders that would take their sun and rain in any other place. In exchange, the whiptails asked only for the bodies of their dead.

"But compacts end or are betrayed. Haddesleys build crushingly heavy houses on wet earth and create a downhill slope that floods some places and parches others. In time, layers of dead sphagnum thicken too much to hold water. Peat dries into soil. Soil admits tall, heavy-leafed plants: rhododendron, alder. The roots make furrows that worms and beetles creep through, eating and shitting until the ground is sweet enough to feed whatever spore or seed might land. Fungi make threads of connection so the new plants can share nutrients. The newcomers grow, and they grow tall. They take the sun and rain from the bogbean, the sundew, the leatherleaf, even the sphagnum. And the whiptails, beneath the surface, go hungry.

"When I was formed, the Haddesley house was already sinking. On firmer ground, white pines were growing. I could see in what direction things were heading. And after a long time, twenty years of wifehood, I realized I too was changing. I began to feel sun-hunger; I began to grow roots from the soles of my feet. I could hear the communications of the trees underground, the longings and distresses passed through fungal wires. Your father didn't understand. I told him. I told him and told him. But he thought this place was dying. He thought I was dying too. When he buried me in the peat, it was because he wanted to hold me still until he could stop this place from changing. Because he thought that would stop me from changing too."

She said, "My children, this place will not survive not changing. *You* will not survive it."

She said, "I have begun changing again; I can feel it. Soon I will be unrecognizable to you. I will lose language. I will lose my feet, my face. I will still be here, but not like before. I have to tell you now. You have to make new compacts. The old ones will not sustain you here anymore."

EDA

After their mother fell silent, the five Haddesley children sat for an excruciating length of time waiting, no one completely certain their mother was finished speaking, no one wanting to interrupt. Their mother had always spoken slowly and softly, but her speech now was fractured by long pauses, her words stretched gently out on the rack of her meaning. As if she were not only searching for words but searching for the way to arrange her mouth and tongue so she could utter them. She was telling them the truth about losing language, Eda thought. She had reappeared only so she could disappear more hurtfully than before, slowly and in front of them.

"How dare you?" Eda startled even herself, her voice shattering and loud against the soft din of the rain. A bird took hurried flight out of the tamarack above her.

"Edd," Wenna admonished, but Eda was too angry to be shamed.

"How dare you leave us and then reappear like this and tell us that we have to do things differently?" she asked. "How would you even know how we've been doing them? It's been eleven years. You were barely here even before that. Always asleep and never around when we needed you. And everyone did need you. They won't ever say it for some reason, but I will. I don't care. I am not going to let you come back here and tell me how to manage this house when I have been holding it together all my life without you. You were never a mother to any of us. I wish you had stayed down there. You should have stayed—"

"Eda, *stop it!*" Wenna planted herself between Eda and their mother. She was close enough that Eda could see her sister's eyes were wet, her shoulders shaking slightly. At their feet, their mother lay still, impassive, indifferent. She wondered if their mother had even heard anything she said. Percy and Nora were wide-eyed. When she met Charlie's gaze, he shook his head slightly, discouraging her from going any further, as if it wasn't worth her anger. She thought Charlie would have been incapable of getting angry even in the course of being stabbed to death. But what about the rest of them? Why was no one else angry?

"Fine," she said. "Fine. I'm going back to the house."

❧

For a long time after she returned home, Eda could only wander the ravaged landscape of rubble and holes left to them by the storm, cataloging the damage done. In every room, the ceilings were caved in or puckering ominously. A thin crust of melting snow became a river that flowed languidly across the slight downhill slope of the hallway toward the back door. The branches of a fallen maple stuck through the front window of the forbidden parlor. Shattered glass and bark littered the divan and the floor. They had no power, and they would have to pump water by hand until the power came back, *if* it ever did come back.

None of this was unmanageable, though Eda did not especially *want* to manage any of it, and, in fact, if she thought about what it was going to require of her, she became so exhausted and so angry at the defiant impossibility of things holding together that she couldn't continue. But she felt that if they let the house stay like this for even a few hours more, they would never get it back. It would stay forever wet and filthy and ravaged, hummocks of rubble and hollows of decay across the floor as if the bog had come inside, and the Haddesleys would have to become the kind of creatures who could live inside it. *You will not live without changing,* her mother had said. But what could they possibly change *into?* The question was too horrifying to consider. She began transferring what was left of their stockpile of peat out of the water-logged great room, piling the least-soaked bricks in the forbidden parlor. Claude and Mathilde's doleful eyes followed her in and out of the room. "I'll get to you," she told them.

When she got to the point in the stack of peat where nothing left was vaguely dry, the bricks crumpling loose into formless clods of mud, she stood in the forbidden parlor with her arms crossed trying to calculate how many weeks of fuel they had left, and how many weeks of cold weather. There was not nearly enough fuel left. Possibly they could cut the trees felled in the storm and burn those, but the Haddesleys were not burners of wood, not ancestrally. She was not even sure they owned an axe.

Across the house, Claude or Mathilde bleated.

"Fine!" Eda shouted.

The goats were angry with hunger, nipping at her clothes, crowding her while she struggled to untie the knots in their wet ropes. She noticed for the first time, as if it had happened overnight, that Mathilde was enormously pregnant. It made no difference; her kid would not live. Eda thought this Mathilde—the latest of many Mathildes, as this was the name the Haddesleys gave all their nanny goats—had never produced a kid that lived. It made no difference to them as long as she kept producing milk, except that when she died there would be no young nanny goat to take her place like there had always been before, *always* of course apparently meaning not time immemorial but a mere hundred years, eight goat generations at most, a meager and unexceptional interval of time when you thought about it, which Eda was not going to, because if she did she would not have the will to go on.

"Come on," Eda said to the goats. She swung the ends of the ropes at them in the wide circular motions that she had seen Percy use to great effect. For her, there was no effect at all. The goats fixed her with steady slit-pupiled eyes and did not come on. She whacked Claude's flank with the frayed end of his rope. She could not quite bring herself to touch Mathilde. Claude's long ears twitched back, deliberating, but he did not move.

"Come *on!*" Eda's voice was loud but unconvincing. She advanced on Claude and smacked him again with the rope, a real lash this time across his hindquarters. The goat lifted his head high and ran forward, pulling the rope out of her hand and pushing past her. His shoulder struck her hip hard, and Eda was thrown to the floor. As she struggled to get her breath back, she felt Mathilde's rope slide through her fingers. She watched the nanny goat trot away through a haze of dots. The swinging pendulum of her belly. The gross prominence of her udders. Eda's heart hammered in her chest. She realized her stomach hurt, a peculiar cramping that meant she was hungry or the baby was dying or both.

The dots in her vision were still clearing when Wenna materialized in the doorway, disheveled and forceful-looking in their father's old coat and a pair of Charlie's overalls.

"You all right?" she asked.

"The goats got loose," Eda said, inadequately.

"I know," Wenna said. "Charlie's got them." She crossed the room to Eda and bent down to help her stand. Her hand was cold and work-firmed, scratchy with callouses. "We should talk," she said, "about all the things Mom said."

Eda's stomach dropped. "Obviously," she said, though she would have preferred not to. She could not conceive of what *a new compact* could possibly mean, other than their eventual annihilation. What separated them from the sun-starved sphagnum, the choked-out whiptails? They knew only one way of living.

She thought of the shriveled tannin-dyed fox they once found adrift in the mire after days of heavy rain, flushed up from the depths. It was a specimen belonging to a species of fox now extinct, their father said excitedly, he and Percy having plunged neck-deep into their field guides. He'd stuffed its body with formaldehyde and paper until its legs went taut and bought twin glass eyes to fill its empty sockets and then displayed its corpse on a shelf in the study. *They used to live here*, he said proudly. *Died out when their preferred prey migrated.* Someday, Eda thought, some interloper would stuff her head with paper and fill her eyes with glass and remember her as a creature whose prey had migrated.

Eda raked her sweater sleeve across her eyes, not wanting anyone else to see that she'd been crying, knowing probably they would know anyway. "Where's everyone else?" she asked.

"Kitchen," Wenna said. "Nora and Percy are making dinner."

Dinner, as Eda had anticipated, was enormous mugs of cocoa. It probably would have been cocoa even if the house had been fully stocked, though, as it was, they had few other choices.

In the pantry, there were dwindling supplies of oatmeal, sugar, baking powder, cornmeal. On the floor were crates of winter squash, sprouted garlic, cellar potatoes brought upstairs two nights ago. The canned goods were entirely gone. Anything left in the freezer would have been ruined by now. *You will not survive not changing*, Eda thought, and she shuddered and closed the pantry door.

The kitchen table had been crushed beneath a pile of rubble, the delicate limbs of the long-suffering brass chandelier sticking like gold spiders' legs out of the crush of stone and plaster. Most of the dining chairs had suffered the same fate, so they gathered the most salvageable furniture from other rooms of the house. Wenna and Percy shared the velvet sofa from the forbidden parlor, while Charlie perched stiffly on the piano bench, having ceded the far-more-comfortable wingback armchair to anyone else. Hesitantly, Eda sat down on it. The leather seat was damp. Every few minutes, wind hissed through the hole in the ceiling and disturbed the debris on the floor. Charlie shivered and then winced as if the motion hurt him.

Nora brought the last of the cups from the stove and lowered herself tentatively down onto the single surviving dining chair as if uncertain whether it would hold her weight. For a moment, she sat stiff-backed, gnawing on her lip, obviously trying to restrain herself. It didn't last. "Why doesn't she eat anymore?" she demanded of no one in particular. "Why won't she eat with us?"

"Oh, Nor," said Wenna.

"She gets food from the ground," said Percy. "And the sun."

Nora swung around in her seat to challenge him, her cocoa sloshing at the lip of the cup. "Why?" she asked. "And how do you *know*?"

"Because," said Percy, tentative now, retreating. "She said. She told us."

"I don't understand," Nora went on, ignoring him, "why she has to be something else. Why she can't stay with us."

"She never wanted to be with us," Eda said. "This is what she always wanted."

"That's not true," said Wenna. "She's never said that."

"Did she have to say it?" said Eda. "She was always trying to get back into the bog since she came out of it."

"Because she didn't ask to come out of it," Charlie said. "He made her do it. He or the bog made her do it. But it was never her that wanted to come out and be his wife."

"But there was a compact," Nora insisted. "Mom said it *was* a compact, between the bog and the Haddesleys." Her voice clung firmly to the word *compact*, as if just its evocation should be enough to force their mother back into the house and back into her assumed humanness. "You were wrong," she told Charlie, accusatorily.

"She said there was a compact between the flies and the sundew too," Charlie answered, a hard edge to his voice. "Would you want to be part of that?"

"Was it like that?" Percy whispered. "Always? Like flies and sundew?"

Who was the fly and who was the sundew? Eda thought. Their father and their father's father and the man before that and the five of them now had spent their lives in pursuit of the approval and devotion of a landscape that had never wanted them for anything besides the bodies of their dead. Who had been eaten and who had been doing the eating was not obvious, from her perspective.

"She was still our mother," said Wenna. "She still loved— loves us, whatever she felt about Dad."

"How do you know?" Eda asked. She really meant it. It bewildered her that Wenna felt so assured. Was there some secret version of their mother only Wenna had known, or was it merely that Wenna's desire to have a different kind of mother than the one they actually had was so strong she had been able to sustain the delusion for twenty-seven years?

"Know what?" asked Wenna.

"That she loves us."

Wenna looked uneasy. "She doesn't love in the way you do, but it doesn't mean she doesn't," she said, which was not really an answer to Eda's question.

"Well, she never loved me," Charlie volunteered.

Something about the way he said it, without a trace of feeling in his voice, as if it were an obvious and not especially interesting fact, cleaved Eda's chest open. She had known, but she hadn't known that he knew. Her brother was a man of thirty-one, but she would never not see him as her firstborn charge, snot-nosed and infinitely vulnerable.

"Excuse me," Eda said, formally. She did not want to storm out again. It was the kind of thing Nora did. But she couldn't bear to be seen crying, and her stomach had begun again to hurt, a clawing nauseous pain that the cocoa had only made worse. She left her cup on the floor and went out the back door.

Outside, she stood on the back step in the last shreds of daylight shivering violently, regretting the direction she'd chosen because she had nowhere to go now. She should have gone further into the house. She wouldn't have minded a ceiling collapsing on her. Their mother's lumpen body lay across the yard like a newly dug grave, a battery-powered camping lantern left on beside it as if their mother could possibly care whether she had light, as if she might want to catch up on her reading. Nora's doing, obviously.

Eda had almost calmed herself enough to consider a strategy for going back inside when the back door opened and Wenna stepped out. She still wore their father's coat, and when she saw how Eda was shivering, she took it off and wrapped it loosely around Eda's shoulders. Eda stood stiffly beneath it, inhaling her father's scent—faded now, barely detectible beneath the newer, sharper scents of wet moss and plaster dust and her sister's fear. After a moment, she relented and drew her arms into the sleeves, resenting that she was being handled, too over-whelmed to think of resisting.

"She never took care of any of us," she said to Wenna, her voice low, mindful that her mother was only twenty or thirty yards from them. It was impossible ever to know whether she could hear what they said. But she needed, urgently, for Wenna to understand. "Never cared if someone hurt themselves or had a bad dream or got in trouble with Dad. And if it were only me she'd done it to, I would still hate her, but I would know it was my fault. But it wasn't only me. It was all of us. You too, Wen. How could she not care for *any* of us? For Nora? For Charlie? Charlie, who had no one, who Dad was always cruel to."

Wenna said nothing at first, and Eda felt certain she would defend their mother like she always did. *How could you make demands of a woman formed out of dead vegetable matter? What did you expect?*

But then she said only, "I know."

"I know you think I'm a tyrant," Eda said. "And I know I am

one. But I've been hanging on to everyone for so long that I'm afraid of what would happen if I ever let go now. None of us know how to take care of ourselves. Even you. When you left, I was so worried about you. I felt sure you would die out there. Mom was disappeared and you left of your own will, but it was you I had nightmares about."

"Oh, Edd," Wenna said. "I was always okay."

"I know," Eda said. She was crying, despite herself. "Somehow you ended up stronger than the rest of us. You can't understand. When Mom said we had to make new compacts, it felt like . . . like she was telling me that I hadn't done good enough before. Like, I already couldn't hold everything together, and now I have to do all of it better, somehow, with a wrecked house and a baby that I'm scared is dying inside of me, and I don't know how I can. I don't think I'm capable of it."

"You're not doing it by yourself," Wenna said. "There are five of us here."

Eda shook her head. "They can't," she said. "They don't know—"

"We can," Wenna said, firmly. "We have to, now."

Eda glanced sidelong at her, longing to believe Wenna meant what she was saying. She had spent so much of Wenna's return—and the ten years before that—being furiously angry with her sister. Yet, for a few weeks during the winter, the household had reached a kind of equilibrium, almost a peace, and Eda had begun to hope it could always be that way. When she'd imagined the future, Wenna had increasingly been part of it. Not at the center of things, necessarily, but *there*: swinging a spade during peat-cutting, crouching low to find bitter pie cranberries at the end of the season, sleeping by the hearth in deep winter, gathering wild ramps in the spring. Holding Eda's child after he was born.

"Will you leave?" she asked, her voice small and hesitating. "After Mom leaves us?"

Wenna stiffened beside her. "You told me to," she said, as if Eda had ever been capable of making Wenna do something she didn't want to.

"Well," said Eda, her eyes on her feet, "I wish you wouldn't."

PERCY

The morning after the storm, after Charlie left him, Percy crouched alone at the bog's mouth with the insensate body of his mother, hearing his brother say again and again, *She never wanted you*. His mouth tasted like decay. He spat until his mouth was too dry to spit as if that would get the taste out, even though he had been the one to spit on his mother's mouth and not the other way around, so the rotted taste could only have been coming from inside of him.

He had a vague recollection, which came to him as if he'd dreamed it, of Charlie coming into the boglands on a wind-torn afternoon and shouting at him, telling him there was no compact and there never had been one. He remembered having felt unconcerned, hearing that. How, he'd thought, could he already be communing with the wife he'd hewn from nothing if there was no compact between the Haddesleys and the land? He'd felt sorry for his brother. But he could no longer be certain, staring at that tannin-dyed corpse with his mother's face. Thinking, *She never wanted you*.

He thought he knew already, but he had to be sure. He crawled away from his mother and returned to the place where he'd spent the winter on the margins of the bog meadow. Crossing the snow-buried landscape, he felt as though overnight he'd lost his rapport with the land. Snow and felled branches made everything unfamiliar. He could not find his old path through the trees; he no longer remembered the texture of the undergrowth, the places where the alder naturally parted to admit the tread of human feet. Everywhere he stepped, he thought he was trampling something. He was afraid he wouldn't be able to find the raised lip of soil where he'd buried the skeleton of sticks and mire, but there was a visceral animal part of him that couldn't not remember. There, that place: between two wizened black spruces, one of them now missing most of its lower branches, in a gentle depression covered by dropped needles, wind-thrown leaf litter, and now a crisp layer of snow three or four inches deep.

Once he found it, he got to work flinging away piles of snow and earth with the spade he used to cut down trespassers. The ground was frozen, resistant to the blade, but underneath, the surface was warmer and more pliant soil: rich dark humus, vibrant with worms and beetles and invisible crawling things even now. Nascent life, waiting to emerge. He inhaled its scent and felt a faint reverberation through his stomach up to his throat like hunger or nausea.

A few inches down, his shovel met resistance with a dull thud. He dug more slowly after that, working slowly around the place from which the thud had come. Finally, he could see, embedded in the earth, the long firm branch that he had conscripted for his wife's spine. Only then did he realize he had already been flinging up pieces of her body, the incidental twigs of her pelvis and fingers and ribs; they were comingled with the loose earth that lay in a pile to his left. What remained of the skeleton, the blocky geometry of wooden head and shoulders and limbs, looked the same as when he'd buried it.

Percy knew for sure, then, what he'd already suspected: there had never been any wife growing underground. The recipe had not worked even partially. It had been *her* down there the whole time; it had never been any woman hewn from nothing. Because if it hadn't been his wife, that many-voiced fibrous presence that had gotten inside of him and brought the insides of him out into the forest, it had to have been his mother, didn't it?

He sat breathing heavily in the empty grave, grieving for the wife he'd thought he was communing with and the now-passed days or weeks (or months?) when he'd felt so connected to someone else that he had slipped loose from the constraints of himself. Despising his mother, who seemed to have appeared out of the bog's mouth like a violent rebuke of his attempt to mend the broken compact. Despising himself for being arrogant and desire-blind enough to think he had been in love when he had only ever been an unwanted younger son gnashing his teeth and demanding sustenance.

He left the empty grave reluctantly, afraid to face the amber-skinned woman that was his mother but had seemed for so long to be his wife, more afraid that if he left her for long she would have disappeared when he came back and he would never have any answers. When his sisters found him, he was relieved to no longer be alone with the impossible thing of their mother's return, but he was also terrified he would at any moment accidentally betray something to them, that just by looking at him, they would grasp by instinct what he had done and respond to him with the disgust and contempt he deserved. As it was, he drowned in humiliation every time he remembered that Charlie knew about the recipe and the months of waiting and the *hearing her.*

And then, hours later, their mother—lying with her fingers stuck in the earth the same way Percy had stuck his own fingers in the earth—said, "I could hear the communications of the trees underground, the longings and distresses passed through fungal wires." And a spark of hope lit in him. Because what she described sounded to Percy like what he had felt. And he began to wonder if it had not been his mother, or at least not only her, that he had communed with when he lived in the boglands that winter. And if he could do it again, even now.

❧

So afraid was Percy of getting a no for an answer that he waited days after their mother's return before approaching her. She lay in the yard, surrounded by a corona of bare earth that Wenna had shoveled out. The rest of the yard was still buried in melting snow and fallen branches. Her fingers and toes were sunk into the earth, her face inclined toward the sun. Percy came hesitantly closer, glancing over his shoulder in case one of his siblings appeared there. They had no reason to be suspicious of him, but he did not want to be overheard. He sat down at his mother's side. *Sometimes she doesn't seem like she can hear you,* Nora said the other night, forcing a buoyant, untroubled tone, *but I think she does.*

"Mom," he said, halfway under his breath.

She did not answer.

"Mom," he said again, and then he barreled on, because even if she wasn't going to answer him or acknowledge him, even if she couldn't hear him, he still had to try to say it, and he thought he'd never get up the nerve again if he didn't do it now. "I have to ask you something," he said. "About the bog. You said you could hear the trees. And I was wondering. Can we hear them

291

too? Are we enough . . . like you? Because," and he hesitated now, tearing restlessly at the grass with his fingers, then realizing that probably she felt that tearing if her fingers were acting as roots in the way he thought they were. Thinking that everything he ever did in the bog had an accidental effortless tinge of violence to it. "I think I heard them," he said. "I think I was connected, when I lived outside."

She said nothing, and his heart sank. "I want to be back there," he said. "I want to be connected like you are."

He startled when his mother pulled her left hand out of the earth. Her fingers were caked in mud and, he saw, trailing hair-thin white fibers that looked like roots. She reached her hand out slowly, without opening her eyes, and found his hand where it was entangled with the starved yellow grass. Gently, she lifted his hand and slipped his fingers into the small gouges where her own fingers had been.

Percy closed his eyes. He waited. And then he was no longer alone. He was hearing, *Feed,* hearing, *Search,* hearing, *Rest,* and obeying with the unthinking ecstatic urgency of instinct.

NORA

When they had first found their mother, Nora had felt the same hopefulness she felt when she first heard that Wenna was coming back. She'd thought, *My animals were sacrificed for this*, and she'd accepted the devastation of the storm as the cost of getting their mother back, of everyone being drawn close like she had wished when she lay awake in Eda's bed. But they were not a family now, any more than they had been a family after Wenna came back and they buried their father and then drifted slowly away from one another into the winter. She was beginning to understand that they never would be. Only a few nights after the storm, Percy returned to living in the forest, although he now came back to the house for meals, which he had not done for weeks before the storm hit; something had changed but Nora didn't know what it was. He wouldn't say. He wouldn't say anything. When she was with him, she felt lonelier than when she was alone, so she tried not to be with him. Wenna and Eda and Charlie, meanwhile, spent their days prodding at the house, standing on ladders and hacking at rubble and mopping floors. If Nora was with them, inevitably she would end up holding a ladder steady as Wenna threw debris off the roof or handing nails to Eda as she fixed old two-by-fours to shattered windows. Nora hated the house now; she could not even look at the house without thinking of her animals crushed in their jars and tanks and cages, so she tried not to be too much with them either. Eda only insisted she come back at night, when they slept in the kitchen where the ceiling had already come down and there could be no danger to them and the wind screamed through the holes in the walls and Nora dreamed of Buz Lukens crushed flat like a rug of possum flesh.

Their mother did not sleep in the kitchen with them. At night, their mother curled onto her side like a dead insect and lay perfectly still until the sun rose again. She was capable of walking, but she hardly ever did. She had told them she was losing her face and her feet and her language and Nora watched as she did seem to lose them, one after another. Most days, she would go out to the yard and sit at their mother's side, making any excuse to stay there where she possibly was not wanted, braiding blades of grass into crowns or bracelets that no one wanted to wear, letting the goats nibble at the dead undergrowth of last autumn. Mostly, their mother lay still with her eyes closed, so Nora could barely tell if she was asleep or awake. Half the time, when Nora spoke to her, she didn't answer. But she would breathe and sometimes she would flinch at the smallest sounds or motions, as if she was painfully aware of everything. It was, Nora thought, as if there were still layers and layers of mire encasing her. As if their real mother—the one who loved them, who used to kiss their flushed-from-outdoors cheeks and admire their cartwheels and hold salamanders in her cupped palms for them to see—was a kernel buried in the center of the motherly body that had come back to them. She seemed to be there, but far away.

Except that Nora knew now: the kernel in the center had never been in the center; it had been only another layer of mire. The real mother was the one that did not speak their language and did not eat the food they ate and did not live inside their house.

The real mother was the one that did not know how to love them.

Nora had felt sad when her mother said how lonely she'd been, sundered from the bog and made to be a human for a while. But she'd also thought: *I feel like that.* She'd thought, *I always feel like that.* And for Nora there was nothing to be unsundered from, nothing to miss. She had never not been alone, and she knew now that she never would be not alone.

§

It was a clear day in the middle of the season, the maples leafing out and wild ramps sprouting in the humus, when Nora went out to the yard and found her mother wasn't breathing.

"Mama," she said, as she usually did. "I'm here."

There was no answer. Not even a small movement, not even an inhalation.

"Mama," Nora said, firmly. "I'm *here.*"

There was no finality in that silence. Nora knew her mother might come back. She might, even now, be listening. Or she might not. There was not going to be any last moment they were together, Nora understood. Unless the last moment had already happened.

She knew Wenna would want to know, but she couldn't bear to tell Wenna yet. Wenna had seemingly not decided whether she was going to leave them when their mother did, and she refused to discuss it—at least, she refused to discuss it with Nora. And Nora suspected this meant she *was* going to leave, that it had already been decided and her sisters had simply judged Nora incapable of holding this knowledge. And she could not bear to lose her mother and Wenna both, not yet. So instead she went first to Percy. Standing in the margins of the forest, she screamed his name until her brother appeared through the narrow trunks of the yearling birches.

"Sorry," he said, coming dazedly out through the wild young undergrowth as if he hadn't heard her.

Nora sat down on the felled tree where she used to leave his dinners during the first weeks of his boglands winter. It sank gently beneath her weight, the wood wet and rotted and weakening. She wanted things between them to feel for a few minutes like they had felt before their father died, before Wenna came back, before Percy thought he was supposed to be the bog's custodian—before, before, before, somewhere past the magical vanishing point where her memory became rosily blurred and she thought she had been happy but she couldn't remember how. For a while they sat hip to hip, passing warmth back and forth between them.

"I think Mom is gone," she said, finally.

"Oh," said Percy, and he didn't sound shocked or devastated or even sad; in fact, Nora thought, he sounded *distracted*.

"Don't you care?" she asked.

Percy hunched down with his elbows on his knees. "Nor," he said. "There's something I want to tell you."

Nora looked at him with suspicion: her brother in his filthy moss shroud, his bare feet sunk in the leaf litter. She thought she barely knew him now. "What?"

He slid back upright. "I think there's a way," he said. "A way to be with Mom."

"What do you mean?"

"Last winter," he said, "me and Charlie, we found this recipe in Dad's memoirs. 'To hew a wife from naught.' Charlie said I could be the one to do it. I don't know why we thought it would work."

Nora shuddered. "Why did Dad have that?"

"Probably to replace Mom," said Percy. "I can't think why else. I shouldn't have used it. But . . . well, something happened. When I was out here."

Nora felt slightly dizzied by the revelation that Percy had spent the winter not plucking trespassers out of the swale but instead trying to get a bog-wife out of nothing.

"I started to feel something. Like I was reading someone's mind. Or, more like, their thoughts were in my head with mine. It was . . . I can't describe it. It felt good. It felt like I was with someone else and not alone out here. At first, I thought it was my wife. I thought it meant the recipe had worked. And then, when Mom came up from the ground, I thought it was Mom. But then, when she was telling about the trees speaking through the ground, I thought: *That's like what I felt.* And I realized I was hearing the forest."

Nora shook her head, uncomprehending. "You hear the . . . forest?"

"It's not really hearing," he admitted. "There's not a word for it. Feeling, but it's not feeling. It's . . . knowing."

Her brother's eyes were wide, his skin flushed. Nora had a sense of the ground widening between them, of being far outpaced. "I don't see what that has to do with anything," she said sulkily. All through the winter, while she had been stuck in the house with her sisters and Charlie arguing over how to fulfill a nonexistent compact, Percy had been embedding himself into the texture of the land, getting closer to their mother than any of them had ever gotten, and not saying anything. She couldn't not feel betrayed.

"Because," he said, "I think you can do it too."

Nora narrowed her eyes, trying to discern whether Percy was playing with her. He didn't seem unserious; her brother was hardly ever unserious. But it was unimaginable, what he was saying.

"Take off your shoes," he said.

Nora did as he said. Percy bent down and gently pressed her toes into the soil, then took her hands and pressed her fingers down too. The earth was cold around her extremities but not forbidding, the ooze grasping her like an embrace. She closed her eyes and braced herself for something, but nothing came.

"I don't hear it," she whispered.

"Be quiet," said Percy. "You have to be quiet. In your head and out of it."

Nora screwed her eyes shut and tried valiantly to make herself quiet. It came sooner than she thought, and Percy was right that *heard* was not really what it was.

Inside her head, where only her own thoughts usually lived, there was a weave of presence, multiple and diverse and yet inseparable, and she, Nora, was suddenly inside that tangle, woven through it. What they said was simple and untranslatable and urgent, and it was what she was saying too, answering them in kind, assuring them *I am here!* and being enfolded by their many simultaneous answers. She felt their needs and their hungers, she knew their carnivorous impulses and their prey responses, she was privy to everything and everything was privy to her. She was seen, known, everything within her.

When she fell out, she was overcome by the bleak, horrific loneliness of the self that she had occupied for twenty-five years of life before those seconds or minutes or hours that she was part of something else. And she understood at once how Percy endured a winter alone—but not alone, not anywhere near anything *like* alone—out here.

"Percy," she whispered, clinging to his shoulder in a futile effort to reproduce the feeling of having his thoughts inseparable from her own thoughts inside her head. His name felt clumsy on her tongue now, makeshift. "Is that what it's like, for Mom?"

"I think so," he said.

"Can we always be like that? Can we . . . would we change like she did?"

Percy lifted his bare feet to show her. There were roots coming out of his arches, firm white cords crusted with soil on the ends. Nora felt the impulse, half-disgusted and half-jealous, to examine her own feet for new protrusions.

"You're going to let it happen?" she whispered.

"We're supposed to make a new compact," he said. "Aren't we?"

"Yes," said Nora, and she hoped that the transformation was a way of going back—beyond the vanishing point, beyond what she could remember, to the fullness and warmth and completion that always eluded her. All her life she had been so lonely. She did not want to be lonely anymore.

WENNA

hen Nora came up to the house one night at dusk with her cheeks flushed, beaming, Wenna's first thought was that their mother must have emerged enough to really talk with her, and she felt a faint murmur of jealousy, because for her their mother had only seemed to drift further and further away in the weeks since coming back to them. But Nora had been more faithful than Wenna could be, sitting in the yard with their mother for hours every day. If their mother was going to say something unambiguous and as longed for like *I love you* to any of them, Wenna thought, it would be Nora that she would say it to, Nora who deserved it.

As her sister came through the back door, she seemed to be trying to choke her joy back, restraining herself. She kicked the mud from her boots against the doorframe and then began unlacing them. Wenna saw her fingers were stained a deep ruddy brown to the knuckles, all ten of them, and something inside her lurched. But she didn't understand, not yet.

"Where is everyone?" Nora asked.

"Working on upstairs, I think," Wenna said. Eda, having found that some of the bedrooms in the east wing were still accessible through a window, had enlisted Charlie in the work of scavenging everything they could from that now-vanished part of their home. Their brother still could not climb a ladder, but he could hold one steady. All day, intermittently, artifacts of their childhood rained down around him: small and wizened-looking leather shoes, toys no one had played with in fifteen years. Ominously, and with pronounced clangs, empty jars and cages that Wenna thought must have been the former homes of Nora's foundlings. She wondered what Eda had done with their occupants, if there were still any.

"Can they come down?" Nora asked.

"If you want," said Wenna. "Why?" She could not help but be suspicious of this sudden compulsion to gather. Since the storm, Nora had been reclusive, sulky, unreadable—not herself. Wenna knew her sister had not forgiven any of them for turning back without Percy, and she especially had not forgiven Wenna for wanting to sell the house.

Nora cast a dismissive, impatient look at her. Then, as if she could not contain herself a second longer, she said, "I know how we can be with Mom."

Wenna's eyes fell to her sister's mud-stained hands. Her heart thudded in her chest, and she couldn't tell whether it was dread or astonishment that she felt. It had become apparent, within only a few days of their mother's return, that she was going to become unrecognizable to them much sooner than Wenna had hoped. She barely spoke now, and when she did, she spoke in fragments, slow and faltering. It was as if she had expended all the words that she had left, that first day. She never stood or walked anywhere. Patches of vegetal-looking flesh had appeared on her arms and chest, tannin-amber ceding to vibrant green. Occasionally, for only a few seconds, her face would twist into a facsimile of a smile, but she had not done that in several days now; sometimes, lately, she seemed to forget to breathe.

"What do you mean, 'be with Mom'?"

Outside, the sun was sinking lower in the horizon, dispersing only milky soft light. By now, Wenna knew, their mother would be retreating further into herself, entering into a sleep deeper than sleep, from which she would not be woken until sunrise. Wenna had learned that there was no point in going to see her after dark. She effectively was not there. Wenna wanted to say that they could not expect anything; they would only be disappointed if they asked anything of their mother now, but she knew Nora must know that; hadn't Nora been there all the March afternoons when the light went golden long before the day really ended; didn't she know that she was approaching their mother *wrong*?

But Nora seemed unconcerned. "Hold *on*," was all she said. "I want everyone."

Everyone meant Eda and Charlie. Wenna saw why, when Nora brought them out the back door to the yard, making her barefoot way through the young moss. Their mother lay where she always lay, her eyes closed, her face restive. There were buds forming on her shoulders, small delicate growths that Wenna thought hadn't been there that morning. Percy lay a few feet away from her, his fingers and toes stuck in the ground. When Eda saw him, she released a stifled yelp, as if she'd been struck.

It was startling to see Percy there. In his moss sheath, he was almost indistinguishable from the terrain around him. Wenna still had not fully absorbed what it meant, that he was there, when Nora lay down at their mother's other side. She twined her fingers and then her bare toes in the earth, working herself into the warm rich soil of the yard.

"We can be like her," Nora said. "Percy found it out. We can do what she does. Hear the trees underground. Be connected. To everything. *Everything* is here. It's like you can see inside of the land. Like you know everything that's going on, and you're inside of it. This is how we live here!" She twisted her head to look imploringly at them. "Don't you want to?"

Wenna didn't answer. She was remembering, with a stark sense of having recovered something lost to her, one of the last days she spent with her mother before the final long tiredness, the strange parka-clad spring, the disappearance. It had been early autumn. They had not cut peat for the year yet. Her mother had stepped close to the bog's mouth, maneuvering delicately across hummocks and hollows, inhaling with open-mouthed drags of air as if she wanted to suck the odor of the rain-wetted sphagnum down inside herself.

"Where were you?" she had asked her mother. "Before the bog made you for us?"

It was the closest Wenna ever came to acknowledging the irreparable loss that made possible her own life. They did not speak of the exchange in the house, not ever. They all acted as if their mother had always been there, the illusion shattered only by the fact that Charlie was already being instructed in the ways of acclimating his own future bog-wife to human existence.

Her mother had looked grateful. As if she had waited twenty-two years to be asked that question.

"Everywhere," she had said, wistfully. "I was everywhere."

"You're not doing this," Eda said now, on the verge of panic. "I don't know what you think is going to happen, but you're not . . . like her. Percy! Get up!"

"But we *can* be," said Nora. "We *can*. And you. Eda, come lie down with us. When you feel it, you'll know."

"I'm not like her," Eda said; she sounded as if she were trying to convince herself. She glanced in Wenna's direction. "Are you . . . ?"

Wenna felt, with an ache in her chest, the longing to lie down between Nora and her mother and stay there until she could no longer get up. To lose her face and feet and language. To cross the chasm that always separated her from her mother, whom she had always loved but whom she could never really know or be known by. Yet she knew for her it would not be a life; it would only be a way of avoiding one. She had always been afraid that she could not return home without being consumed by her family's insatiable needs, their intractable problems, their unspoken and incomprehensible demands. She thought she could not be herself and be at home on Haddesley land. If she lay down with Nora now, that would be true.

She was still finding the words to say no when Charlie stepped forward and lay down to Percy's left. He kicked off his shoes with a violent, urgent motion that sent them flying into the air. Wenna and Eda stood, shocked into stillness, watching him. For a long moment, he lay in the grass, his fingers and bare toes twisted in the earth, unspeaking. And then he crumpled up his body and rose to his feet, wincing at the way the motion hurt.

"I don't feel it," he said—resigned, as if he had known already what would happen. His eyes held Eda's, then strayed to the boglands beyond them. For a moment, there was something desperate in his look, grief and anger together. "I just can't feel it," he said. And then he made for the house, stumbling barefoot through the yard, his shoes still lying a little ways apart from each other where he'd left them.

"Nora, I can't," Wenna said. "I'm sorry."

She braced for her sister to be furious; all their lives, Nora had been clinging to Wenna and Wenna had been pulling away, making small refusals, compromising but never giving Nora what she wanted. But Nora only nodded.

"Okay," she whispered.

"Just . . . there are things I need to take care of. Here. With language, and feet."

She could see, from the corner of her eye, Eda watching her.

"Like Michael?" Nora said, not with the note of snideness that Wenna might have expected from this question.

"Like Michael," Wenna admitted. "But like everything else too."

She sat down between her mother and Nora: cross-legged, her feet drawn up. She rested her hands on the ground, but she did not press her fingers into the earth. On their mother's other side, Percy's eyes were closed. She suspected he had been changing for a while now; she suspected he had begun to leave them before it had occurred to them that he could leave.

"This is what you really want, isn't it?"

"Always," Nora whispered. "What I always wanted."

For a long time, Wenna stayed there with her mother and her sister. At some point, Eda came and sat down beside them. Her feet drawn up, her hands clasped as if she was afraid to touch the ground. Wenna reached out and took her hand, let the reassuring firmness of her sister's grasp anchor them not to the land but to each other.

❧

The letters from Michael to Nora had been lost to the storm; in the forbidden parlor, days after the snow on the floor melted, Wenna found them: wrinkled and torn, blurry words occasionally surfacing from a swirl of water damage. *Wish, miss, only, know.* Wenna couldn't tell what confessions her husband might have made to her sister, what confessions Nora made to him on her behalf, what intimacies passed between them. She could never be certain how successfully Nora had imitated her, whether it had really been Nora that Michael was corresponding with or some half-plausible approximation of herself. But she wrote to him anyway, scratching out a letter on an empty page from Nora's old copy of *Perceval*.

She told him it had always been her sister writing; that she was sorry. She told him she had been bewildered at first, that anyone could confuse them. But she understood she had never really let him know her because she had been afraid of what he would find, if he was ever allowed to look closely. She told him that she wished he would come and see her family home, now that she was its joint custodian. She told him that the land was most beautiful in spring, when everything was changing, becoming more itself, becoming what it had always known it was.

Charlie

he night after he tried and failed to commune with the boglands and his mother, Charlie went back to the study for the first time since the storm. They hadn't even attempted to undo any of the damage there yet, and rubble and wisps of peat insulation still dusted the carpet. The portraits of the Haddesley patriarchs were wind-blasted, sweating moisture. A dead leaf was stuck to the face of Charlie's grandfather, a man whom Charlie had never known, who had been buried in the bog's mouth before Charlie was born but who had been looking down at Charlie from that wall for his whole life, surveilling him through old French lessons and stern talking-tos and the unceremonious washing of his disinherited testicles.

Charlie stood looking at that portrait for a long time, and then he grabbed two fistfuls of peat insulation and scrubbed out the sepulchral face. It felt so good that he grabbed two more handfuls and did the same to his great-grandfather, then to the cockeyed blond patriarch in the next picture, then to that man's predecessor, until he had blacked out the faces of every Haddesley patriarch he could reach. The old peat, delicate with age and still wet, caked beautifully on the canvases.

When he was finished, he went to the bookshelves and filled a canvas shopping bag with books, paying no particular attention to his selections. The leathery, gluey smell of the old volumes flared up into his nostrils. When the bag was full, he filled another. Finally, he lifted the Borradh book from its protective chest and shoved it into a bag with the others. He wanted to hear someone tell him it was worthless, not older than 1897.

He loaded the books into the trunk of the station wagon, taking no special care to be quiet. Then he returned to the study one more time. His father's memoirs still lay open on the desk to the last written-on page, as if someone had left them specifically for Charlie to find, though he thought really it must have been careless happenstance, like most of the other things his family did to him. *Everything to the eldest living son*, the page said, not in their father's hand but in Nora's spidery handwriting. The signature beneath was rough-looking, barely recognizable as their father's.

With a single decisive strike, Charlie crossed out the word *son*, then signed with the looped flourish that he had learned in preparation for becoming his father's heir. If he would not be the last Charles Haddesley, he thought, he would at least be the last one who learned this signature. He hesitated with the pen held an inch above the blank expanse of the lower half of the page. *Don't look for me*, he wrote, at last. *I need to be someone else.*

He would never be able to explain why he was leaving to his siblings, not in a way they could understand. Not Percy, acutely conscious of every mushroom that sprouted; or Nora, foster of three-legged possums and fungus-infested amphibians; or Wenna, who had stood at the door of the station wagon after ten years away and diagnosed immediately the bog's illness with real grief in her voice, as if she were losing someone she loved. Charlie had never loved the land like that. Certainly, it had never loved him. The relations between him and this place had always been poisoned. He could not overcome what Charles Maturin had done on his behalf and his father's behalf and on behalf of every eldest-born Haddesley boy.

For him there could be no new compact. There could be no staying here.

§

The road down to Marlinton was so familiar that Charlie could think of anything else as he drove, so long as he remembered every few minutes to punch the accelerator. People drove fast on that road, impatiently. In the rearview mirror, he could see a rust-eaten pickup gaining on him. He let it pass on the right, holding his pace steady. There was a veneer of unreality on everything. He punched the radio on. "They're just pouring in," said the man on the radio. "Nothing stopping them." He thought: *It's like that. Pouring in. Nothing stopping it.* Though he didn't know what the man was referring to. He rounded a tight downhill corner into a patch of dense forest and the radio dissolved into static, fragments of speech intermittently fighting their way to the surface: "You wouldn't even know," the man said. "The birth rate. It's almost too late." Charlie changed the station. Classical always came through.

A symphony carried him down to the interstate, and down the interstate to Winchester. He slept in his car until the antiques dealer opened, then carried his bags inside and laid them down on the counter. He did not let himself be intimidated by the tortoiseshell cat. The woman at the counter had her hair in a gray braid still. She seemed to recognize him but to feel that she shouldn't say so. Charlie didn't remind her, not wanting the specter of his last sale hanging over this one. She asked if he wanted to wait while she appraised things or come back. "I'll wait," he said. He listlessly browsed aisles of junk while she stood at the counter scrutinizing his father's beloved possessions. She put the ones that she would buy in one pile and the ones she didn't want in another.

"I've never even seen this language," she admitted, holding the Borradh book to the light.

"You can toss whatever you won't sell," he said.

The Borradh book disappeared in one of the piles that she carried out to the dumpster, but he didn't see the moment she threw it away. It wasn't as gratifying as he'd hoped it would be. But still, he walked out of the antique shop with twelve hundred sixty-seven dollars, having spent thirty-three on a vintage Western shirt with pearl buttons and a dark line of sequins across the shoulders. He couldn't explain why it was that shirt he'd wanted. Only that it felt right to him, truer somehow than anything he'd worn in his thirty-one years of feed-store overalls and hand-me-down fisherman sweaters. In the car, he crouched his head low and changed his clothes, throwing his father's careworn flannel into the back seat behind him.

After that, he drove without a direction, his heart occasionally pumping a jagged few beats of nervous exhilaration when he remembered what he was doing. He drove for hours on the interstate. Out here, in the lonely land between Charleston and Pittsburgh, it was mostly him and semitrucks. He found he liked driving here: the breakneck wobbly pace that the truckers set, the bizarre loneliness of the billboards that screamed ADULT VIDEO, AFTER TWO WEEKS BABIES HAVE HEARTBEATS, SEEK HELP FOR YOUR GAMBLING ADDICTION into the darkness. When the car pinged imploringly, he took an exit ramp and filled the station wagon's tank using a pair of twenties. The station wagon was, he had realized sometime since learning to drive, a deeply inefficient car. He had thought sometimes of trying to buy another, one with better gas mileage, one that could handle more than an inch of snow, one that held none of the essence of his father or his father's father or any other Haddesley liar. Maybe he would, soon.

On impulse, he did something he usually forbade himself and lingered in the gas station convenience store. The fluorescents and crowded shelves with foil-wrapped mass-produced foods held an appeal for him that he couldn't explain. He could feel the teenaged cashier and wall-mounted security cameras on his back as he perused the Corn Nuts. He felt deep regret when he determined, too fast, that he was definitely going to buy the alluringly blue Cool Ranch flavor.

He ate the Corn Nuts as he drove, one after another, cringing at the gritty sensation of the powder on his fingers. At some point he crossed into Pennsylvania. The sun began to sink, and the road filled with commuters, then emptied as night washed out the horizon. Charlie kept driving, past the Pittsburgh exits, into the featureless hills of southwestern Pennsylvania and through a toll booth that took his picture, leaving an irrevocable mark of his presence. Now he was the first Haddesley man to appear in a photograph since Charles Maturin, thought Charlie, and he wondered what address they would send his toll fee to. He wondered what his siblings would think, if it came to them and they opened it and understood that he was not only gone but had left them for someplace else.

After Philadelphia, he changed his direction, realizing that he was coming up on the coast. He was in New York now, a state he had never seen, though he found it was as full of discouraged-looking roadside slush and barren trees as Pennsylvania and West Virginia, that he could buy the same brand of Corn Nuts when he went into a convenience store, although now he could also buy handles of liquor and he would have paid three dollars more for cigarettes, if he'd wanted them. He contemplated having a drink, then remembered that he had no ID. It dawned on him that he would have to get one—and then suddenly hundreds of things dawned on him, and he wondered how Wenna had done it: how she had managed, at only seventeen, to reconstruct herself in a way that seemed to him now utterly terrifying, impossible. But he had gone too far to turn back. When night fell, he pulled over at a motel whose sign flashed orange from the interstate.

"Do you have a room?" he asked the clerk, emboldened by his pearl-buttoned shirt and his twelve hundred dollars.

"Name?" said the clerk, and at first Charlie didn't understand, but then she pushed a sheet of paper toward him and he said, "Oh." Then—decisively, taking the burden of his family's hundred-year-old founding lie upon himself—he said, "Charles Maturin" and exchanged fifty-two dollars for a key tied to a thin wooden paddle.

He felt a faint exhilaration when he twisted the key in the lock and the door opened to reveal to him a room dusty with cigarette traces and heater exhaust but belonging singularly to him. This was the first significant thing he had ever done alone, not at the behest of his father or the needling of his sister or the primal obligation of the defunct Haddesley compact but because he wanted to and he could. He examined himself in the mirror above the sink and tried to see himself without seeing his Haddesleyness, the sharp chin and deep-set eyes and dark-blond hair that he shared with the rest of them.

"My name," he said aloud, practicing, "is Charles Maturin.

My father owned a tract of land in West Virginia. But he's dead now, and I chose not to inherit."

He took a shower, the first shower of his life. Dark rivulets fell muddily down his legs and into the drain. His hair was coarse with grit. He thought he had never in his life actually gotten clean, and he stayed in the shower stall behind the vinyl curtain until the water ran cold, scrubbing the bog out of his scalp and armpits and navel and tree-riven genitalia until his skin was rawly red and smelled only of motel soap, medicinal and slightly waxen.

Afterward, he sat on the end of the motel bed and turned on the TV and his lips formed again and again the name Charles Maturin as he sat in the soft glow of a commercial for a metastatic-lung-cancer medication that would extend your life by six or even possibly eight weeks.

EDA

They made their new compact slowly, without ever consciously entering into it, as the days lengthened and the frosts thinned and firm orange buds appeared on the branches of the maples. At night, Nora and Percy slept on the margins of the bog meadow with their mother. Percy came up to the house in the mornings sometimes for a cup of coffee, but Nora never did. Charlie did not come back from wherever he had gone in the car. They cleared felled branches from the yard and the forest and the meadow, letting the ground breathe. Some of the branchless trees died but others healed themselves slowly, gathering strength, at last sprouting stubby new limbs.

In the middle of the season, it rained for a week straight and the ceilingless kitchen flooded and they began sleeping in the goat shed. They shoveled out the manure and mopped the floor with well water; they swept away the cobwebs; they hung blankets on the walls. They let the goats wander the yard. At night, they shut the door and lit a single candle and shared a single heap of covers. Wenna cooked oats with fat-stemmed ramps and white mushrooms and wild radishes gathered from the forest. Eda made a garden plot from rich forest humus and got last year's seed packs out of the potting shed and planted squash, carrots, potatoes, nasturtiums. Charlie did not come back. Percy and Nora opened their mouths and closed their eyes when it rained.

The ceiling caved in the kitchen and they stopped going back to the house. They dug a firepit and cut the trunks of storm-felled trees for firewood and cooked vegetables on the coals. Wenna resolved to get a battery-powered hotplate. Nora and Percy and their mother ate sunlight and water and the nutrients that swam through the soil to reach them. New maple and pine sprouts came up, delicate and finger-thin in the sedge. Lines of orange mushrooms unstitched the boundary between bog meadow and bog forest. Heavy rains fell and the bog's mouth swelled open and the ground absorbed the moisture and the bog's mouth shrank nearly to closing. They shoveled earth into the swale, then planted rows of pine saplings on top like restitution. Their mother's flesh became woody; her arms stiffened and stretched out; her eyes and nose and mouth seemed to recede back into her face until her face was featureless and flat. Charlie did not come back. On warm afternoons, Wenna sat between Nora and her mother and closed her eyes and Eda could see that she was feeling whatever they felt: the worms nosing hungrily through the humus, the fungi questing after tree roots, the earth knitting together, the bog becoming forest. And her chest always hurt when she saw her sister there, her throat tightened, but Wenna never spoke of it, so Eda didn't either. At night, they sat in the yard and read the romance of *Perceval* to each other, the only one of Nora's romances they managed to recover from her room upstairs.

The last clumps of their mother's amber hair fell out and lay on the ground around her. Wenna gathered them up and braided them and hung them around their mother's woody neck. The black spruces on the margins of the bog forest regained their waxy needles. Mathilde crouched in the yard and labored for fifteen hours and delivered a stillbirth. Wenna and Eda buried it among the birches, where the soil was becoming rich and hungry. In the yard behind them, the nanny goat wailed deep grief-stricken wails. They got a rag wet with warm water and rubbed the blood and amniotic fluids from her inflamed skin, released the milk from her heavy superfluous teats. She lay with her head in Eda's lap as if she were a human child. Afterward, Eda sipped hot goat's milk and held her belly with one hand and did not say that she was terrified of labor. "It won't be like that for you," Wenna said, and she read *Perceval* to Eda and to Eda's baby and to weary grief-stricken Mathilde.

The young pines in the bog forest grew to the height of Eda's waist. Turtles hatched in the bog's shrinking mouth. Charlie sent money to the house in an envelope with a note that only said, *For your needs—C*, and no return address, so they could not send it back; they could not even tell him that they had no easy way to spend money now. Eda stood in front of the mailbox and sobbed, then came back and hung the money on the walls like decor. Every night, it rained. They read *Perceval* until they came to the abrupt last lines and then began again because they both agreed that the ending did not feel like it had ended.

Near the bog's mouth, the first cranberry blossoms opened. Another envelope of cash came from Charlie. A trunk sprouted from their mother's woody chest. Buz Lukens or a white three-footed possum identical to Buz Lukens appeared one night in the goat shed. Wenna looked at him and laughed. "Do we make him leave?" she said.

"I don't think we can," said Eda. They made a bed for him out of pillows from the forbidden parlor. The next day, they carried him down to Nora and set him on the ground beside her half-vegetal form, and there the possum lay down and rolled, exposing his belly, but he didn't stay. He preferred the humans and their scraps and their couch cushions.

The days became long and heat-muddled and lazy. They ate handfuls of serviceberries that stained their hands magenta. Flies hung lethargically over the sedge. Between rains, the bog closed its mouth. On a warm and full-mooned night, Eda went into labor.

Wenna supported her out to the margins of the encroaching forest, where she lay down beneath the three slender trunks of her mother and Nora and Percy. She lay stiffly at first, feeling unprotected, feeling alone, and then when a well of pain crested over her, she gouged her fingers into the earth like she was hanging on. And she felt, for the first time, the land braiding her into itself, every tendril of vegetable life in the nascent forest sharing nutrients, sharing strength, sharing anxious and hopeful anticipation.

On the moss-made earth, above ten thousand years of buried history, she gave birth to a girl.

They named her after no one.

Acknowledgments

Thanks to my editor, Dan López, and the rest of the team at Counterpoint Press, including Dan Smetanka, tracy danes, Nicole Caputo, Megan Fishmann, Vanessa Genao, Rachel Fershleiser, and Kira Weiner, Barrett Briske, and Mikayla Butchart, for giving this novel a warm and nurturing home. Thanks also to Daniel Carpenter and the Titan Books team for bringing *The Bog Wife* to the U.K.

Agents Laura Cameron, Amanda Orozco, and Lisa Rambert-Valaskova provided vital feedback on the manuscript and shepherded it to publication. Thank you for believing in this book.

Thanks to the park rangers and staff at Cranberry Glades Botanical Area and Tannersville Cranberry Bog Preserve for protecting and providing public access to the boreal peat bogs that inspired this book. Particular thanks to the Nature Conservancy guides who lead the bog walks at the Tannersville Cranberry Bog. Thank you also to Karolina and Aaron Segal for the road trip.

The Bog Wife took inspiration from folklore as well as ecology; I am especially indebted to the books *The Bog People* by P.V. Glob, *Ecology of the Northern Lowland Bogs and Conifer Forests* by James Arthur Larsen, *The Biology of Peatlands* by Håkan Rydin and John K. Jeglum, *From Ritual to Romance* by Jessie L. Weston, and *Purity and Danger* by Mary Douglas. All errors in bog representation are my own.

Finally, thanks to Joe for patience and support.

© Caroline King

KAY CHRONISTER is the author of *Thin Places* and *Desert Creatures*. Her short fiction has appeared in *Strange Horizons, Clarkesworld, Beneath Ceaseless Skies, The Dark,* and elsewhere, and has been nominated for the Shirley Jackson and World Fantasy awards. She lives outside of Philadelphia.